S[illegible]
FOR
CHEFS

Edited by
Rachel Loosmore

Published by Accent Press Ltd – 2005
IBSN 0954489985

Edited by Rachel Loosmore

Printed and bound in UK
By Clays Plc, St Ives.

Cover illustration by Richie Perrott
Desert Point Illustration.
www.desertpointillustration.com

Acknowledgments

'Party Peace' by Sue Houghton appeared in *Woman's Weekly* December 2004. 'The Way To A Man's Heart' by Sue Houghton appeared in *You Magazine* (South Africa) in June 2004. 'Honeymoon' by Della Galton appeared in *Woman's Weekly Fiction Special* in July 2004. 'Summer Rose' by Liza Granville appeared in *Active Life* in August 1995. 'Picking Cherries' by Sue Johnson appeared as 'Telling Fortunes' in *Woman Summer Special II* in July 2004. A version of 'Doing The Cooking' by Jane Wenham-Jones appeared in *Woman's Realm* in August 2000. 'Perfect Timing' by Daisy Jordan appeared in *Woman's Weekly* in January 2003 under author Lynne Barrett-Lee. 'Recipes For Life' by Sophie King appeared in *Woman's Weekly* in April 2005. 'Tea And Sympathy' by Adele Parks appeared in *Woman's Own in Summer* in 2003. 'Trapped' by Linda Povey appeared in *Take A Break's Fiction Feast* in March 2003 and *New Idea* (Australia) in Oct 2004. 'Brief Encounter' by Jill Steeples appeared in *Espresso Fiction* in May 2005. 'Nice Work' by Ginny Swart appeared in *Woman's Day* (Australia) in April 2004 and *You Magazine* (S. Africa) in May 2004. 'Setting The Scene' by Ginny Swart appeared in *That's Life* (Australia) in April 2005 and *You Magazine* (S. Africa) in August 2005.

Contents

Desserts

Foreword

Food, love and charity are important to us all and all can be found is this exciting and fun new collection of short stories and recipes which I hope you will enjoy. The money raised for Breast Cancer Campaign will be spent researching *the cure*.

One woman in nine will develop breast cancer in her lifetime in the UK – this could be *your* mother, sister, aunt, friend or colleague. Men too can develop breast cancer; they account for around 300 new cases a year, in the UK.

Together we can all help to beat it.

Warm wishes,

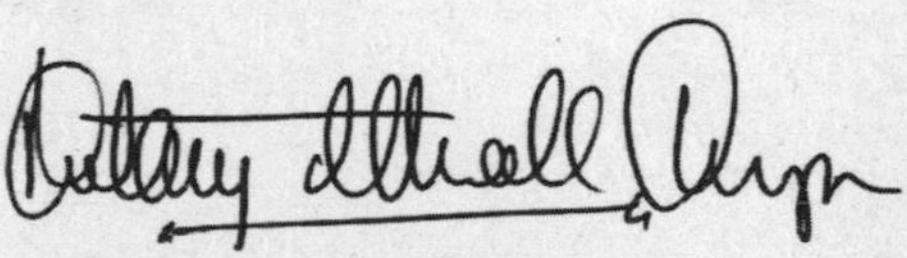

Antony Worrall Thompson

Table Manners
by Kelly Florentia

I knew he was Italian from the very first moment I set eyes on him. He had those dark, penetrating eyes and that moody expression. I remember the way he looked at me as I approached the counter, through long, luxurious, black eyelashes. When he spoke in a husky accented voice, I wasn't disappointed.

"Ciao, Bella, what can I get you?" Alright, it was a corny line but who was complaining? I ordered a mozzarella and tomato panini and a large decaf, skinny latte. "Come on," he teased, "you don't need a skinny Latte, you already a skinny lady." If only, I still couldn't get into my favourite pair of jeans despite constant dieting. But Italians like their women curvy, don't they? So, I took it as a compliment with a sprinkling of humour from a very dishy Italian chef.

Six months later, I walked into the same café, wearing my favourite pair of jeans with room to spare. But I didn't need to place my order. I just sat at 'my table' as Luigi endearingly referred to it. I waited while he prepared something low fat and delicious for me.

Sometimes, when he isn't too busy, he joins me at 'my table', sips Espresso and tells me stories about his childhood in Sicily and I listen with total abandonment. Luigi has this special gift, you see, he can make any woman feel like a princess, regardless of age, shape or size. Only, I'm short of one thing… a prince charming, but hopefully that's all about to change. I'm feeling a bit jittery about taking Luigi home to meet mum. Who'd have thought that, after all those dates, Luigi would be the one to fit the bill? Doubtless, she'll have her reservations, she always does, but he's the only one who passed 'the food test', so she can't complain about that. Let me explain. Mum has this theory about eating habits.

"You can tell a lot about people by the way they eat their food, Lucy, all you have to do is learn how to read them," she said over Sunday lunch three weeks ago.

"What, you mean like tarot reading?" I teased, knowing that mum hated anything to do with predictions.

"Oh, don't be so ridiculous," she took a sip of wine then fixed me with one of her looks and I knew I wasn't going to like what was coming next. "That speed dating thingy you're going on with Carol?" My eyes narrowed suspiciously, I was wondering when we'd get round to this.

"Yeah, go on," I said, cutting into my roast chicken a little harder than intended.

"Well, I was wondering if you'd do me a favour?"

"What kind?" I asked guardedly. Surely she didn't want to come with us now she was single again?

"Have dinner with each man who contacts you on your list, study their eating habits then report back to me. I swear I'll pick out your prince charming for you." I let out a sigh of relief. And I dubiously agreed. What harm could it do? And it would give me a peaceful life.

Dinner date number one was a pompous bore and to be honest I couldn't wait to get rid of him, so I made my excuses before dessert and escaped.

"You're back early, was he that bad?" Mum asked sympathetically. "Mum, he ate like a horse and bored me to tears." I said kicking off my shoes.

"Greed," said Mum, "not a good trait, cross him off the list." And I was only too happy to. Dinner date number two went fairly well.

"Well, how did it go?" asked Mum eagerly the next day.

"Not bad actually. He barely touched his food though, just fiddled around with his main course while playing footsy with me under the table."

"Oh, that's disgraceful," Mum retorted, "Dining out on a full stomach. Mean and sex mad, ditch him!"

By dinner date number three I was tiring of it all and beginning to think that Mum was right, this kind of introduction was a waste of time. I arrived late and there didn't seem to be anyone waiting for me outside the restaurant. To be honest, I was half pleased. With folded arms I leant forward on the sole of my foot and peered through the restaurant window.

"You're late," came a voice from behind me. Startled, I spun round and there he stood. My Prince Charming. All six foot two of him, his blue eyes shining against his tanned skin and black, vibrant hair. A smile swept over my face as my eyes fell onto his broad shoulders and rippling muscles veiled beneath an expensive looking pink cotton shirt.

"I'm Danny," he held out his hand and when I took it he drew it to his mouth and softly brushed his full lips against my fingers, sending all kinds of sensations down my spine. Why couldn't I remember this gorgeous man at the speed dating night? Mind you, chatting to over thirty men, with a three minute per man limit, under the influence of quite a few glasses of Pinot Grigio might answer that.

Inside the restaurant we sat at a cosy table under an alcove. We dined on the finest food, drank heavenly wine and exchanged intimate glances. For dessert he fed me spoonfuls of chocolate ice cream across the table. I was smitten, only the next day Mum wasn't impressed.

"Darling, if he left his favourite food on the plate till last then he's a procrastinator, too easy going. It'll be a job getting him down the aisle I can tell you, chuck him before it's too late." I was disappointed to say the least but I carried on crossing the men off my list to see if mum really could pick out Mr Perfect.

Dinner date number four cut his food into equal portions. Mum's analysis was 'fastidious and hell to live with'. Number five was even worse. He mashed most of his food up with the gravy.

"Yuk," said mum, "do you want to live with a slob for the rest of your life?" I was at the end of my tether, and list for that matter. Then I secretly had dinner with Luigi but told mum he was number six on my list.

"So, you're saying that he ate his favourite bits first?"

"Yes, Mum, and I did ask him why."

"And what did he say?" she asked, rubbing her hands together.

"That he eats the best bits first in case he fills up on the rest of the food and misses out."

"Darling, he sounds perfect. That means he seizes life, enjoys the moment. Bring him home for tea."

So here we are. Luigi sitting on Mum's floral sofa looking as handsome as ever, his dark eyes shifting from me to Mum. And Mum looking uncomfortable under his penetrating gaze.

"Well? Isn't he gorgeous?" I whisper excitedly in the kitchen.

"Yes, darling, but isn't he a bit…old?" Luigi's head appears around the door.

"Need any help, Mrs Bennet?"

"Ah, Luigi," Mum blushes, "no, you sit yourself down, we've got it all under..." But he's already taking the lasagne out of the oven. "Bellissimo, Mrs Bennet, this smells fantastico," he kisses his fingertips and shoots them out into the air like a star. "And what is this for starter? Oysters!" he growls playfully. Dinner is perfect. Luigi entertains us with Sicilian stories, his arms waving in the air expressively. I haven't seen Mum enjoy herself this much in years.

"You know, Mrs. Bennet,"

"Oh, call me Linda, for God's sake," She pours more wine, a good sign.

"Linda, you did fantastic job bringing up Lucy," Mum and I shrug smugly and exchange glances. "And I'm so glad she says you need a man." I take a deep breath and watch mum's horrified expression.

"I beg your pardon?"

"Mum, this isn't how it seems," I interrupt.

"Che?" Luigi shrugs with open palms, "I say wrong thing?"

"No, Luigi but…"

"Mrs…Linda, when Lucy had dinner with me last week and said, 'Luigi, you'd be a perfect match for my Mamma', I was…how you say in English? Shock. But now I see you, Lucy was right, you are a bella donna." Mum looks at me wide-eyed and aghast while I try hard to stifle a giggle. I come clean.

"Mum, Luigi's your blind date." I say flatly. OK , maybe it was a bit sneaky of me but she's been so lonely since Dad went off with that younger woman. And poor Luigi, so much zest, so much passion and widowed at the age of thirty-eight. Wasn't it a shame that two beautiful people should walk the path of life alone?

Soon we're all laughing and Luigi stays for coffee and Tiramisu while I slip away quietly. I've a date with Danny at eight. No food theory is going to make me pass on a dish like him. Besides, I too always save the best till last.

Fresh Oysters

Allow 6 oysters per person

Ingredients

oyster knife
salt and pepper
tabasco
red wine vinegar
french dressing
tartare sauce
horseradish
worcestershire sauce
crushed ice
lemon wedges
buttered brown bread

Method

Place oysters on a bed of crushed ice and surround with lemon wedges. Open or shuck them with an oyster knife just before serving, ensuring that the shells are clean and that no pieces of shell are piercing the oysters. Clean away any broken bits from the lower shell. Season with salt and pepper and if preferred add a dash of garnish, i.e. Tabasco, Worcestershire sauce or any other from the list above – serve with buttered brown bread.

Take It Away Man
by Jill Steeples

I love working in Quick Bites. To some people, I suppose, it may seem mundane, but to me it's the best job in the world. Creative in a way, too. Slapping down the thick slices of bread, smearing them with butter, dressing them with a yummy topping and popping the end product in a fresh, crinkly bag. It's immensely satisfying.

There are three of us behind the small counter and most of the time we're working flat out. We move like sequence dancers dodging between one another as we reach for the various fillings.

I have this theory about the sandwich someone chooses. I think it reflects their underlying personality. Here comes a customer now. He's grey-suited, bespectacled and brief-cased, a traditional, home-loving type by the looks of him. Definitely a beef man, I'd say.

'What would you like, Sir?' I ask.

He looks up at the blackboard, his eyes darting across the different options.

'I'll have a roast beef with horseradish, on white, please.' See, you get to know these things after a while.

I start spreading the butter quickly, my other hand reaching for the wedges of meat. A generous dollop of sauce and then I press the other slice down firmly on top, before easing the knife through its centre. Another satisfied customer.

The best thing about the job is all our lovely regulars. Some of them you can set your clock by. There's the site foreman, who comes in early and is relentlessly cheerful. He's a cheese and pickle on white.

Then there's the young girl from the solicitor's office across the road. She's an English salad with marmite on wholemeal. Deadly earnest. No butter, no mayonnaise. No wonder she's rake thin.

But my favourite of them all is George. Not that it's his real name, of course, it's just what we call him. He's gorgeous.

Dancing dark eyes, silver flecked hair and a gorgeous grin, he's the nearest thing to George Clooney that will ever grace our shop. The girls know I've a weak spot for him.

'Put your lippy on Jen,' they say, 'lover boy will be in soon.'

He reminds me of Tom, I suppose that's what it is. Same build, same easy manner, same dreamy effect. And Tom was my first love. You never forget your first love, do you?

Each day during the lunchtime rush I get a bit tingly knowing that at any moment George may walk in. When he does, the girls push me forward to serve him. He stares at me, a little half grin on his face, as I flutter behind the counter, feeling the heat of the kitchen rise to my face.

He's a cheese combo man. That's grated cheddar mixed with sweetcorn, spring onion and mayonnaise. On granary. Funnily enough, it's my favourite sandwich too. I knew then that we were meant to be together. It had to be some kind of omen, a sign of our potential compatibility.

'All right, darling? he says in that drawling lilt of his and my stomach performs a leaping pirouette.

Our hands touch briefly over the glass top counter as I hand over his cheese combo and for a lingering moment our eyes lock in recognition of something else, something infinitely more substantial.

Then, a couple of weeks ago, without any warning whatsoever, he stopped coming in. At first we thought he might be on holiday or even that he'd changed jobs, but Tina spotted him one day as she was grabbing a can of drink from the window display. Bold as brass he was, walking into Maria's sandwich bar across the road.

Well you can imagine how I felt. Our sandwiches are the best in town so what could he possibly be getting from Maria's that he couldn't get from our shop?

'What have you done to upset Lover Boy, Jen?' the girls jeered.

I tried to laugh it off, but I was more hurt than I was letting on. Seeing George was the highlight of my day. He was the reason I twirled so smoothly across the linoleum floor in a flush of spring-like anticipation, greeting each customer with a genuine desire to please.

I couldn't just let him go as easily as that. I had to do something about it.

The next morning I made one of his special sandwiches, taking extra care to use all the best ingredients and a more than generous helping of mayonnaise. When I spotted him walking into Maria's I grabbed the sandwich from the side and hurried out of the shop and across the road. Sure enough, five minutes later he came out clutching his carrier bag, looking a tad guilty, I thought, when he noticed me.

'Hello,' he said. That smile of his floodlit his features.

'Hi,' I said, as casually as I could muster, 'we've not seen you in the shop for a while.'

'Um, yeah,' he said sheepishly. 'It's Maria,' he gestured towards the shop behind him. 'She said I was being disloyal.'

'Maria?' I asked.

'Yes, she's my…' he paused, his gaze drifting down towards my shoes.

'Oh I see' I said, not knowing what else to say. I thrust the cheese combo into his hands and turned away before he had a chance to notice the embarrassment pricking beneath my skin.

How could I have been so stupid? Someone as good-looking as George was bound to have a woman and I certainly couldn't compete with the likes of Maria. Titian hair piled high on her head, thrusting pert breasts and her own sandwich bar to boot. What man wouldn't be tempted by the lure of her exotic flavourings? She had them all. Tangy lemon chicken, mango and shredded lamb, sushi specials. Why should George be interested in me and my extra mature cheddar?

I hurried back to the shop, sniffing back the stinging tears brought on by the cool spring air, feeling for all the world like a fool.

'George won't be coming back,' I told the girls.

They were very good to me. Did their best to cheer me up and made sure they didn't mention his name again. They even encouraged me to befriend another male customer, but I didn't like the look of him and what with him being partial to a tuna roll, well, I knew there could be no future in it.

I'm a one-man woman. Always have been. Ever since Tom. And there was I was thinking George was my man of the moment. Some things are simply meant to be.

Thankfully the following days passed in a whirl of activity. That's the thing about working in the shop, there isn't time to get bored. But I always had one eye on the door hoping that George would have a change of heart and come back. I wouldn't forget him, I couldn't.

And that's what thought does. Yesterday I was washing-up in the back, my arms elbow deep in a bowl of suds when Tina called through to me.

'Someone here to see you, Jen.'

I walked out drying my hands on my pinny. My heart gave one of those funny little lurches when I saw George standing there, smiling at me with that special twinkle in his eye.

'Hello,' I said, 'thought you'd given up on us.'

'I've tried,' he said, 'but I realised I miss the cheese combos too much and more than that I've missed you too.'

The girls swooned in unison behind me.

'I wondered maybe, if you'd like to, we could have some lunch. Perhaps share a sarnie together?' he shuffled self-consciously from one leg to the other.

What was there to think about? I had my coat on in a jiffy while Tina rustled up a couple of combos for the pair of us.

In the promise of that brisk afternoon, we walked close together, clutching our paper bags, until we reached the park bench in the middle of the blossom-carpeted square. Perching on the wooden slatted seat, our knees gently touching, my curiosity got the better of me.

'What happened to Maria, then?' I asked, nonchalantly.

'Maria?' he smiled. 'Oh, she'll come round. Lovely girl, my daughter, but when it comes to making a decent sandwich she's got some funny new-fangled ideas.

My heart soared in relief, as we laughed together in understanding.

'If her mum were still alive today, she'd have a thing or two to say. I mean, what's wrong with a simple cheddar roll.'

A plain talker, that's what I like. Just like my Tom, God rest his soul.

Smiling, I unwrapped the cheese combos from their greaseproof wrapping and passed one over to George.

He gave me a sexy little wink as together we bit into our succulent sandwiches.

Somehow I think George and I will get on together just fine. In fact, I think we'll make the perfect combination.

Cheese Combo

Ingredients
2 slices granary bread
butter
2 tbsp grated extra mature cheddar
2 tbsp cooked sweetcorn
1 spring onion, chopped finely
1 tbsp mayonnaise
black pepper

Method
In a bowl, mix together the cheese, sweetcorn and chopped spring onion (adjust quantities to taste). Add the mayonnaise and black pepper. Gently stir. Butter bread and spread mixture onto bread.

Cut in half.

Wrap in greaseproof paper.

Nice Work
by Ginny Swart

Alison stood in front her stove, waiting for the pastry cases for the vol-au-vents to reach golden perfection before she took them out. While she waited, she beat some double-thick cream into the cheesecake mixture and put it in the fridge for later.

She turned her attention to her feet – which shoes to wear with the silky blue outfit she'd bought for *the interview*. Horribly expensive, but the trim little box pleats and belted waist said 'serious and career minded.' She decided her old navy heels would do, once she'd polished them.

Ever since she'd seen the advert for a receptionist at the Harcourt Hotel, home-from-home for the rich and famous, she was sure this job was meant for her. She'd made it through the first round of applications and was on a short list of three.

Alison could see her glamorous future rolling out in technicolour, registering important guests, directing them to their suites and confidently advising them on the best restaurants in town. 'Client liaison' it was called and she knew she'd be good at that.

"I suppose I couldn't persuade you to join me for dinner?" purred Tom Cruise, leaning enticingly over her reservation book, "Even the perfect receptionist has to eat sometime."

As she gazed coolly into Tom's green-flecked eyes he added, "At a table for two in a private room?"

It could happen.

The oven pinged obligingly and she removed the fragrant pastry shells, carefully transferring them to the wire tray to cool. The chopped chicken breasts with ginger and lime sauce stood ready to be spooned in, and as soon as she was back from the interview she planned to take the pastries and cheesecake round to Moira for her dinner party that evening. The mushroom and smoked-mussel soup was already in the container and she'd made the Malay-style lamb curry the evening before, to give the flavours time to meld together deliciously.

She was always surprised that so many of her friends found cooking difficult and were so pathetically grateful for her help.

"Why not go into catering, Alison?" Moira had said, "You're a natural born cook."

But she preferred the security of a cheque at the end of the month. If she got it right this morning, she'd be earning a very nice salary behind the wide marble front desk of the Harcourt Hotel.

Alison badly needed this job. Five weeks without work was more than she'd bargained for when she'd impulsively resigned from the dry-cleaning shop to follow the sun. Two weeks in Greece had left her with a beautiful tan but a savings account that was running dangerously low.

It was pouring with rain as she set off, and with the pavement under water just outside her gate, she was forced to detour onto the street. Trying not to wet her shoes, she stepped gingerly across the gutter that was streaming with water.

As she did so, a little red car sped around the corner, straight through a deep puddle and sent up a great whoosh of dirty water. In one icy second, Alison was drenched to the skin. And as she jumped back, her heel caught on something and she sat down hard in the gutter.

This can't be happening, she thought, scrambling slowly and painfully to her feet. Not today.

"I say, I'm terribly sorry. Are you alright?"

It was the driver of the car, concern written all over his face.

"No, I'm NOT alright," she snapped furiously, "Thanks to you. How could you go through that puddle as such a speed? Look at me! I'm a disaster!"

The suspicion of a grin increased her fury.

"I'm on my way to an interview. Now I've probably lost the best job I was ever going to get."

"I feel terrible about this," he said sincerely, helping her up. "The least I can do is take you home to get a change of clothes."

She scowled.

"I haven't got a change of clothes. This is my interview outfit you…you idiot! I can't apply for a job at the Harcourt Hotel in a pair of jeans!"

"The Harcourt? That's a coincidence; I work in the kitchen there. What's the interview for?"

"It was for receptionist" she said pointedly. "But now you've totally ruined my chances, you…you…dish-washer."

His mouth twitched.

"Oh, that's right, I heard they were looking for someone. Look, I know the hotel housekeeper, and she could dry everything and have you looking good as new."

"How? My dress is filthy and wet, and my hair…"

"Jump in," he said firmly, opening the passenger door. "Mrs Nichols can work miracles."

She glared at him.

"I don't even know your name."

"Sorry." He held out his hand, which was surprisingly firm and warm. "Rick Williams."

"Alison Andrews."

She sank squishily into the front seat.

"Look on the bright side," said Rick, "You're very lucky I didn't run you over."

Alison cheered up and looked critically at her driver. He had a thin, humorous face and a gold earring gleamed under his dark hair which curled over his collar and added to his slightly raffish look. Maybe I was lucky after all, she thought, I'll definitely have to get to know him better when I'm working there. On the other hand – front office personnel and the kitchen staff? They might not allow it.

Rick ignored the splendid curving drive up to the pillared entrance of the Harcourt Hotel and parked around the back.

"Staff entrance," he smiled. "Not quite as grand, is it?"

It certainly wasn't. The lobby smelled of wet boots and badly need a coat of paint. From a room off to the left came a crashing of pots and impatient, raised voices.

"The kitchen," he explained, "Things get a bit hectic here at this time of day, they're just preparing lunch."

Lured by the smell of rosemary and something else she couldn't quite identify, Alison peered around the door. About ten men with white coats and funny hats, intent on stirring and chopping, didn't look up from their work.

"Venison for lunch?" she enquired, sniffing appreciatively.

"Right." Rick stared. "You've got a good nose."

"Venison with rosemary sauce – Nigella Lawson!" she exclaimed.

"Clement Freud, actually."

"Ah, but she took it from his book on Irish cuisine and changed it a lot. Put in the juniper berries and used loads more wine. It's the sauce that makes that dish, don't you think?"

She grinned at his puzzled face.

"I like to cook." she said simply, "Now, where's that miracle worker of yours?"

He led Alison through a maze of dark, narrow passages to the small housekeeper's room on the first floor, where a motherly person was counting towels..

"Mrs Nichols, my friend Alison needs some help," said Rick. "She's a bit wet."

"Caught in a shower, were you dear? Might take more than a miracle, but let's see what we can do," said Mrs Nichols, heaving herself off the stool. "Off you go, Mr Williams."

Alison wrapped herself in a bath towel, watching as Mrs Nichols sponged and ironed her skirt and top. She rubbed her hair dry in front of a heater and started to relax. She still had five minutes before her interview.

"Got a special date, have you dear?"

"I'm applying for the job as receptionist here," said Alison.

"That's nice. If you can handle those demanding guests."

"I'll manage," she said, thinking of Hugh Grant walking up to her desk, looking lost, needing her help. Hugh Grant, demanding? Never. "Is my skirt dry yet, do you think?"

"It'll do," said Mrs Nichols, "I've got most of the mud off. And this little tear at the back won't show at all."

"You're a darling, thank you so much. Now, how do I get to the manager's office?"

"Turn left at the end of the passage, and through the glass door," said Mrs Nichols. "Good luck."

Alison fingered her lucky rabbit's foot nestling inside her bag. "I'll be OK." she said confidently.

There was no mirror in the housekeeper's room, but she dressed hurriedly, twisted her hair into a knot on top and hoped for the best.

The Harcourt Hotel she recognised started on the other side of the glass door. A thick blue carpet paved the way across the foyer to the marble-topped reception desk, where a smartly dressed woman was seated.

As Alison approached, she looked up and her bland expression changed to one of distaste.

"Yes? Can I help you?" Her icy voice had undercurrents of however, I doubt it.

"I have an appointment with Mr Adams, the manager. Um…about the job."

Get a grip, girl, where's your confidence, she thought crossly. Then she caught sight of her reflection in a big gold-framed mirror and clutched the edge of the desk in horror.

Her blue skirt, which had seemed so right that morning, no longer said 'serious and career minded'. It had shrunk so badly it now screamed 'cheap and nasty' and the polka-dot top cheekily bared her beautifully tanned midriff for all to see. The cute little navel ring that had seemed such fun on the beach at Rhodos twinkled maliciously. Not the Harcourt Hotel style at all.

"I…it's all right, I'll phone him later," mumbled Alison, and she turned and dashed blindly back through the glass doors to the staff quarters

She took her treacherous rabbit's foot out of her bag and hurled it angrily into the corner, then took a deep breath and re-traced her steps down the passage. She was about to walk past the kitchen when Rick appeared.

"That was quick," he said, "How'd it go?"

"It didn't. I'm out of here." She yanked angrily at her skirt. "How could I possibly see the manager looking like this?"

"That's a very fetching frill," he grinned. "Old man Adams would have loved it. But I take your point. Look, at the very least, I owe you a coffee and I'd like a word with you."

He took her arm and led her into a small sitting room furnished with comfy old arms chairs.

"Staff lounge," he said "And quite good coffee. I can recommend it"

She sat down while Rick poured them each a cup.

"Shouldn't you be toiling in the kitchen?" she snapped.

"Oh, I'm allowed a minute or two off," he smiled. "Tell me, wouldn't you rather be cooking than listening to complaints all day long?"

"Yes, of course, but there's the small matter of my rent."

"Okay, now don't think I'm crazy, but what sauce would you use if you were preparing whiting?"

"I'd try a Maltaise," she answered promptly. "But I'd use fresh Seville orange juice instead of lemon. It's subtler and works wonderfully with whiting."

"And what would you do to cheer up roast lamb?"

"A sauce? Not boring old mint. OK, so let's assume you've roasted it with lashings of fresh rosemary and slivers of garlic…hmm, maybe a caper sauce? With that flat-leafed parsley and loads of black pepper. And stir in some thick cream just before you serve it."

She swallowed hungrily. Breakfast seemed a long time ago. "Why do you ask?"

"You want a job, right? And you obviously know your way around a kitchen. How would you like to start as assistant to the saucier here?"

"The what?"

"He's the chef who makes the sauces. Monsieur Reynard. He's nearly seventy and desperately needs an assistant. I think you'd be very good. You're creative."

Alison stared at Rick. Tom Cruise wasn't ever going to find his way down that gloomy passage. On the other hand, working with this totally gorgeous man every day could have its attractions. And she did love to cook.

"Great perks, too," he added. "Good staff lunches. On-the-job training from one of the best sauciers in the country. You can wear jeans to work every day if you want, although with legs like yours, that'd be a crime."

He gave her a look of pure appreciation and she bit her lip.

"Cheeky. So what are you, then? You don't wash dishes."

"I never said I did. I'm the Executive Chef. So I do the hiring and I think you'd be just what I'm looking for."

Exactly what I was thinking about you, she thought, then blushed crimson in case he could read her mind.

"You'd be my boss?"

"Not exactly, you'd be answerable to Monsieur Reynard. I don't interfere in his department."

Yessss! She thought, looking into his deep brown eyes with a little shiver of anticipation. Dating the boss is never a good idea.

Smoked Mussel And Mushroom Soup

Ingredients

2 tins mushroom soup
1 punnet fresh mushrooms
1 tin smoked mussels
half pint of cream
wine glass sherry or red wine
Sprig of fresh thyme (optional)

Method:

Slice mushrooms and fry them gently in butter for a couple of minutes.
Heat the soup to almost boiling, add the mushrooms.
Drain and chop mussels finely, add to soup.
Lightly beat the cream and mix it in to the soup. Lastly add the sherry.
The sprigs of thyme make a nice garnish.

Let's Pretend
by Ruth Joseph

Let's pretend we are back in college. I met you when you were running for a lecture and almost crashed into you with my bicycle. The sky had been darkening since sunrise and now it hung with clouds sodden like a filthy duvet. Suddenly spears of rain fell full and relentless. Your head was down, shoulders almost screwed into your neck to avoid the onslaught and in your arms a pile of files and unprotected papers.

I was riding towards you but you came headlong into my path. I managed to stop before you were hurt. But the papers were not so lucky. They flew out of your arms and landed in the growing puddles. And, as I alighted from my bike and tried to help you, stooping to retrieve the soaking manuscripts I noticed your handwriting. When you raised your head, for a second, I looked into your eyes and laughed, and your frustration turned to laughter as you looked at me. You scanned your watch.

"I'm so late… it's hopeless now… I've missed half my lecture," you grimaced.

"And he's so angry if you disturb him in the middle…"

I glanced at your notes. "Is it Blight, physiology? Damn…better pull a sickie than walk in in the middle."

"But all the work, so many pages to rewrite…"

"No problem…Come on now, we'll have coffee and then I'll type them up for you…but come now…please?"

I looked at your face – olive-skinned like mine, black hair hanging in wet strands: a drop of water hanging like a crystal off each tip.

"Please, please come…I promise..."

We made our way to one of the coffee shops on the High Street and found the favourite leather couch that overlooked the view of the river. The coffee shop was virtually empty. That time of day – too early for the serious shoppers and the students that later would crowd and drag the chairs into a gaggle, wanting double portions of big toast and soup.

Now it was quiet. I watched as you peeled the damp coat off, hung it on the hook behind us, and rubbed your cold-reddened fingers together. Then you shook your shoulders in a shiver. You sat down beside me. I wanted to hold you then, but I stopped myself. The bundle of papers had now regressed into dampened pleats.

"OK, let's look at the damage…use this table. Let's spread it all out to dry."

As you laid out the papers, I realized that it was, in fact, the work I had done two years previously.

"I can help you…it's easy…I have this piece of work. Old Blight's a stickler for lateness but his memory's not so good and I can print out my documents on…and give them to you later. Haven't you got a computer?"

"Yes, but it's very old, second hand, and I've had trouble with it. It's difficult to borrow one from the college."

As we were talking, my coffee arrived. You had hot chocolate. I'd persuaded you to have the marshmallows and the whipped cream and you dipped the long silver spoon into the rich liquid, relishing every tiny taste. How extraordinary, I thought. Every girl I'd ever met had sucked up the frothy liquid like soup.

"Do you like it?" I asked.

"Oh it's wonderful. I've only had a couple of chocolates like this,"

It was still quiet in that corner with husky sounds of some mellow jazz singer weaving a gentle harmony with a saxophone. Outside, through the window, the river was a grey flooding rush of water.

I so wanted to stare at you. Finally, I took a deep breath and gazed intently, watching as your hair was drying into dark coils in the warmth of the coffee-shop. You lowered your eyes, maybe in modesty, but certainly as if you couldn't cope with my scrutiny. We could have been from the same family. Very dark hair…your complexion was clear and your nose covered with freckles – die sommersprosssen they call them in German – summer sprinkles. I would tell that you sometime. And then when you returned my gaze, your eyes were green like the river in the summer when it is slow and holds the reflection of the willow trees.

"I'm sorry, I'm staring at you," I said.

"No…no…it's OK. It's been good…I should leave…"

"Your mobile number? I'll print off those notes. In fact, you can have the whole year's notes then, maybe we could take another early morning like this?"

"But Mr Blight?"

"He won't know. Please will you come out again?" I pleaded.

You laughed. "It would be good."

And, after that, it was as if we had always known each other: as if we had been part of each other's lives. We huddled together under my black umbrella when the weather transgressed. And when we were apart, it felt so wrong so that we counted the hours until we were together again. I invited you back to my home but the boys wouldn't stop teasing, so you invited me back to your place and made me a rich soup full of tomatoes scented with coriander, paprika and chillies, and nestling in a covered basket were flat breads filled with chopped herbs, ground cumin and coriander seeds and decorated with sparkles of sea-salt. That time, you and I sat with dusk stealing the light, two contented people eating soup in our own world.

Our relationship grew. I managed to get you a cheap lap-top that one of the students was discarding and began to think of you as part of my day – you held my nights. It seemed only a matter of time before I would ask you to be with me – always.

I'd planned the perfect moment. I would prepare the most sensational picnic and then I'd ask you. Yes, of course there were doubts. Every other moment they flooded my mind. Whether my parents and yours would be happy for us. How we would manage the simple practicalities of our shared life, and then I'd ignore the bad thoughts pushing them away like a pile of unopened bills. It would be alright. We'd cope somehow. I forced my mind to return to the picnic and its reality.

I'd spread out a blanket – the birds of course would be singing and the earth underfoot would be firm from lack of rain. Oh Lord, I was even expecting the elements to oblige. Then I spent hours running through favourite recipes in my mind. Pasta? Not good cold…tends to go sticky. Pizza – also gluey cold – unless I bought it but that would spoil the moment. It had to be something that I could lift out of a bag in small dedicated containers and, as I prised open the lid on each specially prepared food, you would gasp and say, 'Yes, I love that! You know how much I love this!' Then after some wine, chilled of course, maybe rose, and some strawberries, placed in a basket and picked that day from the local fruit-farm heady with fragrance, you would find a small leather box with a ring at the base of the basket.

Crazy, crazy, what to cook? Something so redolent of good times. Then I remember how you talk of hummus – not the supermarket wallpaper-paste stuff but a real rich chick-pea dip. Yes, yes, that's better, and olives from our favourite corner shop and a quick pickle, and harissa – a hot spicy dip and a cucumber salad to cool the heat and falafel – chick pea balls –I can make them myself, the night before, in the apartment and I will heat them up just before I leave. And I will buy a paper tablecloth and serviettes and we will pretend that we are sitting next to the best damask linen and the bottle of cheap rose will be our champagne.

I cannot afford a ring – a proper ring – but I so need a ring. I hassle the owners of the second-hand shops for something I can use – it has to be gold or silver. Finally, the day before the picnic, Mr Oliver in the old bookshop says that he's had a ring with some books for payment. It is small but your fingers are tiny – it's the thinnest nine carat gold and a very small ruby twinkles from a small setting. It's not a good stone. I know that. But I feel that it has been worn with love.

It's the day of the picnic. I am nervous – more anxious than I can ever remember. It has rained all night and the ground is too wet to lay a blanket. I have to think of somewhere else. Then I remember Mrs Worthington's fire-escape. The old lady – the wife of an ex-lecturer who kind of adopted me when I came as a first year's student – a raw state of stammering anxiety. She'd found out about me at a students' supper and used to invite me with a few others for high tea. I was crazy about her slices of fruit bread – thickly sliced and heavily buttered. And on dark days when the sun had forgotten to emerge, I'd relish an invitation to sit beside a real fire with flames licking smoky over a handful of logs and toast crumpets on an old antique fork. Then we'd slather them with butter and eat through the charred outsides to reach the soft saturated insides. In the summer, Mrs. Worthington would often open the door to her fire-escape, leaving just a soft muslin curtain that caught the wind and hung over her pots of herbs and a honeysuckle that grew rampant over trellising.

Yes, yes, the perfect place. I rang her, explained my plan and she was more than happy for me to use her space.

'Would you like me to make some Bakewell tarts?'

'No, no – that's very kind, please don't trouble…I will bring everything.'

Finally, we reached the strawberries and the small leather box – not blue as I had imagined but a rich shade of maroon. You gasped as you opened it and slipped it on your middle finger.

"No," I said, "No." And placed it on your engagement finger.

"I want you to be my…"

I stared into your dark eyes lined with tears.

"But how…it's impossible with our fathers living on either side in countries which fight each other?"

"We have to… somehow…" I said

Now I see you every day stumbling over stones to reach the border between your country and mine to work with me in the same hospital and care for your people and mine – in a place of no barriers. I pray that one day there will be no wars and that your father will embrace my father and we will eat at the same table together.

One day, you will wear my ring.

Hummous

Ingredients

1 tin of chick peas, (approx 400-450g), save most of the salty water
1 tbsp of tahini
1 tsp of ground cumin seeds
1 tsp of paprika
handful of fresh thyme leaves plucked off the stalks or
1 tsp of dried leaves which are much stronger.
5 twists of black pepper
fresh coriander, fresh parsley

Method

Blend all the ingredients together in a food processor. Serve with a light sprinkle of cayenne for a hot taste or paprika for a milder taste chopped coriander and parsley and some good black olives.

Pitta Bread

Ingredients

500g Extra Strong white bread flour
1 sachet of easy blend yeast or 15g fresh yeast
1 tsp sugar
2 tsp salt
4 tbsp good olive oil
1 tsp mill ground cumin and coriander seeds – not essential but gives a spicy flavour.

Method

Sprinkle a little polenta on 2 baking sheets. Put a little of the flour in a bowl and whisk it with approx 300ml warm water (not hot), the sugar and the yeast and leave until it bubbles. Then add the olive oil and the salt to the rest of the flour, then combine the two mixtures. Knead into a silky ball and leave to rise in a warm place, covered with a tea-towel .When mixture has risen, punch back and divide into small pieces and roll each with a rolling pin into a pitta shape. Place on baking sheets with space to rise and leave until well risen again. Bake in a hot oven for 10 minutes until they are puffed and golden.

The Last Supper
by Christine Field

"Did you say the Dobsons are coming to dinner tonight Mum?" Lydia asked.

"That's right dear, about seven, I'd better get on".

"Dreadful people" Lydia muttered, helping herself to a slice of camembert.

I remembered how I used to love preparing dinner and having friends round when John was at home. I was still Mrs Jacobs then but we had lived separately for some three years now.

It all began when John, a barrister in chambers at Lincolns Inn, announced he was going off to Switzerland on a skiing weekend.

I hadn't questioned the trip; I was used to John's impetuosity after all he worked hard and was an excellent husband and father and I had no reason to suspect anything.

Success had come early to John and he had done very well. We led affluent lives, and John wouldn't have minded me doing something similar if the occasion had arisen.

I don't work now, but when we met twenty-three years ago I had been a social worker with the local Borough Council and whilse I enjoyed the work I had not been averse to giving it up when the children started to arrive. Marty, now twenty-two, Angharad, nineteen and Lydia, seventeen.

I can vividly recall the moment I found out about John's affair. It was the Sunday after he had been in Switzerland. There had been a telephone call for him from a woman, a stranger. I didn't think much about it at the time and forgot to mention it to John on his return. Unusually he had asked whether there had been any calls for him. I'd told him there had been one but she didn't leave her name. "Didn't you recognise the voice?" he'd asked and seemed to attach more importance to it than I had.

As the months passed, I noticed John was staying at work late into the evening more and more often, some weekends the family wouldn't see him at all. I was concerned about this but not suspicious.

The denouement, came about one hot summer's day in July. He arrived home and announced he was leaving. I didn't understand what he meant, but it was simple, he was having an affair and he wanted to leave me and the children and go and live with another woman. So that's what he did – and he's still away, I'm not sure whether the affair is still on.

John and I still speak on the phone, he visits the children but we never mention *it*.

Because, of John's affair, I had a breakdown and spent several months in hospital being treated for severe depression.

It was at this time that Delphine and Eric Dobson came into my life. I had vaguely known Eric in my social worker days, and it was whilse the Dobsons were visiting a relative in the same hospital that we struck up a friendship. I was glad of their company and looked forward to their visits. John too had visited me in hospital and also met the Dobsons at least once. After my release we stayed friends and I invited the Dobsons round for dinner on several occasions.

"What's on the menu, Mum?" enquired Lydia.

"Well, I thought we'd start with an aperitif, probably Vermouth, followed by crayfish bisque"

"Oh, is that what I can smell?"

"Yes, you probably remember Delphine's a fish person – for the main course bonito steaks, black potatoes, green aubergines and Julienne carrots with a parsley sauce"

"Bonito?" queried Lydia.

"Yes dear, it's a large oily fish of the tuna family. I've only tried it once before and it was delicious."

"I suppose I'll be managing on a cheese sandwich?"

"Probably dear, but I do have a good selection of cheeses."

"Are they getting a pudding?"

"Oh yes, *my* favourite, Tiramisu and if there's still a void I shall serve amerettinis with a dessert wine. What do you think?"

"Oh Mum, why do you always go so over the top whenever the Dobsons come round? What's so special about them anyway?"

"Nothing, it's just that they were so good to me when I was in hospital. And I do enjoy their company".

"But they never invite you for a meal do they?"

"No, but that's not the point."

"You still miss him terribly, don't you Mum?" Lydia asked.

"If you mean your Dad, of course I do dear, he was wonderful company and loved us all to bits."

"So why did he do it?"

"Have an affair? I don't really know, I suspect we still loved each other but were no longer in love there is a difference. Anyway I must get on and you've probably got something to do, too?"

The old grandfather clock in the study struck seven. I was just putting the finishing touches to my hair when the doorbell rang. "Can you get that for me, Lyd?" I called.

I could hear voices and came downstairs to welcome my guests. As I did so, my heart missed a beat, my hands felt clammy and I felt myself blush. "John? what are you doing here?"

"Thought I'd call round to see how things are, if that's OK? You look lovely Sue, are you going out?"

I just happened to be wearing John's favourite dress, a simple little scarlet chemise.

"No, just having a couple of friends round for dinner"

"Oh right, I'll be off then, perhaps we could get together sometime? Maybe go out for a meal, what do you think?"

"Yes, that would be nice" I replied.

Just then the doorbell rang again. I opened it and the Dobsons stood in the porch each with a bottle of wine.

"How lovely to see you both, do come in" I said. As they walked into the hall I glanced at John – he had turned the colour of my dress. Instinctively, I looked at Delphine who was also looking strange.

"John, you remember the Dobsons?" I asked.

"Yes of course, hello" said John.

After three years, I was pretty sure I knew who the other woman was.

Crayfish Bisque

Ingredients

1lb crushed crayfish shells
3 pt fish stock
1oz butter
1 tbsp olive oil
1 large carrot
3 shallots
2 celery sticks
1 leek
1 fennel bulb
1 garlic clove
1 star anaise
1 strip of orange zest
basil leaves
tarragon leaves
pinch soaked saffron
2fl oz brandy
4 tomatoes
1 tbsp tomato puree
½ bottle white wine
salt, black and cayenne pepper

Method

Dice all vegetables, crush garlic and quarter tomatoes. Melt butter with olive oil. Add diced vegetables, crushed garlic, star anise and orange zest, basil and tarragon. Add the pinch of saffron. Allow to cook on a medium heat for 10-15 minutes. Add crayfish shells, cook for a further 10 minutes. Add brandy and cook until almost dry. Add tomatoes, puree and simmer for 6-7minutes. Pour over white wine and reduce by half. Add fish stock and simmer for 20-30 minutes.

Liquidize mixture and strain to remove shells. Season with salt and peppers.

Recipe For Success
by Pam Weaver

As the Daimler slowed to a halt outside the chapel, she looked up and their eyes met. Marcel, Head Chef of the Première Hotel, waiting in line with the escort party, felt his heart lurch and his pulse quicken. As always whenever she turned to look at him, he was rooted to the spot.

A veil, which fell in blue smokey clouds from her broad-brimmed hat, covered her face. All the same, he caught just the hint of a smile as she ran the edge of her tongue along the bottom of her delicately coloured lips. Even in grief, he thought, she is so beautiful. The diamonds suited her so well.

"My mother-in-law had such beautiful jewellery," she'd once told him wistfully, and with a sigh, "but my husband always puts the restaurant first. I've only got a few trinkets."

Marcel had kissed her tenderly. He remembered how her eyes lit up when he'd given her the diamond earrings.

The black-coated funeral director crept slug-like between them and opened the car door. "This way, Madam..."

Chantelle took his outstretched hand and stepped out. Immediately, Marcel was consumed with jealousy. Why hadn't he thought to open the door and offer her a hand, damn it? If he'd been a bit quicker, he could have touched her one more time. How he longed to touch her – just one more time.

Their last meeting had been when they'd laid on the four poster bed in the Presidential Suite under a canopy of muslin curtains the day after the restaurant had finally made it to the five star billing. In that little room, they had both risen in an ecstasy of pleasure more wonderful than creating the lightest soufflé.

An involuntary groan escaped his lips. It had been so long, too long. Far too long. His throat tightened with desire and he forced himself to look away. As he turned, he accidentally trod on someone's foot. Marcel gave his victim a nod of apology but Pierre, the vegetable chef, hadn't even noticed. His eyes were on the grieving widow.

The pallbearers were lifting the coffin out of the hearse. Chantelle opened her handbag and appeared to be looking for something. She sniffed delicately.

Snatching his handkerchief from his top pocket, Pierre stepped forward and held it out for her. She took it with the briefest of smiles and he felt his knees turn to water.

She was wearing the diamond pendant he'd given her the last time they met. He would have liked to say something, but of course he couldn't. Her perfume hung in the air as she walked behind the pallbearers. Breathing deeply, Pierre followed, the small distance between them seeming more like a thousand miles. He watched the back of her silk dress caress her thighs and longed to give her just a crumb of comfort.

He'd always looked forward to those times when she opened the doors of her home to the staff, Madam Chantelle was the perfect hostess. She made everyone feel most welcome and she was the soul of discretion. No one knew of the honour she'd done him but being with her on the red leather chesterfield in the study was as dangerous a position as being under the feet of the Maitre 'd when the cauliflower is slightly over-cooked. He'd never known such a wonderful woman. So giving, so exciting, so needy.

He'd begged her to leave her husband but she was too loyal. It would harm the hotel team morale she said. She was old fashioned that way.

When he'd given her the necklace, costing half a year's salary, she'd cried, "Is this for little me? I can't believe you'd be so kind!"

The rest of the family melted into one long procession as the coffin was carried shoulder high into the crematorium. Pierre slid noiselessly into a pew, accidentally knocking someone's hat onto the floor as he shuffled to the end. Picking it up, he handed it to a rotund little man who nodded his head sharply.

Smith, the kitchen porter was beginning to feel embarrassed. He shouldn't have come. He knew that now. It was just that he wanted so badly to be there for Madam. He saw her looking round at the all the mourners and their eyes met. She touched her hat veil and his heart soared. She was wearing the diamond ring that once belonged to his great-great-grandmother on the little finger of her left hand. Wearing it for him! What a cracking woman she was! A real lady.

Smith began turning his hat round and round in an agitated way. He couldn't help it. He longed to dash out in front of all these stuffed shirts and say, 'Don't you worry, m'darlin'. I'm 'ere. I'll look out to you.'

As the first hymn began, he found his mind drifting back to the time when they'd begun their secret tryst in his porter's lodge. At first, he couldn't believe an amazing woman like her would be interested in someone like him. Maureen from the pub said he was 'a silly ol' fool,' and she was havin' a good laugh, but Madam, (he could never bring himself to call her Chantelle) made him feel like a million bloody quid. Their first meeting had come about after she'd popped out of the back entrance to buy her husband a surprise present. They'd bumped into each other and from that moment on he never complained when he had to empty the kitchen bins. If she was there, his heart would race and his knees would turn to jelly, especially if she gave him that certain look.

That's why he'd given her the ring. It was the only thing of value he'd got. It had been handed down through generation after generation of Smiths. She'd protested of course, but he'd insisted. He told her he'd be honoured if she'd wear it, and here she was, on the day of her husband's funeral, still doing her best to make him feel special.

Smith willed himself to concentrate on the eulogy, now being delivered by the head wine waiter, Jackson-Browne.

"Sir Reginald was a brilliant businessman," Jackson-Browne was saying, "He built up the reputation of The Première as the place to eat. Sir Reginald always had the well-being of his staff in mind..." His voice trailed off.

How could he say this stuff? Jackson-Browne shifted his feet, feeling very uncomfortable. Chantelle was looking straight at him. He tried to tell her how he felt with his eyes. 'My own dear Poppet, this must be hell for you...'

He noticed just the flicker of a smile on her lips and it gave him the courage to go on. She looked fantastic wearing the diamond brooch he'd given her last week. After what happened between them last night on the boardroom table, he'd buy her a bloody boatload if she'd let him. What a pity Sir Reginald never really understood the needs of a fantastic woman like her.

Jackson-Browne wished with all his heart that he could soothe all her pain away, but later on he'd have to watch her being hurt all over again. He'd heard about the old boy's will. What on earth had possessed the man? What did it mean? Why on earth, had her husband, a man only interested in the well-being of his staff, written a codicil which bequeathed his wife to The Première Hotel?

Marcel's Cheese Soufflé

Ingredients

25g butter
25g flour
150ml milk
½ tsp salt
½ tsp mustard
pinch cayenne pepper
3 eggs
75g cheese (either all Cheddar or half Cheddar half Parmesan.)

Method

Melt butter, add flour and cook gently over a moderate heat in a saucepan. Gradually add the milk, stirring all the time. Remove from heat and add salt, cayenne pepper and mustard.
Add the egg yolks and stir.
Stir in grated cheese.
Using another clean bowl, beat the egg whites until they stand in a firm peak.
Fold the stiffened egg whites gently into the soufflé mixture with a metal spoon.
Pour into a greased soufflé dish.
Place in oven set at 190ºC375ºF/gas mark 5. Cook for 30 minutes and serve with green watercress and lettuce salad.

The Watercress Wife
by Tamar Hodes

Hundreds of green butterfly wings tickled the roof of Gideon's mouth, the paper petals of exotic flowers torn from their stem. Watercress, the sensuous nothingness in his mouth, and then the sting it left on his tongue afterwards. His mother grew it in chalky ponds and ripped it in bunches for him to eat in salads. Or she'd boil it in water, push it through a mesh sieve and puree it, with cream stirred slowly in. Gideon sat at the huge kitchen table, sipping his soup from a white porcelain bowl. Through one square of the window frame, he could see his father, a small figure in the distance, feeding corn to the chickens or tying hay bales and loading them onto the tractor.

Behind him, the pine dresser was laden with jars of pickles and chutneys, which his mother had made and labelled. Onions glistened like whole moons in vinegar, marmalade heavy with orange rind, lemon curd the colour of sunlight.

On spring days, Gideon and his mother took a basket and collected wild flowers, which grew in clusters around the farm. Wood anemones and meadow cranesbill, willowherb taller than his head and field woodrush. The names alone were poetry to him. Back home, they'd empty their basket of gatherings onto the kitchen table, shake the grass seedlings away and then press the petals between giant sheets of blotting paper, soaking up the flowers' sap. The layers would be placed under heavy books and hidden until the winter. Then, beside a log fire, the pages would be uncovered and there, between the sheets, pressed and faded, were remnants of spring, flattened but preserved. These were stuck in a book and recorded so that Gideon and his mother kept an album not only of their lives but of the changing life of the farm and of the land itself.

When it grew dark and Gideon was tucked up between clean cotton sheets, his mother gave him hot cocoa and read to him. Gulliver's Travels, Alice in Wonderland, Daddy Longlegs, Arabian Nights, so by the time he fell asleep each night, his head was swimming with magic and satin and purples and gold. His father sat downstairs and sharpened tools by the fire.

Leaving Mother and the farm was a terrible blow, one that Gideon had dreaded many times but luckily he was extricated from it by necessity. His father died, a stranger till the end, and his mother moved into sheltered accommodation. Gideon did not know that the farm was only rented to them, had never thought of such things and therefore there was not much money left. Gideon and his mother could not bear to look back as the removal van pulled away from the farm and towards the nearest town. They both knew, without saying so, that they had left paradise and that they could never re-enter.

Gideon was lost: taste and smell and love were dead to him. In the town library where he worked stacking shelves, Gideon passed the day, trying to focus on the wording on the spines and where they should go and to push from his mind thoughts of their former home. The dresser with the gleaming jars, the chickens pecking at the ground, the tiny flowers dotted in the grass, these flooded his head and the pleasure they brought was too much to bear.

Back home in the evening, he'd cook himself a simple meal and then go to visit his mother. She was frail now but seemed quite happy in her little flat, with its modern kitchen and bathroom and tiny bed-sitting room. In this new home were memories of the farm – a framed watercolour of the house which Gideon had painted as a child, the album with its pressed flowers, now faded and flat, books of farmhouse recipes which his mother would never make again. The page edges were floury and egg-stained. Like the album, its contents seemed to lack energy and life.

Nowadays, Gideon read to his mother but she had been a better reader than she was an audience. She often fell asleep when Gideon read to her and he'd take his coat and slip quietly away.

Gideon had few friends. There were Carl and Annie who had lived in the neighbouring farmhouse whom he occasionally saw, but, once they had moved away, he lost touch with them.

Then Gideon met Jilly. She often came into the library where he'd now been promoted to working on the desk, a job he didn't feel suited to as it involved answering so many questions. He didn't mind pointing out the guides on birds to an older lady or stamping the books that were being taken out but he didn't feel easy with articulate children from nearby villages who demanded recent publications or young women who asked him questions in what he felt was a flirtatious way. Gideon had never thought of himself as good-looking, he had never considered it but women did seem to be drawn to him. He wondered if it was his mother's influence, maybe they felt he understood women.

Jilly, some years older than Gideon, didn't flirt; he liked her serious attitude to life. She worked in an office in the high street but would come in during her lunch hour to choose books. She liked reading fiction but often went to the reference section too, if she wanted to look something up in an atlas or find out the name of a flower she'd seen. She wanted Gideon to serve her even though he was not a trained librarian and the other members of staff knew much more than he did.

Jilly, it seemed, was a fast reader as she would take away a pile of books and return with them a few days later with a variety of cast-iron verdicts on them: one was disappointing at the end, another was hard to believe, the third poorly paced. Gideon found her so critical that finding books to please her was a challenge. He'd set them aside during the week with a reserved sticker on them, a special pile for Jilly. She seemed pleased although she was never exuberant.

When summer came, she asked Gideon to have his lunch break with her. He brought his own lunch from home, she brought hers and they would walk out together and find a park bench to sit on. Gideon had pies in his lunchbox, salad and fruit but Jilly had white bread with cheese in the middle. He noticed how plain everything to do with Jilly was: her clothes, her speech, her food. Nothing was ornate. However, they talked easily together. Gideon described his childhood on the farm and Jilly talked about her work and the novels she liked to read.

After Gideon's mother died, he found himself asking Jilly to marry him. It seemed a necessary next step, not an event which inspired him with excitement or gave him wild dreams but the next logical progression in their relationship.

The wedding was simple and small as neither of them had much family and afterwards they moved into a rented cottage with a garden which backed onto a stream. It reminded Gideon a little of the farm as did the many mementoes which his mother had left him: the paintings, the photographs, the recipe books, the album.

He knew that Jilly thought him sentimental. She kept nothing of her late parents with her, nothing of her past, as if she didn't have one, as if she started afresh each week with each new batch of library books. She never looked forward or back. She lived each day as it arrived.

It was soon after their wedding that the differences between Jilly and Gideon came to light. Gideon's love of home-made food was sneered at by his wife who felt that food should be plain and functional. She stared dismissively at the pile of chutney at the side of his plate or the way he picked wild flowers and put them in a jug on the table. She did not say so but she sometimes thought him effeminate, his attention to detail, his desire to pretty the cottage with floral curtains and painted plates on the walls.

When they first married they made love sometimes, neither of them with a desperate desire and without great satisfaction. It gradually petered out. It didn't mean enough to either of them to initiate and so it remained dormant, a slight stirring in Gideon's loins which he ignored, in Jilly, a lack of interest.

Their early years were marked by mutual indifference. Neither had the impetus to leave and there seemed no reason to but they lived as lodgers in the same house more than husband and wife. However, as the years passed, Jilly began increasingly to mock her husband and his gentle ways.

"How many men do you know who look at albums of pressed flowers in the evenings?" she'd ask.

"They remind me of the farm," said Gideon. "Mother and I used to…"

"You always talk about your mother, not your father. Where was he, for goodness sake?"

"Working on the farm. It was just Mother and me and the meadows and the fields."

And he kept his mother alive in his way of life, the flowers, his love of food.

After a few years, Gideon and Jilly had earned enough to buy the cottage. Feeling the land to be his in a way that he had assumed the farmland was his, Gideon began to grow vegetables, sow wild flowers in the meadows. When the first batch of plums ripened, he picked them and made jars of spicy plum chutney which he labelled and stored on the shelves. All this while Jilly looked on, sneeringly. He didn't mind as long as she left him alone. She was a presence, at times an irritating one, but he was stuck with her and he could manage. He gained his pleasure from work and his garden, his cooking and, increasingly, his painting. There was enough for him to enjoy. Like the smell of damp in their cellar, Jilly could be overlooked.

But over the years, she not only mocked his hobbies, she started to deny him the pleasures he had.

"You're spending too much money on plants," she told him. "What do I indulge in? My books come from the library, my clothes are second hand. Why should all our spare money go on your cooking and your plants?"

"But you could have something if you wanted." said Gideon.

He looked at his wife's sour face. She was getting worse as she grew older, her health deteriorating.

"I want you to give up the excess," she said.

"What excess?"

"The frilly things. The… the watercress. The flowers. Why must everything with you be so excess to requirements?"

Gideon was hurt at first. Then he was resigned. He would renounce something; maybe he was too self-indulgent. He gave up watercress. He tore up the small patch he had grown before it had begun to spread wildly and ate one last feast of it: green flutter on his tongue. Sheer delight.

But that didn't satisfy her. Jilly's health was bad, her moods almost deranged.

"Stop it," she'd cry out so loudly that Gideon was ashamed of what passers-by would think, "give up the silly little jugs with wild flowers. Give up the labelling of jars. Give them all up."

And he did, partly frightened by the violent shaking of the head and her delirious fits and partly because she made him ashamed that maybe he was not a whole man. Maybe she was right.

It was only in Jilly's last few months that Gideon actually grew to loathe her. When the doctor came and diagnosed a weak heart, Gideon thought to himself, "I didn't know she had one" and when he took his wife a bowl of soup in bed, he found the sight of her repulsive. Her face was small and grey above the white sheets, the skin on her hands shrivelled and veined like blue cheese. He wished that she would die, so that he could fill up his drained life with water and joy again. She had denied him everything: physical comfort and beauty and pleasure and love. Every gift Mother had given him she had taken away.

When Jilly died in her sleep, he was relieved. Her death felt like his rebirth.

And he flourished. His garden was full of colour and life, frilly lettuces and bushy potato plants, bloodshot tomatoes and plump pumpkins. And he cooked and he painted and he grew back again, like a pruned bush.

At the bottom of the garden, near the stream, Gideon built a pond. The ground was chalky and the running water supply made it a perfect site for growing watercress. In the centre of the pond he put a statue. He had seen it, grey-stoned and harsh, in a garden centre and it reminded him of Jilly, the tight mouth, the cold stare. He placed it in the centre of the watercress which grew in abundance around it, a huge circle of green petals.

And whenever he wanted to, Gideon went down to the pond, lay stomach down on the grass in the sunlight and ripped bunches of watercress. He let the leaves fall on his tongue and melt into his throat. The sting lay on his tongue for seconds and he relished it, looking up at the stony, unsmiling face of his wife.

Watercress Soup

Ingredients
2 bunches watercress
1½pt chicken stock
salt & pepper
single cream

Method
Sauté the watercress in a little butter. Add the chicken stock, some salt and pepper and bring to the boil. Simmer for about 20 minutes. Liquidise. Then add a swirl of cream before serving.

Trapped
by Linda Povey

I was clearing away the remains of the salad and finger buffet, to make room for the sweets, when I felt a hand on my shoulder. I automatically shook it off before turning to see who it belonged to. A stocky, middle-aged man stood there leering at me.

"Best part of these conferences, the food and drink," he said, his voice close to my ear. He smelt strongly of alcohol. I took a step away.

"Well, I'm glad you enjoyed the food," I said. It paid to be polite to customers, whoever they were.

"You responsible for all this?" he asked, gesturing towards the tables.

"I'm the outside caterer, yes," I told him.

"Is it a sign of age when the caterers seem very young?" he asked with a smirk.

"No, I am very young," I said, "I opened up the business almost as soon as I left school."

"Doing well?"

"Yes, very well. I've always got a full diary." I kept my face expressionless, but couldn't resist a little bragging. I was proud of my achievements. From a very early age, I'd been given lessons in cooking by my mother. Bless her. She'd brought me up single-handed and made a good job of it, though times had been hard. She'd never enjoyed good health and wasn't able to go out to work. I was glad to be able to afford lots of treats for her now.

"I must say, you're an extremely pretty caterer." The man leaned towards me.

"Thank you," I said stiffly. I made my exit as quickly as I could and did my best to avoid him for the remainder of the afternoon. Lecherous drunks I could do without.

I was the last to leave – but then I usually am. I like to make sure everything is nice and tidy before the cleaners come. No cake crumbs on the tables or half-eaten sausage rolls lurking in the corners. I hadn't built up my business by being sloppy.

I balanced my cardboard box of dishes and utensils on my knee as I pressed the button for the elevator. As it arrived, I heard footsteps behind me and a voice say, in rather slurred speech, "Well, well, it's the pretty caterer. Can I help you with that?"

I looked over my shoulder and recognised the drunkard from the conference. He was even worse for drink now.

He took my box off me before I could reply. There was nothing for it but to go through the doors, though I could've thought of people I'd rather share an empty lift with.

The elevator, like the building, was old. It moved downwards at a slow pace. I was uncomfortably aware that the man was eyeing me up.

"I thought everyone had gone," I said.

"I popped into my office to pick up a couple of things."

"You work in the building then?" I asked.

"I'm Executive Managing Director of Wilkinson Distributions."

'Get you,' I thought but said, "That's nice."

He stood next to the controls, the box in his two hands. I shall never know whether it was by accident or on purpose, but his elbow hit the STOP button as the lift gave a sudden jolt. We came to a halt.

"What have you done!" I cried. I leapt forward and pressed the ground floor button. Nothing happened. I began pressing the other buttons, with the same result.

The man put my box down. "No point in panicking, love, that won't get you anywhere." He gave an ominous laugh. "Anyway, I can think of worse things than being stuck here with you. I'm sure we can find some ways to amuse ourselves."

I ignored the insinuation. "We'll have to shout for help," I said.

"Go on, then," the man told me.

I shouted and screamed, "Hello! Hello! Is anyone there!" as I banged on the sides of the elevator and on the doors.

He stood watching, a stupid grin on his face.

"Aren't you going to help?" I asked.

"You seem to be making enough noise for the two of us," he said. "Relax. The cleaners will be here soon. Might as well make ourselves comfortable while we wait." He put his arm round me and tried to pull me down with him onto the floor.

"Leave me alone!" I cried. I sprang away from him. In his inebriated state, he was too slow to stop me.

He sank down clumsily on his own. "Please yourself," he said. I moved well away to discourage him from trying any more tricks like that.

The next few seconds passed in silence as I prayed for the lift to start moving. When it didn't I began pressing buttons, then banging and shouting again. All to no avail.

"I think you'll have to resign yourself to waiting for the cleaners," the man said.

I went and sat in the corner furthest from him. It was still too near for my liking. The lift was very small.

The man kept his eyes on me. I was uncomfortably aware that he was studying me from head to toe. I pulled my skirt over my knees.

"You really are an attractive girl," he said in a low voice. "Got a boyfriend?"

"Yes," I said, though I hadn't. "Married are you?"

He guffawed. "You could say that. Doesn't stop me having a bit of fun now and then." He lowered his voice. "I'm always very discreet, you understand. My wife thinks I'm the perfect husband."

I shrank further into my corner. "Do you have children?" I asked.

"Two. That I know of." He laughed out loud. "Could be more. Had a bit of a misspent youth too."

"What do you mean?" I asked.

"Got around a bit." He winked. "To tell you the truth, I know at least one of my ex-girlfriends had a baby by me."

"And what did you do about it?" I asked, anger suddenly taking over from fear. He'd touched a raw nerve.

"Nothing. She tried to get me to marry her. Huh, as if I'd want to throw my life away on the likes of her."

"And did you support the child?"

"Did I hell! How do I know it's mine? I said. Though to be honest, I was certain it was. I'm pretty sure she was a virgin before we met and she was too besotted by me to play around while we were seeing each other."

"What did she have, boy or girl?" I asked.

"No idea. I made myself scarce before it was born. But I gave her fifty quid. She should have been grateful."

I stared at him. "My father did that."

The man frowned. "Did what?"

"Gave my mother fifty pounds when she got pregnant with me. Then left her."

"Well, that's a bit of a coincidence. Still, I suppose..."

"She never saw him again and he never asked about me. I know his name, though."

The man fingered his collar. "Oh, yes, and what was that?"

"Kenton. Kenton Fernley."

I hadn't seen anyone go pale like that before. His previously red cheeks were now chalk-white.

"That's...an unusual name," he said faintly.

"Isn't it? I was given my mother's surname, I'm pleased to say. Wouldn't have wanted to be associated with *his*. Mind you, I've often thought of trying to find him. I got the impression he wasn't short of money. Perhaps I could twist a bit of cash out of the swine." I narrowed my eyes. "Yes, maybe I will do that. Probably get quite a bit out of him. I imagine it would be greatly inconvenient if his family found out about me."

The effect this had on the man was quite a revelation. His mouth dropped open and he literally squirmed in front of me. But he was saved a reply when the lift gave a lurch and began to move. "Oh, thank God for that!" he cried, jumping to his feet.

I stood up, slowly. "I thought you were enjoying the experience," I said with a smile.

The doors opened when we reached ground level and a woman in a cleaner's overall stood waiting.

"Oh, hello Mr. Fern..."

"Just off now, Jenny, " he interrupted. "Well, bye then, Miss er..."

"Taylor," I said, picking up my box. "Susie Taylor." I turned as I walked away. "I never did ask your name either?"

"John Smith," the man replied hurriedly. The cleaner gave him a strange look.

I walked towards the car. My mother had been abandoned by my father before I was born. That much was true. Not the rest. Still, I hoped my words would give that wretched man an uncomfortable time for a bit longer. Until he realised that the name tag he'd worn for the conference was still attached to his lapel.

Main Course

Home-grown Talent

by Rachel Sargeant

January 1st

Okay so Christmas dinner wasn't perfect. Four sherry-fuelled hours I spent in that kitchen. Anyone can forget to switch on the oven. The turkey was fine in the end, nothing a little surgical amputation and a microwave couldn't fix.

It's just that Gerry always finds something to pick on. Fancy hiding the mince pies and telling me my love handles are getting too loving. It's all right for him, so lean and handsome. I'll show him. I'll make next Christmas one to remember.

January 9th

Have signed on for "Fun and Fasting with Fiona" – there's a contradiction in there somewhere – and "British Cookery for All Seasons". Nigel, the cookery teacher, seems friendly but I doubt he'll stay all year. He's a chef and he's good-looking so he's bound to land a Reality TV contract by April. Fiona the Faster is all right, too, in a half-starved kind of way.

Gerry's not keen on the British cookery idea. He was thinking more Italian. Tortellini and trimmings for next Christmas, then?

January 16th

I was wrong about Fasting Fiona. She's not nice at all. She's banished butter and ice cream and chocolate. Is she nuts? Oh, no, she's banned them, too. At least she would have approved of tonight's cookery lesson. We made winter soup packed with low calorie onions, turnips and carrots. Nigel the chef said he didn't know anything about its slimming qualities. It was just something hefty to stoke up our insides on a cold night. It worked for me.

Gerry was out when I got back so I did FF's homework and cleared out the kitchen cupboards. No more crisps, biscuits, pastries, pickles and salad cream.

January 17th
I'm in the doghouse. Gerry's furious that I've binned his Parmesan cheese. He isn't the one with the problem. I should have just exercised self-control.

February 14th
My first weigh-in with FF. Don't ask!

In a change from our usual Valentine's night out, Gerry invited his new PA, Maria, to dinner. She's stick thin but nothing a square meal wouldn't fix. And I did my best on that score. I served up the Lancashire Hot Pot I made at yesterday's lesson. I'm supposed to be off red meat but what can you do? Nigel really knows how to make a sauce, all rich and dark, and thick enough to coat the back of his spoon. The five fluid ounces of white wine helped. (That would be 150ml in Italian money but the wine was English, crisp and zesty). I'm not sure whether I preferred the aroma of the hotpot or the new aftershave that Gerry has taken to wearing. He was the perfect host, chatting to Maria all evening. Apparently she prefers a Neapolitan diet. I should have shoved Lambrusco in the stew.

March 12th
No weight change. Fasting Fiona, owner of the same broken record collection as Gerry, says I lack willpower.

Gerry working late, so I stayed on after cookery to eat my Sticky Toffee Pudding with Nigel. My, my, we did get our fingers in a mess.

I was wrong about Nigel. He's not really a chef. He's a metalwork teacher. He got into cookery after his girlfriend left him but, cooking for one, he piled on the pounds. He looks fine to me, better than those wiry guys you see about the place.

April 16th
Have just had an out-of-this-taste experience. Nigel's Caramel Slice. One bite and I hit Nirvana. After chewing through the smooth gooiness, there was the most delectable aftertaste as the hardness of the biscuit base crumbled. Nigel said he likes to see a girl enjoying her food. I managed to save a box of slices for Gerry. Don't know what he's done with them.

May 14th

Had to miss the weigh-in (hooray) and cookery (boohoo) because Maria came to dinner. Gerry said I could go anyway and he'd manage without me. But I could hardly let him cater for Maria all on his own. What kind of hostess would that make me? I phoned Nigel. He gave me the recipe in advance: country-house fish pie. Maria said she would have preferred Linguini with it. She doesn't like British food apart from cakes. She said she was given some homemade caramel slices recently, quite tasty. Perhaps she'd like to try Glazed Lemon Tart. It's so her.

June 11th

I've lost two pounds. How on earth did that happen?

Been practising my Victoria Sponge as a surprise for Gerry. Phoned his office to check what time he gets back from his conference but no-one is sure as his PA is away too. Took the cake to the cookery lesson instead. Nigel said it oozed with the best sweetness he'd ever tasted.

July 9th

I've been reunited with my missing pounds, and they've brought a couple of pals along with them.

Tonight we made trifle at cookery. Nigel is so cutting edge. The recipe said four fluid ounces of sherry but Nigel said rules are there to be broken.

August 31st

Gerry at another conference, this time in Naples of all places. No courses this month but I've been trying out a few recipes – Colcannon, gammon in cider, steak and kidney pudding. Lots of phone calls to Nigel. Such a great mentor.

September 10th

Maria came to dinner. She's looking well. Great sun tan. Nigel popped round to help me prepare the beef stew. When I'm with him I feel I can be just a little adventurous, so I mashed the potatoes with fresh thyme and piped them into nests. Nigel went one better and added chestnuts to the dumplings. Gerry and Maria thought the nutty taste was "interesting". They were quite constructive in their way, suggesting a few new dishes I could try next time, like torta verde and polpi affogati. I looked that one up – drowned octopus – they're welcome to it.

<u>October 29th</u>
Gerry is out at his office Halloween party. He said he wouldn't dream of pressurizing me into going with him. Far be it from him to ride roughshod over my interests. So I went to the weigh-in. My new weight? I forget.

Bumped into Maria on the way to cookery. Nearly didn't recognize her in her black rubber mini dress and witch's hat. Stayed on for bubble and squeak and pumpkin pie with Nigel. Those two pickled cucumbers really perked up the Wow Wow sauce. I felt quite sustained afterwards.

<u>November 21st</u>
Must make the Christmas pudding but my heart's not in it. According to FF, it's lettuce and low fat yoghurt for me this yuletide. Wonder if I can substitute Slimma margarine for suet. Must ask Nigel.

Gerry is still dropping hints about going Italian this year. I suppose I could use panettone breadcrumbs in the pudding but I draw the line at stuffing the bird with pesto.

<u>December 1st</u>
Nigel phoned. So masterful. He says there's no such thing as a low fat Christmas. He's given me a list of ingredients for the next course. It's going to be Roast Bubbly-Jock. That's turkey Highland-style with a shot or three of Scotch in the gravy. It'll be a great rehearsal for Christmas lunch. I'm getting it right this year. Even Gerry won't complain. Hope he doesn't make me swap the Scotch for Frascati.

<u>December 10th</u>
Fasting Fiona tried not to look too relieved when I didn't sign on for next year. At least Gerry's stopped asking about the weigh-ins. He doesn't seem hung up on my figure these days. He's so much more considerate in many ways. It's the office Christmas party tonight but he's letting me go to cookery instead. He looks dapper enough in his dinner jacket but I'm going off the aftershave.

December 11th

Got home very late last night, stayed for chat with Nigel and lost track of time. Do you know that you should cook turkey on its side to let the juices run down the breast to keep it moist? Thought provoking.

Gerry home even later. He's invited Maria for Christmas lunch and he's insisting on Italian.

December 26th

Had the best Christmas dinner ever. We fed each other on just-right juicy turkey, honey-roasted parsnips and chestnut sprouts, all crunchy and soft at the same time. Each tender forkful carried a hint of bread sauce, fired up with peppercorns. And, yes, all coated in whisky gravy. Then we stuffed ourselves senseless on mince pies with double cream brandy butter.

Gerry and Maria had Italian. At least they will have done if Gerry remembered to defrost the tiramisu. The pizza could be cooked from frozen.

Must stop now. Nigel is bringing me breakfast in bed. That's a full English breakfast.

Nigel's Bubbly-Jock

Ingredients

1 x 5kg (12lb) turkey
100g (4oz) butter and oil
1 carrot
1 onion
1 bunch of mixed herbs
1 glass of whisky (the recipe says a small glass but you know Nigel)
1 tbsp cornflour
150ml (¼ pint) double cream

Method

Preheat oven to 170ºC, 325ºF, Gas Mark 3.
Spread butter and oil over turkey and place it on its side in the roasting tin. Roast for 30 minutes, baste occasionally.
Turn on to other side, roast for another 30 minutes, baste occasionally.
Finish cooking breast upwards for approx another 3 hours.
(Allow 20 minutes per 450g (1lb) for the total cooking time.)

Gravy

Boil giblets in pan with 1.7l (3 pts) of water.
Skim.
Simmer with carrot, onion and herbs for 90 minutes.
Strain.
Take the fat from the turkey tin and pour in the whisky.
Boil strongly for 2 minutes.
Stir in cornflour. Keep stirring constantly.
Gradually add the strained stock, stirring constantly.
Pour in cream and stir to obtain a smooth gravy.
Serve with your favourite seasonal trimmings.

The Birthday Party
by Rosemarie Rose

Cottage pie was one of my favourite meals, but Matthew's announcement had completely ruined my appetite. I stared miserably at my plate as he scribbled down the recipe for tomorrow night's dinner party.

Marriage to a chef-turned-restaurateur who criticised my every meal was bad enough; but, even worse, he refused point blank to cook at home, insisting that somewhere deep within me and every other woman on the planet – lurked a budding Delia. What he really meant was that he had better things to do with his free time, like golfing with his mates. And now, horror of horrors, he expected me to cook posh nosh for his snooty mother's birthday.

He slid the recipe across the table. "Pork fillet braised in French cider and Calvados. Served on a bed of crushed celeriac, with red onion marmalade and asparagus hollandaise." He kissed the tips of his fingers with vomit-inducing drama. "Even you should be able to manage that."

It was that scornful *you* which finally pushed me over the edge.

"Stuff your recipe!" I threw down my cutlery, splattering the snowy cloth with gravy. "Your family ate here for the last time on Sunday. I've had enough of your mother's and grandfather's insults!"

Matthew's grandfather, a Michelin-starred chef trained in France, had taught Matthew the business. In my view, their posh restaurant with its overpriced cuisine attracted folk with more money than sense. What on earth was wrong with traditional British food?

Matthew's jaw dropped. "You cooked roast again, for the third Sunday running! And the potatoes were burnt to a crisp! Of course they complained!"

But there was no stopping me now. "You listen to me for once, Matthew Jones. This house is not a restaurant. The potatoes were fine. *My* parents didn't complain, and neither did your father. But the chef gene clearly skipped a generation there – he likes normal food, has perfect manners, and hates playing stupid games with metal sticks and dimpled balls!"

Matthew gaped, incredulous. "And what does he like? Playing stupid games with paints and easels!" His eyes narrowed. "Stop being childish, Sara. It's not their fault Henri's place burnt down last night. And our own chef's snowed under with bookings. There's nowhere else half-decent for fifty miles. They're eating here and that's that. Dad said he might be late so I've deliberately picked a dish that won't spoil if he is. I know how you panic and cock things up when guests don't turn up on time."

"Oh thank you so much for your consideration! But I'm telling you now, if I have to cook this pork and cider crap…"

"*Porc au Cidre,*" corrected Matthew, impatiently waving the recipe under my nose. "Can't you read?"

I glared at the man I'd once loved with a passion, the man who'd stolen my heart on my first day at *A Jones & Partners, Solicitors*. Matthew had dropped in to quiz his father on some legal matter concerning the restaurant and Cupid's arrows had found their marks (my heart and Matthew's groin). To his mother's horror – county set I'm not – we married less than six months later.

I drew a deep breath and began again. "As I was saying before I was so rudely interrupted, if I have to cook this crap myself I swear I'll poison the pair of them!"

"Sara!" Matthew slumped back in bewilderment. "What on earth's got into you?"

"Three years of you and the twins from hell pick-pick-picking on me, that's what! And I'm surprised you haven't found fault with this yet!" I snatched up my knife and repeatedly stabbed my cottage pie.

Matthew's face lit up. "Now you mention it, purple garlic would have improved this boring dish no end..."

Fighting back murderous thoughts, I leapt to my feet, grabbed Matthew's dinner plate and held it over his head. "Matthew! I'm warning you...!"

Gravy dripped from the rim and plopped into Matthew's wine. His face turned the colour of pickled beetroot. "Sara, you idiot! That's vintage Bordeaux!"

With an exasperated scream, I upturned the plate. Gravy slithered down Matthew's face like molten lava, closely followed by carrots, onion, mince and mash.

Grabbing my mobile phone from the sideboard en route, I fled into the garden and threw myself on to the rustic bench in the rose arbour. I rang Alex, my closest friend and the only person who would understand.

"I can't stand it another minute!" I wailed. "I have to get out of here before I go insane…" My voice wobbled and the floodgates opened.

As always, Alex eventually managed to calm me down, and before long I was laughing. Alex had hatched the perfect plan.

The following evening, I stood and admired the dressed dining-table. Even Matthew's picky family couldn't fail to be impressed.

The doorbell chimed. I opened the door to the hall to find Matthew greeting his mother and grandfather. Pinning on a brilliant smile, I joined them.

"Happy birthday, Muriel. Evening, George."

Muriel, Matthew's mother, was tall, thin and chic. She looked me up and down with undisguised disdain. She must have been beautiful once, in an ice-queen sort of way; but too many face-lifts meant she now bore more than a passing resemblance to a shrink-wrapped skull.

George, Matthew's grandfather, was even taller and thinner. He sniffed noisily, like a pig foraging for truffles. "Can't smell a damn thing. Seems your cooking's lost its aroma as well as its flavour!"

I winced as the hallway rang with their laughter, Matthew joining in with accustomed enthusiasm.

"Oh, George!" Muriel gasped, dabbing at the corners of her surgically-elongated eyes with a tissue. "You're such a comedian!"

I sighed. How Matthew's father had put up with them for so long was a mystery. Working for him, I'd soon found out how different he was from the rest of his family. Sadly, his father and wife had pooh-pooh'd his artistic talents and pushed him into a legal career he hated. But like most of his colleagues, who were happy to cover for him, I knew he'd secretly rented an artist's studio in Cornwall a long time ago, in order to preserve his sanity.

As a result, fictitious legal seminars in far-flung corners of the world were a regular event.

Muriel composed herself. “Burnt beef again, is it, Sara dear?” she asked, checking her mascara and eyeliner for laughter damage in the hall mirror.

“Oh, much better than that, Muriel dear.”

“I hope so,” growled George, peering in the mirror over Muriel’s shoulder and fingering his neat, grey moustache. “Sunday’s roast potatoes were the worst I’ve ever eaten. Even in this house.”

I shrieked with mock laughter. “Oh, George!” I mimicked. “You’re such a comedian!”

Three heads swivelled towards me. Their amazed expressions said it all: where was the mouse they’d reduced to tears again last Sunday?

Matthew recovered his composure first. “Dad’s been delayed at work again. But he won’t be long so you can get the asparagus on. And Sara – no longer than six minutes before you test it, please!”

I gave his arm a soothing pat. “Don’t panic, darling. Everything’s under control. Now come with me…”

I ushered the dumbstruck trio into the dining-room. Silver gleamed and glassware sparkled in the candlelight. “*Porc au Cidre*,” I announced with a smug smile at Matthew before indicating the large covered serving-dish in the centre of the table. “Enjoy your meal. I’m off.”

Tyres crunched on the gravel drive outside the window as I exited the room through a brief, shocked silence. Then everyone spoke at once.

“Sara! Where the hell do you think you’re going?”

“It’s PMT – she’ll be back.”

“I expect that’s your father – let’s eat.”

As I collected my packed suitcase from the hall cupboard, my mother-in-law’s scream echoed from the dining-room. Despite the need for a speedy withdrawal, I couldn’t resist a final peek and I stuck my head around the door.

Matthew, holding the lid of the silver dish aloft, stood silent, eyes bulging, mouth flapping open and closed like that of a distressed trout on a riverbank. I watched gleefully as Muriel and

George reached into the dish and drew out a string of raw pork sausages and a bottle of cider.

"Do-it-yourself *Porc au Cidre*," I called. "Enjoy!"

Laughing, I left the house for the last time, slamming the front door behind me with a flourish. I found space for my case in the back of the waiting car and slid into the passenger seat.

"Alex, it was brilliant! The looks on their faces…!"

Alex laughed. "Tell me all about it later, when we're safely underway."

Wheels spun on gravel and the vehicle shot along the drive. As we bounced onto the main road, a mouth-watering smell reached my nostrils. I greedily sniffed the air.

"Oooh, Alex…! Is that what I think it is?"

Grinning, Alex changed gear and stamped on the accelerator pedal. Tyres squealed. "The carrier bag on that pile of canvases on the back seat – fish and chips and a carton of mushy peas. I guessed you might be hungry."

I grabbed the carrier and tenderly kissed the corner of his mouth before settling back in my seat. "I love you, Alex Jones! No more fictitious seminars for either of us. Cornwall here we come – for good, this time!"

Macaroni With Sardine And Garlic Sauce

(Serves 4 to 6)

Ingredients

450g macaroni
150ml olive oil
50g butter
2 large cloves garlic, coarsely chopped
100g tinned sardines, drained and filleted
4 tbsp fresh parsley, finely chopped
275ml dry white wine, cider or lager
ground black pepper and grated nutmeg to taste
3 tbsp fine breadcrumbs

Method

Cook the macaroni. While it cooks, make the sauce.
Heat the oil and butter in a large pan. Add the garlic, sardines and parsley. Break up the fish and cook the mixture gently for 5 minutes. Drain the macaroni and rinse quickly in cold water. Add to the sauce and stir well. Then add the wine, pepper, nutmeg and breadcrumbs, and stir with a fork until the macaroni is completely covered with the sauce. Serve at once.

Setting The Scene
by Ginny Swart

Abby paused in front of the frozen section of the supermarket. Crab patties for starters or seared aubergine with goat's cheese and olives? This dinner was going to be her final assault on James's uncommitted heart and no expense was too great. She popped both into her basket.

Abby had been dating James for six months and she was in love with every bit of him. Apart from all the sterling qualities in his character, she admired the way he played the guitar and his way of telling a joke, sort of hesitant but laughing so loudly half way through she could hardly hear the punch line. And his deep brown eyes and the way his face broke into a grin at the slightest provocation. And he was a great kisser too, the best she'd ever known. He could work her into a frenzy just by nibbling her ear.

This was the man Abby wanted to spend the rest of her life with. But cuddling on her sofa was not getting him any closer to asking her to marry him and Abby had decided it was time to jump a few squares forward, using the tried and tested way to get a man on his knees with a proposal.

"Guys don't do that any more, silly," said her mate Maureen. "These days it's mostly the girls who do the asking. If they get married at all, that is."

"Nonsense. Under all his macho exterior I know he's a closet traditionalist," smiled Abby confidently. "I'm going to set the scene like one of those old movies. Scented candles and soft music and me wearing something madly seductive. And I'm going to cook him the most fantastic meal he's ever eaten and ply him with the best wine I can find and after that James will be putty in my sensual hands."

"Not too much wine or it won't matter how sensual your hands are," grinned Maureen. "What sort of food? I've heard oysters are really powerful stuff. For men, I mean."

"Right, I get them. How do you cook those?"

"You don't cook them silly, you eat them raw. Just swallow them down with a squeeze of lemon juice."

"Oh yuck. Well, I'll serve them to him anyway, and watch admiringly. And then I thought I'd do a curry – he loves curry – and for afters…?"

"You!

"Exactly!"

Abby was pleased with her lamb curry, which was fiery hot, just as James liked it. She was less certain about the oysters, which smelled like old seaweed and didn't look like something anyone would want to eat. But they cost such a fortune they had to be good, and she was sure James would be suitably impressed.

She spent most of the afternoon perfecting the ambience for the evening. She threw an old gold velvet drape across the sofa and arranged some fragrant white jasmine blossoms in a bowl. Then she set candles on every surface, small ones, fat ones, tall thin ones and a couple shaped like Father Christmas which she found in the back of her drawer.

Finally after soaking in a bath heady with jasmine oil, she dressed in the wickedly expensive red dress she'd bought and sprayed herself liberally with perfume.

Irresistible, she thought serenely.

Just before James was due to arrive, she pulled the cork on the wine, allowed Julio Iglesias to croon softly in the corner and started to light the candles.

Abby was still lighting the candles when James pounded up the stairs and rang the bell.

"Hi, sweetie," he said giving her an enthusiastic hug. "Mm, something smells good."

"Moi?"

"No, I meant the curry. What's the problem here, power failure again?"

"These candles are meant to be romantic, you fool."

"Oh. Right. Romance is good. And you're looking very good too."

"Thanks. Would you like to pour us some wine?"

"None for me tonight, love. I've got the finals tomorrow. I'll stick with water, but here's one for you."

Damn! She'd forgotten his Club tennis championship match. Well, this meal could still be a sensual mating ritual without wine, couldn't it?

She brought out her first piece de resistance, dainty little crab patties arranged on a bed of rocket and parsley. She was dismayed to see his face fall and remembered his big appetite. A cook's joy, her mother called him fondly.

"Don't worry, this is only the starter," she said hurriedly. "I'm treating you to a four-course meal tonight."

"Phew. I thought this might one of your diet evenings," he joked, wolfing them down like crisps and looking up expectantly. "Four courses? Wow, my lucky night."

'You don't know how right you are,' thought Abby.

The velvet textured crème caramel she'd made for desert waited in the fridge and promised to be deliciously sweet and creamy. It would make the perfect end to the overture before the main symphony of the evening began.

But she was starting to have her doubts about the oysters. James had pretty conservative taste in food and to be honest these didn't look like his kind of thing.

Presentation was all.

"Ta-da!" she announced, producing the plate of greyish objects with a flourish.

"What are these? Oysters?" James looked horrified. "These are the things you're supposed to eat raw, aren't you?"

"Yep," she said confidently. "Just tip up the shell and swallow it down. They're delicious. I believe."

James watched her as she nonchalantly lifted a shell to her mouth, trying not to look at the contents.

"You too," she said.

"You first," he said firmly. "They don't look like something I'd eat unless I was shipwrecked on a desert island. But if you tell me they're good..."

Abby couldn't do it. The oyster stared at her balefully, cold and grey and raw.

"I just remembered I don't even like sushi," she grinned, "But I thought all men were supposed to love these things."

"Not this one. I'm a meat-and-potatoes man myself, love."

I should have known, she thought. We've had enough meals of steak and chips for me to know his taste by now. Together they tipped the oysters into the kitchen bin and James lifted the lid of the bubbling casserole, sniffing appreciatively.

"That's more like it," he said. "Your curry's the best."

"So I'm not just a pretty face, then?"

"Never said you were," he said lovingly, kissing her neck.

She allowed his hands to wander upwards hopefully and was overcome by a familiar weakness of her knees. She nearly turned round in his arms and suggested they continue on the sofa instead of in the steam from the curry. Be strong, girl, she told herself.

James nibbled her ear tenderly. "You're a woman of many parts and all of them talented, all of them gorgeous and – what's that smell?"

The wispy net curtains above the elegant long candles had caught fire, with flames leaping up the wall. James went into take-charge mode and emptied his glass of water at them, followed by the wine. The fire sizzled out in a fog of black smoke, the wallpaper behind charred and stained with red. The room smelled dreadful.

James blew out the rest of the candles and switched on the lights.

"Let's eat, I'm starving," he said. "I'll get those curtains down afterwards. Then I've got to go, I need an early night to be ready for the match."

So much for this romantic meal, she thought sadly, and decided to keep the fabulous dessert until the next day.

"How about we have a picnic down by the river tomorrow, after your tennis match?" she said as she kissed him goodnight. "I'll bring a quiche and salad and something nice for afters."

"Sounds good," he said. "I'll bring the beer."

Abby made a mental note to include some chilled wine. Beer was not the right thing for romance by the river.

"You'd better take a nice big rug," said Maureen when she phoned her next morning. "You don't want a nasty grass rash in an embarrassing place. Definitely real wine glasses and china plates, and a tablecloth. You'll need a touch of class to lift this picnic from a lunch-time sarmie to something more…memorable.

"I'm buying a cheese and onion quiche," said Abby defensively. "No sandwiches."

"I read somewhere that real men don't eat quiche," said Maureen dismissively. "James is more a pork pie kind of guy, isn't he?"

Abby didn't like the image this conjured up but she had to admit James had been known to eat five of them in one evening.

"I'll get some of those as well," she said. "And we'll need music! I'll take my portable CD player."

"It's got to be the right sort of music though," said Maureen. "I'll lend you my *50 Songs for Swinging Lovers*, if you like."

"Iglesias works for me, thanks," said Abby. She hoped it would work for James too; he'd hardly had time to listen to the music last night. "I've got to hurry, I promised him I'd watch his match."

"This was a great idea, my love." James murmured. He was lying on the grass with his head on Abby's lap, his eyes closed. "That was a smashing meal. Mm, it's beautiful without that fellow groaning away. Listen to the birdsong."

"We've still got the dessert," she reminded him, running her fingers through his tousled hair and thinking what a very nice face he had. And what a very nice man he was. When he'd won match point after a long gruelling battle on the court, he'd bowed in her direction and blown a kiss. Just like the Wimbledon champions did, and she'd felt all the tennis club members watching enviously.

With such a public declaration of love, surely he'd be in the mood for suggesting something permanent this afternoon?

She was answered by a gentle snore.

I suppose that's what five sets in the hot sun does to a man, she thought ruefully, and the pint of beer he'd insisted on pouring into the silver trophy and then downing in one go hadn't helped either.

She relaxed against the tree trunk and opened her magazine, resigning herself to an hour of solitary reading.

But the insect buzzing around her head wouldn't go away, no matter how much she flapped her hand. Finally it settled on her arm and she triumphantly gave it a whack, realizing too late that it look horribly like a bee.

"Ye gods! What's happened?" James leapt to his feet at her shriek of pain.

"I've been stung!" she whimpered. "Ouch. It's really, really sore."

"My poor baby." He rubbed her arm and kissed it better, but that didn't help. As they watched a nasty red line seemed to travel up her arm under her skin. At the same time her mouth went dry and she had difficulty breathing.

"I – something's wrong," she croaked. "I can't breath."

"You're allergic to bees stings," he said immediately. "You're going into anaphylactic shock. We'd better get you to hospital right away."

He picked her up and ran across the lawn to his car. He's really good at taking charge, she thought, enjoying the comforting sensation of being carried in his arms. He practically threw her onto the back seat, slammed the door and roared off down the road.

"Hang on," he shouted, "I'm going to burn rubber, OK? My sister's allergic to bees too and I know what can happen if you don't get an injection in a hurry."

"What can happen?" But her throat had closed up so much she couldn't speak and by the time James reached the hospital she was slumped unconscious against the door.

"You're a very lucky girl," said the doctor's voice from somewhere above her head. "You've had a major allergic reaction to a bee sting which could easily developed into something worse if it wasn't for the fast work of this young man."

James squeezed her hand and she opened her eyes. Abby was aware of him sitting next to her but she could hardly see and her whole face felt peculiar and tight.

"Don't worry, facial swelling is quite a normal reaction. It should start to go down by this evening. I've prescribed some anti-histamine tablets for you, but please don't argue with a bee in future. Next time could well prove fatal." The blurry figure of the doctor disappeared from her line of vision.

"James? Do I look a terrible sight? My face feels so weird."

His lips twitched. "Sort of like a pink pumpkin with little slitty eyes. No change, really."

"Oh – you." She tried to punch him but her arm was too painful and had swollen to almost the size of her leg. "Please don't look at me. I feel awful."

"You gave me a heck of a fright," he said seriously. "Disturbed my beauty sleep too." The picnic and the river and the birds… suddenly it all came back.

"Oh no! Your beautiful silver cup! We've left it by the river."

"It's just a cup, love. I'm more worried about our pudding. Someone's bound to eat it."

"You daft thing." She smiled weakly but it felt as though her face was splitting in two.

James gently stroked the hair from her forehead, gazing at her in an odd, intense way with his usual half-smile wiped from his face for once. She recognized it as concern. Or maybe love. Or both.

"Abby, sweetie..." James cleared his throat. "I think it would be a good idea if we got married. Don't you?"

"No!" she said through swollen lips. "Not like this, James!"

"No, well of course we'd wait a bit, until your face has gone down. I don't mean today. But do you agree in principal? With marriage, I mean? To me?"

"I mean, don't propose like this!" she mumbled through numbed lips. "Of course I agree, silly. But I'd like a bit more – you know – romance when you propose. The whole traditional bit."

"Oh, right. Hang on…" His head sunk to the level of the mattress.

"What on earth are you doing?"

"I'm on my knees," he said, "Abby my darling, would you do me the honour of becoming my wife?"

She started to giggle hysterically and searched for a tissue to wipe her eyes.

"Could you answer quickly," he said. "My knees hurt."

Just then the door opened and in came a nurse.

"Oh my goodness," she gasped, "Have I interrupted a proposal? How lovely! Even though you're so…oh isn't that romantic!"

"Yes," gasped Abby.

"Yes that's romantic or yes you'll marry me?" asked James, rising unsteadily to his feet.

"Yes to both," said Abby.

If she wanted James and romance, there was always the honeymoon. Wasn't there?

Abby's Very Tasty Good Hot Malay Curry

Serves 6

Ingredients

2kg mutton pieces
6 tomatoes, skinned and chopped
5 potatoes, peeled and quartered
4 onions, chopped
1 cup frozen peas
5 cloves garlic, crushed
thick finger of green ginger, peeled and chopped fine

Spices

1 tsp turmeric
1 tsp curry powder
1 tsp ground cumin
50mg oil
3 cinnamon sticks
8 whole cloves
5 cardamom seeds
bunch of fresh coriander

Method

Cube the meat and sprinkle with turmeric, curry powder, coriander and cumin.

Using a heavy bottomed casserole dish, brown the onions and garlic in the oil, add the ginger.

Toss in the meat and add cardamom, cinnamon and cloves. Add tomatoes and about 250ml of water and cook very gently for an hour or until meat is tender. You might need to add more water.

Add the potatoes and cook until tender, and toss in the peas five minutes before serving with finely chopped green coriander leaves sprinkled on top.

If you prefer a VERY hot curry, add a red chilli finely chopped to the meat.

The Way To A Man's Heart

by Sue Houghton

According to this recipe book, *Cooking with Nature's Bounty*, preparing a meal for your man should be a sensual experience; one that he will find highly arousing.

Let me tell you, the way Mark's licking his lips has less to do with passion and more to do with his desire for second helpings.

"How's the steak?" I ask.

He lets out a hearty belch and a drop of gravy oozes down his chin. "It's a bit tough," he lies. Compliments don't fall easily from his lips these days – unlike onion gravy.

"It's organic. Best there is. I got it from the butchers in High Street."

"What do you want? A round of applause?"

"What about the mushrooms? Not too much garlic? Not over-seasoned?"

"What is this? Twenty questions? Leave me alone." And he piles more of the mushrooms from a side dish onto his plate.

"Bon appetit," I say, settling myself at the table beside him. I open my book again and wait in pleasurable anticipation.

That reminds me. What was it my mother was so fond of saying? Ah, yes.

"Anticipation is the better part of pleasure. You remember that, Lou," she'd say, "and you won't go far wrong."

It was her way of saying don't let a bloke smooth-talk you into bed, but she was far too polite to say so. We were in the kitchen the last time she said it. A place she considered sacrosanct

"Let me tell you," she said, separating the fat off the gravy (because that's the way father likes it) "it takes more than passion to keep a relationship together."

"Next thing you'll be saying is the way to a man's heart is through his stomach."

"Your dad's never complained. And don't sigh like that, young lady. It may be old-fashioned, but it's sound advice."

Yes, the same advice she'd been spouting since she found out I was seeing Mark. And I was tired of it.

Mum stopped spooning butter into the mashed potato and wiped her hands on her apron. She cupped my face in her hands.

"Lou, I'm only trying to protect you. I mean, how much do you really know about him? Be honest."

I'm ashamed to say, I pushed her away. "Oh pur-lease, spare me the lecture, Mum."

"Okay. Just promise me you won't rush into things. I couldn't bear to see you hurt."

"I love Mark, Mum. And he loves me. He'll never do anything to hurt me."

"But you've only known him a little while."

That much was true. But it was long enough to know I wanted to spend the rest of my life with him. Oh, I'd heard the rumours. I knew he had a reputation; maybe that was part of the attraction.

He was generous back then. Flowers, chocolates, jewellery. We wined and dined at Le Figaro, his favourite haunt. Always, he'd order for the both of us. In French, of course.

"You must try the wild mushrooms in garlic, Lou. They're picked straight from the forest floor. Simply delicious."

I did sometimes wonder where the money came from. When I asked what he did for a living he said he dabbled in the equestrian scene. He certainly had the body of a polo player. He liked to keep fit, he told me, as we hiked miles through the countryside. He amazed me by pointing out and naming wild flowers. We picked berries from the hedgerows and he laughed when I confessed I didn't know a sycamore from a bluebell.

"Don't touch that!" he yelled, when I stooped to pick a mushroom, on one of our walks. He took me in his arms, his lips brushing mine.

"It's a poisonous Death Cap. You really are a little townie, aren't you?" His hand caressed my breasts through the softness of my blouse then slowly he unbuttoned it. "I can see I'll have to educate you in the country ways." And he did; on a bed of warm woodland fern, the feathery branches of a young oak tree filtering the noon sun on our naked bodies.

And all the while he made love to me I was imagining my mother force-feeding my father roast dinners.

What did a woman whose only thrill was watching her husband wolf down her treacle sponge know about passion?

I told her that when I got home. We had a huge row and I announced I was leaving. Mark had asked me to move in with him and nothing she could say or do would make me change my mind.

It was a lie. Mark hadn't even invited me to his flat, let alone asked me to move in with him. But I was certain if I turned up on his doorstep he wouldn't turn me away.

I was right.

"Make yourself at home." he said, taking my suitcase.

Home? A far cry. I hadn't expected his place to be so…grotty, was the only word for it. Mark didn't seem concerned that it smelled of damp dog, that the wallpaper was peeling and the furnishings stained and tatty. Empty wine bottles littered the floor and dirty laundry was heaped over an ironing board. Not the chic bachelor pad I was expecting at all. He must've seen the shock register on my face. He waved a hand at the mess.

"Don't worry, love. Things aren't what they seem. This is only temporary. I've got the builders in at my other place. I'm buying one of those conversions down by the marina. There doesn't seem much point spending money here."

He placed his arms around me and nuzzled my neck. "Don't suppose you could rustle up some dinner could you? I've had a really hard day. Oh, and there's nothing in the fridge so do some shopping. Yeah? You pick up the bill and I'll straighten up with you later. And maybe you could run the vacuum over when you get back."

"Um, OK," I said. Though I'd expected our first night together to be a bit more romantic. Still, we were together and that was all that mattered. Or so I thought.

"Maybe we could tart the place up a bit," I said, when weeks later, I couldn't stand the sight of those dirty walls any longer. "A few tins of emulsion shouldn't cost much. I know the new apartment must be costing you a fortune, but it'd be money well spent because you'd get more for this place when you sell it."

"Sell it?" He was lounging on the sofa in front of the TV. The racing page open on his lap.

"To move into the new place."

"New place? Oh, didn't I mention? It's fallen through."

Alarm bells should've rung. But love was deaf as well as blind.

"Shame," I said. "Still, all the more reason to tart this place up. And this carpet's seen better days. If we're to stay here a bit longer…"

"If you want to decorate, then do it yourself," he snapped. "Now if you don't mind, maybe you could leave me in peace. I've got a wager on the two-thirty."

"It'll only cost a few pounds for the paint," I said, anticipating he would stump up the cash. He didn't. So I did.

And I paid for the new carpets and curtains too. And a cooker, as the restaurant visits had ceased and there's only so many microwaved meals a person can stomach. Mark's idea of a treat became a pizza purchased from the take-away as he staggered home from some club, usually with his mates, half drunk and spoiling for a fight.

It was the morning after one drunken episode that Mark flipped when I asked if I could invite my parents over. We were having breakfast – Mark insisted I cook him a meal before I went to work, even though he was 'working from home' as he called it.

"I could cook us a special dinner," I said. "I know. How about your favourite? Steak and wild mushrooms like we used to have at Le Figaro."

I thought it might prompt him to suggest we book a table, but instead he went into a sulk.

"These eggs are under-cooked," he said, waving his knife at me. "What are you trying to do? Poison me? Can't you get anything right?"

For a moment I thought he was going to throw it at the walls. I had visions of the lovely new wallpaper, a delicate cream with tasteful border, splattered with a full English – tomato sauce mingled with egg yolk and a rasher of bacon caught up on the tassel fringe of the table lamp.

"I try my best," I sighed.

"Then try harder."

After he left. No doubt to visit the bookmakers – it hadn't taken me long to work out that this was the equestrian scene he was involved in – I phoned work and told them I wouldn't be in. Then I went to the supermarket and, afterwards, spent a few hours in the library. Mark was right. My cooking wasn't up to scratch. I needed to look up a few recipes. Something special. Something he wouldn't forget in a hurry.

It seemed my idea worked. Mark picked up his wine glass and shook it at me. "Any more?"

I put down my book and poured him another glassful.

"You not having anything to eat?" he said, swiping the back of his hand across his mouth and then resuming his attack on the steak.

"I'm not hungry."

He looked me up and down. "Suppose you could do with losing a few pounds, anyway."

I ignored his remark. I've become used to his childish jibes.

"What's that you're reading?" he asked.

"This? I got it from the library." I flashed the book cover at him. "You remember you said you were going to educate me in the country ways? Well, I thought I might do a bit of swotting up myself. It's really interesting. Did you know a person could rely entirely on the fruits of the forest to survive?"

He scraped the last bit of food from his plate and sat back in his chair, rubbing his swollen belly.

"This coming from the same girl who can't tell a sycamore from a bluebell," he scoffed.

Then he gripped his stomach and his face contorted in pain. I hadn't imagined it would happen so quickly.

"Hmm. You could be right," I said. "It took me all afternoon to gather those mushrooms. I forgot to take this book along with me, you see. For reference. Trouble is…looking at this," I point to a photo of 'extremely poisonous' fungi. "I may have got it wrong, after all."

His eyes snapped open. "What?"

"Silly me. They looked similar, but now I'm not so sure. Tell me, how do you feel?"

The colour drained from his face and he gripped his chest as if he's about to suffer a heart attack.

I got up and went into the hall and collected my already packed suitcase. I threw my keys on the table. "It's as you said, Mark. Some things aren't always what they seem." I checked my watch. "I'd estimate you've got about six hours and then mercifully, it'll all be over."

"I didn't think I'd be able to pull my plan off," I told Mum when I arrived back home. "It took an awful lot of garlic to hide the taste. But he shovelled it in so fast, he didn't notice."

"You really shouldn't have done it, Lou. You could get into serious trouble."

"I did have doubts at the last minute, I admit. And the look on his face…I almost felt sorry for him. But it had to be done." I looked at the clock ticking the seconds away on the mantle-piece. "I hope the stomach cramps aren't too severe."

Then we both burst into laughter.

Don't worry. He'll be fine. He'll have the sweats for a few hours until he realises he hasn't been poisoned. Least, I don't think they sell dodgy mushrooms in Sainsbury's. Now, as for laxatives…

Browned Onion Gravy

Ingredients

1 tbsp safflower or olive oil
1 large onion, halved and sliced
1½ cups water
2 tsp vegetable seasoning
½ tsp dried tarragon
⅛ tsp sage
¼ tsp chervil
dash of nutmeg

Method

Heat oil in a large skillet. Add onion slices and sauté over medium heat until onion wilts and begins to brown. Add water, vegetable seasoning, tarragon, sage, chervil and nutmeg. Bring to a boil and lower to medium-low heat. Cook until gravy is reduced to about ¾ cup. Delicious served with mashed potatoes.

Lucky Thirteen
by Elaine Everest

"Here's the shopping list Meg, you will get all the ingredients, won't you? This is so important. Nothing must go wrong!"

My best friend Sally looked worried. "Salmon fillets, ginger, garlic, lemon grass, double cream and some smelly cheese." I sighed and licked my lips. "This is one extravagant meal. You're certainly pushing the boat out!"

"Nigel's worth the effort. It's taken me six months to get his attention. Now he's noticed me I don't intend to let him go."

"Do you think that inviting him to dinner will keep him? You're not exactly a cordon bleu chef. You usually open a can or telephone the Chinese take away."

"Meg, if you weren't my oldest friend I'd slap your legs. I'll let you know I've practised this recipe until it's perfect."

I peered into the recipe book, "Salmon in a Thai sauce served on a bed of noodles. It looks tricky. How many times have you practised it?"

"Don't laugh, tonight will be my thirteenth attempt. The first three were terrible, even the cat turned up his nose. The next four resulted in my needing a new set of saucepans and a fire extinguisher. But the last few attempts have been spot on. I've even served noodles that haven't welded together in a large glob!"

I sniffed, "no wonder your flat's smelt of burnt fish for the past fortnight. It must have cost a fortune practising for tonight. Why bother, it's only Nigel from Accounts?"

"Only Nigel from Accounts! Meg, he's a dreamboat. All the girls in my department are head over heels in lust with him. He went out with Clare from Sales for a week. He dropped her after catching food poisoning from a seafood risotto she bought at the supermarket. He told me he could never be serious with a girl who served convenience foods."

"Don't tell me, you told him you had a cookery diploma and invited him to dinner?"

"Yes, more or less. Luckily he's been away on a course which gave me time to practise."

I laughed. "So what's for starter and dessert, have you practised that as well?"

"Darren told me to keep it simple, serve soup for starters with strawberries and cream for dessert. I mustn't forget a decent cheese board either."

"Who's Darren?"

"Darren owns the delicatessen in the High Street. He has a great fish department and the most delicious cheeses. He's been really helpful and ordered in the salmon fillets specially. I've bought so many in the past weeks. He showed me how to dice the salmon neatly and chop the best parts of the lemon grass. He even managed to find fresh coriander for me. Have you ever seen fresh coriander in Grantley before?"

I stared at my friend in wonder; she's never had any inclination to cook before. I'm surprised she even knows her way around the kitchen. The only thing I've ever seen in her fridge was a collection of nail varnish and her best silk stockings – the cold's suppose to stop them from laddering.

Sally looked at her watch. "You will remember to ask for Darren at the Deli won't you? I'd go myself but I must get ready."

How could I refuse? I was longing to meet this paragon of the cheese board. I glanced down the list once more.

"A kilo of onions – seems a bit excessive?" I frowned.

"It's for the starter, French Onion soup with croutons. I have a kilo here, but I'm sure to need more."

I felt the first stirrings of panic, "are you sure it will go with a Thai main course? More to the point can you make it? Why not buy an expensive can of soup and add some herbs and a blob of cream for effect?"

Sally, glared at me. "I'll have you know that French onion soup was the first meal I ever made in cookery lessons at school. My teacher said I had a knack."

Sally forgets that we went to school together and my recollection was a little different. Our teacher's comment referred to her knack of making more mess than any other student in the room!

I shrugged my shoulders; there's no point in arguing with Sally when she's set her mind on something. I picked up the shopping basket and headed for the high street. Nigel was arriving in three hours. I wanted to be on my way home by then.

Darren's Deli was a delight. It was like stepping back in time as I walked into the shop. No self-service here, all the goods were laid out for inspection on marble counters and tiled shelves. The assistants, waiting with a smile on their faces, wore straw boaters and long white aprons. Spicy aromas blended with rich fragrant coffee that was being ground to order and wrapped in small brown paper parcels.

"Can I help you?"

I jumped, I'd been so engrossed in this tantalising shop I hadn't noticed the man standing nearby. "I have an order to collect." I said gazing up into the most beautiful brown eyes I'd ever seen – really this shop was getting to me!

He looked at the list I held out and laughed. "Tonight's the night then is it?"

"What?"

"Sally's big night – the meal for the important date?"

"Yes, but how did you know?" I faltered.

"I'm Darren, this is my shop and I'd recognise Sally's shopping list a mile off. It must be the tenth time I've made up the order."

"Thirteenth," I replied, and we both laughed. I held out my hand, "I'm Meg, Sally's friend, I've been roped in for the final preparations."

"Pleased to meet you Meg, why not have a cup of coffee while I get this order ready? We have a small coffee shop at the rear of the store. It's the latest addition to the business."

"This is the strangest Deli I've ever been in – not that I've visited many," I added as Darren led me through the shop to the rear of the building.

"I agree, it started as a deli but then I bought the shop next door. We introduced the fresh fish department and now with the extension just finished we have our own little coffee shop as well! Here, I'll show you our selection of coffee beans. We have a great range of cream cakes as well. I'll just get one of the staff to make up Sally's order then I can take a coffee break with you."

That was fine with me I thought, as I watched Darren instruct his staff. He looked back at me as I was watching him. A smile spread over his face making me blush and look away shyly. I'd only just met this man and he made me feel like jelly. This has never happened to me before.

We spent an hour sipping rich strong coffee and nibbling at exquisite walnut cake. I'd completely forgotten about Sally and the meal until my mobile phone bleeped loudly, making me jump.

"It's Sally," I said to Darren as I jumped to my feet. "She's cut her hand chopping vegetables. She's not good with blood and feels faint. Thanks for the coffee and cake but I've really got to dash."

Darren was already pulling off his apron. "Don't be silly, I'll come with you. If she's badly hurt I can patch her up until we get her to hospital. Let's grab her order and get going."

We got back to Sally's flat in record time to find her sobbing uncontrollably. It turned out not to be as bad as we thought. Sally was more concerned about her dinner date.

"It's a mistake, how did I think I could cook a meal like this?" She blew her nose on the kitchen roll she was using to stop the flow of blood from her thumb. "Nigel will be here in just over an hour, the meal's not ready, I've cut my thumb and I stink of garlic!' she wailed.

I looked towards Darren for help. He was busy unloading the groceries.

"Why don't you take Sally and help her get ready for her date. I'll start preparing the meal."

"Would you really do that, Darren?' Sally gave him a nervous smile and sniffed loudly.

"How could I let my favourite customer down in her hour of need?" he flashed her a knee-wobbling smile.

I was surprised as a stab of jealousy hit my heart. Was I falling for a man I'd only met that afternoon?

We didn't need any more prompting. Sally showered as I ironed her little black dress. Luckily her injury only required a plaster and a glass of wine. As I blow-dried her hair we could hear Darren whistling away as he worked in the kitchen.

"He's nice Sally." I whispered. "How long have you two been friends?"

"Ever since I bought my first salmon fillets," she whispered back, and we both giggled at the silliness of the situation.

"He likes you though," Sally said and was instantly hushed by my stern look.

"Don't be daft, I hardly know him."

"How long do you have to know someone before you fall in love? With me it was just a glance across the photocopier and I knew Nigel was the one for me."

I didn't want to burst my friend's bubble. Nigel was no doubt gazing at another female member of staff by the water cooler at the same time. I'd just be there when she needed a shoulder to cry on.

With Sally crimped and preened to perfection we joined Darren in the dining room. The table looked beautiful, candles glowed in the glass holders and a starter of melon was intricately set out at each place setting.

"I thought it was best to start with something simple." Darren said as he folded the napkins. "Besides there was blood in the chopped onions."

The ringing of the doorbell interrupted our laughter; Sally flapped her hands in panic. "It's Nigel, we're not ready – what shall I do?"

Darren held her hands still and looked her in the eyes; she visible calmed as he spoke to her clearly and slowly. "Everything is ready, go answer the door. The strawberries and cream are in the fridge. Once we've finished the main course we can let ourselves out and Nigel will be none the wiser. Go have a great evening."

Sally pecked him on the cheek and gave me a quick hug. After handing us a bottle of bubbly she rushed to open the door. We slipped quickly into the small kitchen and closed the door.

Darren opened the bottle and poured us both a glass of wine. "To work, assistant, pronto!"

I saluted him and chopped lemon grass under his careful instructions. The room was small and he constantly brushed against me as he went from the oven to the table.

I was very aware of the proximity of his body. The hairs on my neck were prickling as he whispered instructions in my ear.

With the salmon cooked to perfection and a bowl of noodles being kept warm we peered through the slightly open door. Sally was feeding Nigel pieces of melon as he looked adoringly into her eyes.

Darren took my hand and kissed my fingers. "I think our work's done here, are you hungry?"

"Are you cooking?" I asked, as he pulled my coat around my shoulders and held me close. It seemed the most natural thing in the world to do, as my arms reached round his neck and our lips met.

"I know the perfect place for oysters and champagne?" he murmured.

"And dessert?" I asked as he released me from his arms.

"I'm sure you can think of something sweet and tempting," he smiled.

I took his hand and lead him from the kitchen; "I most certainly can…"

Thai Salmon And Noodles

Serves 2

Ingredients

1 tsp olive oil
2 cloves garlic chopped
1 red pepper sliced thinly
1 yellow pepper sliced thinly
1 small onion chopped finely
1 carrot cut into thin sticks
50g lemon grass chopped finely
1" fresh root ginger grated
250g salmon fillets cubed
60g sugar snap peas
baby corn on the cob
3 tbsp light soy sauce
2 tbsp of sweet chilli sauce
1 tbsp chopped fresh coriander
1 lime
150g thin noodles

Method

Heat the oil in a wok until hot.
Add the garlic, peppers, onion, carrot, lemon grass and ginger and stir for three minutes.
Add the salmon, sweet chilli sauce, peas, sweetcorn and soy sauce and stir until the salmon is cooked through, making sure not to break up the salmon.
At the same time cook noodles as per packet instructions. Drain and divide on to two plates.
Serve the salmon on top of noodles.
Sprinkle with the fresh chopped coriander and a wedge of lime.

Delia! Help!
by Kath Kilburn

My mother's never going to be mistaken for Delia Smith. It's not only that she's small and round, with white hair and rimless glasses. It's also that she can't cook. I mean, absolutely can't. Mum's Sunday roasts are dry, her pancakes stick to the pan, her jellies don't set. She's not in the same universe, food-wise, as Delia.

While my friends' mothers churned out casseroles and fish pies without ever looking at a recipe, poor Mum would pore over the battered Trex cookbook, closely following the instructions. But something always went wrong. I never invited friends over to eat with us but spent many evenings at their houses, happily munching whatever was on offer, wondering whether I dare ask for a doggy bag.

"Don't you get fed at home?" their parents would tease, as I eagerly accepted fourth helpings.

Dad had his main meal at work, followed by something inedible at home for tea. Enough to stave off starvation. On Sundays he'd cook us all a big breakfast – sausage, fried bread, mushrooms, eggs, bacon. Mmmm, I can still smell it, still taste it. Mum thought of this as a treat for her. Dad and I knew it was the only way we'd get a weekend meal worth eating.

"Dad," I'd hiss, "this is the only good meal I ever get. Can't you do something?"

"Don't know what you mean," he'd always reply, grinning, loyal to the last. "And don't you go upsetting your mum. She does her best."

Dad never complained and Mum seemed totally unaware. I spent a lot of time munching secret Mars Bars in my bedroom.

When I was a teenager my dad died suddenly. We were heartbroken, Mum and I, and from then on it was just the two of us facing the burnt sausages and undercooked fish. About that time, too, it started to matter and I made sure she knew. I was embarrassed at the cake she presented to accompany my first boyfriend's cup of tea. I was mortified at the scones she offered my super-cool friend Shelley when I'd finally persuaded her to be my pal. I blamed mum's stupidity – "Sorry, Julie, I thought it was sugar, not salt" – when Shelley moved on to another classmate soon after. My mother didn't seem to think she was much of a loss.

My husband thinks Mum's great. She is. I've realized that talent in the kitchen isn't everything. When I look back now, I remember she read with us, took us to the park, kissed us better, was nice to our friends and generally, apart from the food thing, looked after us well.

I have a daughter too. Poppy. She's thirteen this year. I feed her the hotpots I was denied and she glowers, telling me she's going vegetarian. I make biscuits – brandy snaps are my speciality – and she's on a diet. I plan the menu for her first teenage party and her bottom lip juts forward. "All homemade?" she asks. I have to stop myself from shaking her and shouting that at her age I'd have been grateful if Granny could've produced a lovely buffet for twenty, confident that no-one would contract food poisoning. But what's the use of arguing with a child in bittersweet adolescence? I let it go.

My mother meanwhile has taken to filling her widowhood with afternoon adult education classes. She can throw, and paint, a decent pot. But she still can't manage a good cup of tea to fill it. I'm not sure even Delia's covered tea-making for one.

But these days I make the tea while she's still putting away her easel or yoga mat. It takes me a while to find the stuff sometimes as she's re-designed her kitchen and put up extra shelves with help from a guy in the joinery class.

"Donald, his name is," she confided.

"And…?"

"And he's good at shelves."

I wondered whether there was any chance Donald would be storing his toolbox next to Mum's sometime soon.

It turned out Donald teaches the joinery class, and is organizing a fun-day to raise funds and promote the college. Mum told me, with a self-satisfied grin, that he'd put her on catering duty. I wondered how well he knew my mother. If public health was in danger he should be warned.

"Don,' I said, 'you know my mother's a disaster in the kitchen?"

"She set fire to the boil in the bag fish last week so I was starting to have my suspicions." He smiled at me.

"But you've put her on refreshments for the fun day?"

He looked puzzled for a minute, then smiled again. "Refreshments? Well…it'll be fine. No need to worry."

We arrive as they're setting up and Mum takes me aside. I'm expecting her to ask for help with the food.

"It's about Poppy."

"Poppy?"

"Her birthday party spread - she's upset. She asked me not to mention it but she'd really like a take-away. It's more *cool.*"

"Oh!" I'd been so looking forward to feeding all these youngsters – feeding's part of nurturing, caring, looking after. All that stuff parents do.

My mother took my hand. "Julie, she's growing up. She's benefited all these years from your home cooking but now she wants to impress her friends. I could never make lovely meals but remember, there's more to caring than cooking. You long to give her what you wanted, but maybe she wants something different?"

She became brisk "Anyway, I've things to do…no, I don't need any help, thanks. You go and enjoy yourself. I'll see you later."

I watch her trip away, and go in search of the others. The sun filters through wispy clouds as we wander round buying raffle tickets, watching the prettiest pup competition and buying pots of fresh herbs to line the kitchen windowsill. I don't see Mum again until we spot every teacher's nightmare – the old-fashioned board with holes for heads to slot through, and there at the side, my mother smilingly supplying the custard pies ready for throwing. Poppy and I laugh as she hastily and inexpertly pipes shaving foam (or something!) on to cardboard plates and hands them over. I've never been too sure what those pies are made of, but my mother's doing a splendid job, even without Delia's help.

Doing The Cooking
by Jane Wenham-Jones

Maggie looked like something from the glossy lifestyle pages. Tanned and relaxed, she lay back in her garden chair and stretched out a hand for her drink. "Mmm" she smiled at me as she sipped. "I love summer – so restful."

I looked from the pile of magazines by her side to her glowing skin.

"I love summer too" I said, pulling a mirror from my handbag and peering at my own harassed reflection, "but it's not any more restful in our house than at any other time of the year. Still all the cleaning and shopping and cooking to get done."

"Cooking!" said Maggie in horror. "You don't want to cook in the summer…" She sat up and reached for the exotically packaged coconut and lotus flower suntan oil and proceeded to smooth it down a long golden leg. "Summer is for soaking up the sunshine, having chilled wine and lots of good sex…" She dabbed a little moisturiser on her luminous cheeks, "all those endorphins – so good for the skin." She gave me a wicked smile. "Forget the cooking…"

"Well, yes," I said uncertainly, "but you can't just live on salad all the time"

She laughed. "Who said anything about salad? Yes – chuck some in a bowl to go with it but I'm talking about melt-in-the-mouth lamb, marinated chicken, succulent ribs, spicy bean burgers, speciality sausages – all without you moving from your chair."

"How?" I leant forward eagerly, wondering if she was having a rampant affair with that rather gorgeous young man from the Turkish take-away.

"Very simple. Three easy steps and all your cooking will be over till the autumn."

"Well go on then!" I said, breath bated, allowing myself a brief and delicious fantasy of him having a hunky brother who ran the new summertime home-delivery service.

"How? Buy a barbecue!"

"Oh," I sat back again, disappointed. "Have they invented one that does it all on its own then? Before it shags you afterwards?"

Maggie giggled. "Trust me," she said. "You'll be a new woman – you'll be chasing Ian round the kitchen." I raised my eyebrows. Usually by the time I'd finished in that particular room of the house I was in no mood to pursue anyone, least of all my husband.

"Stuart and I did it twice last night," said Maggie smugly. "I think it's the high protein diet that's doing it!" She winked. "You just have to follow my three-point plan."

I had to admit Point One was most enjoyable. It involved sitting in Maggie's garden all afternoon with our husbands and children, drinking wine and eating the most delicious char-grilled food I'd tasted for ages.

"Thank you!" I said fervently to Stuart as we left. "And thank YOU," I murmured to Maggie as I hugged her. She kissed Ian and winked at me over his shoulder. "Have a relaxing summer!" she called as we all went down the path.

The minute Ian and the kids had gone the next morning, I was off to the garden centre to view a confusing array of shiny new barbecues in various shapes and sizes. Half an hour later, point two complete, I was staggering to the car under a weight of charcoal. I was tempted by the range of shiny tongs and slices and meat probes but I remembered Maggie's advice and walked firmly past.

The minute my teenage son returned from school, I hauled him outside. "Quick help me with this before your father gets home. I held up the two bolts and small metal flap which for some reason had been left over after my six hours of home-assembly that was supposed to take twenty minutes.

"Do you know anything about barbecuing Mum?" he asked doubtfully as I tipped up the sack of charcoal and grasped the lighter fuel.

"No" I said cheerfully.

The timing was perfect. Ian arrived home just as I'd managed to create an evil-smelling, smoking black heap and was about to balance a sausage directly onto the charry pile.

"No!" he shrieked from the kitchen doorway. "Don't do that!"

I turned in hurt surprise. "You said you loved it at Maggie's." I positioned myself between him and the plate of raw meat and looked at him from beneath lowered lashes. "You said, when you came home, that you loved me…"

Ian dropped his briefcase and rushed past, ignoring the last part of my sentence.

"But there's an art to it," he explained, agitated, "you can't just stick some charcoal on and start cooking." He moved me to one side and took his jacket off. "You need to know what you're doing. Here," he took the fork from my hand and shook his head sadly. "and we should have the proper tools." He turned to put his arm around me and said kindly: "I think you'd better leave it to me."

It wasn't at all bad for a first attempt. Ian had obviously picked up quite a few tips from Stuart during the hours they'd spent huddled over the barbecue at Maggie's. And my hasty instructions to the children paid off. "Brilliant Dad!" said Alex, between mouthfuls. Even Lindy who had reeled in shock at the sight of her father cooking for the first time in her life, made a rapid recovery and enthused. I gave her a nudge under the table. "Can you do ribs? Dad?" she asked

"Ribs?" cried Ian heartily the next night clutching the barbecue tools he'd bought on the way home, "I can do anything you like…"

"It's amazing," I said to Maggie a couple of weeks later as we sat in my garden looking at the row of hooks Ian had put up on which to hang his shiny new cooking implements and the sexy chef's hat I'd bought him. "He just loves it. I've filled the freezer to the brim and now he barbecues almost every night. Won't let me anywhere near it. "

I laughed. "He was ever so nice. Said that it wasn't my fault I couldn't do it – it was a bloke thing!" I grinned at Maggie. "Stuart told him you'd never managed to grasp the rudiments either!"

"Told you it would work," she said smugly, closing her eyes and tipping her face up to the sun. "He's become all macho about it, you've got time to lie around feeling sensual and I bet…"

"Well, yes…" I said blushing as I nibbled at a little cold meat ball left over from the night before."

"Excellent," said Maggie, licking her fingers, "Now, have I told you how to be really hopeless at ironing…"

Hot Sizzling Ribs

Serves 4

Ingredients

2kg (4lb) pork spare ribs – try and choose meaty ones.
For marinade
2 tbsp of sunflower oil
2 tbsp white wine vinegar
4 tbsp tomato ketchup
1 tbsp Worcestershire sauce
2 tbsp runny honey
2 large cloves garlic crushed
½ tsp each of chilli powder, ginger, cumin, coriander
½ tsp sea salt
ground black pepper
For glaze
2 tbsp of honey
1 tbsp of lemon juice.
2 tbsp tomato ketchup
pinch of cayenne pepper

Method

Lay the ribs in a shallow dish
Mix all other ingredients together in a bowl and spoon over the ribs, ensuring the meat is thoroughly coated. Cover and refrigerate for at least two hours, or overnight if possible, turning the ribs occasionally.
Before cooking, scrape off excess marinade and discard.
Barbecue over hot charcoal till tender and browned, turning frequently and basting with a glaze made of the honey, lemon juice, tomato sauce and a pinch of cayenne pepper.
Serve with a green salad and wet wipes

Signature Dish
by Veronica Henry

Rachel Harper had always taught her son Michael not to judge a book by its cover. People deserved the benefit of the doubt, she told him. It was, after all, usually insecurity and lack of confidence that brought out the worst in people. Given time, even the prickliest of customers usually mellowed.

When she met her prospective daughter-in-law, however, she made an exception and broke her golden rule. She loathed Justine Webb on first sight. She tried to tell herself it wasn't because Michael had proposed to the girl before asking her advice, for she was adamant that her son didn't need her approval as to his future wife. She had, after all, approved of all his past girlfriends, and the last thing she wanted was to be branded interfering, or controlling. But to her mind, Justine was vain, pretentious, grasping, cold and calculating – everything that her warm, shambolic, generous-hearted, vague, forgetful and impulsive son wasn't. Rachel was more than proud of Michael. From the moment she'd looked at his dear little face, still covered in blood and vernix, she had sworn to protect him for ever. She would still die for him.

Not only that, she would kill for him.

Justine was standing here now in her kitchen, immaculate in camel trousers and a cashmere twin set. The disdainful look on her face said it all – was she risking salmonella or gastro-enteritis by agreeing to eat anything that had been cooked in this hovel? Rachel was a firm believer that dirt and germs were a good thing. This was where Michael had been brought up – he'd done his homework at the pine table, learnt his alphabet from letters fashioned out of pastry – and he was rarely ill. Living proof that hygiene was over-rated.

Her cooker bore a range of cast iron pans that were never washed; just wiped with a paper towel. Shelves were crammed with pots and jars of jewel bright spices and muskily-scented herbs, bottles of essence and elixirs and sauces, threads of saffron, star anise, vanilla pods. Strings of onion and garlic and dried chillies hung down from the beamed ceiling; baskets filled with bulbous ginger and elegant lemongrass jostled for position on the counter; pots of tarragon and basil and flat leaf parsley spilled along the window sill. There were eight jars of mustard, five types of honey; countless oils: virgin and extra virgin, cold-pressed, pumpkinseed, walnut, oils infused with garlic and lemon and chilli. And vinegars: cider, wine, raspberry, three sorts of balsamic of varying age. Rachel could usually put her hands on any ingredient called for in any recipe, and if not she was a good enough cook to be able to improvise.

Rachel could just imagine Justine's kitchen. A stainless steel abattoir, with gleaming, shining, harsh black granite surfaces; not a single food item on show except a pyramid of waxed lemons in a pristine glass bowl. A place where food wasn't prepared lovingly and extravagantly, merely extricated from its layers of Styrofoam and clingfilm to be reheated and turned out onto matching Villeroy and Bosch.

Why on earth was this sleek, pampered Italian greyhound marrying her great shaggy sheepdog of a son? Michael, who made a freshly ironed shirt look as if he'd slept in it two minutes after he put it on. You didn't need a degree in psychology to work it out, decided Rachel wryly. She remembered an ironic joke she'd once heard: "So, what was it that first attracted you to millionaire screenwriter Michael Harper…?"

Rachel didn't want this woman to marry her son. She wasn't going to provide him with the warm, loving, nurturing environment he needed. Their marriage would be all about Justine and her needs – the pressure she was under as a copyright lawyer. She would be too busy leaping onto transatlantic flights to check that he was eating and sleeping properly, that he took plenty of breaks, that he realised there was another world outside the one he was creating. No – Justine would be power-breakfasting and networking over dinner, Michael secondary to her career and her ego. She would be too self-absorbed to realise that, as a writer, he needed encouragement and reassurance. That despite the air of affable eccentricity, his genius didn't always come easy, that the process sometimes bordered on torture.

"Has Michael told you what I can and can't eat?"

Rachel snapped to attention, and managed a reassuring smile. "Don't worry. He's told me about the fish."

She would normally have served bouillabaisse at an occasion like this, rich and ruby red, bubbling with tomatoes and garlic and swimming with monkfish and langoustines and served with dollops of aioli. That was Rachel's signature dish. But today she was doing Thai chicken curry, in deference to Justine's life-threatening allergy.

"He only told you about the fish?"

Rachel looked at Justine sharply. She was looking suspiciously coy.

"It's not just fish. I can't eat unpasteurised cheese. Or liver. Or pate. For the time being, any way." She gave a conspiratorial, girly shrug, managing to disguise her triumph as sheepishness.

Rachel felt Justine trying not to recoil as, still clad in her food-splattered apron, she gave her a hug of congratulation to demonstrate her false delight. Michael wandered in with a rueful grin, swinging a bottle of chilled Laurent Perrier in one hand and holding three champagne glasses by the stems in the other.

"Only a teeny weeny drop for me," said Justine primly, and Rachel tried not to roll her eyes. Her generation had drunk like fish all through their pregnancies. It certainly hadn't done Michael any harm.

Later, as she put the finishing touches to the lunch, Rachel reluctantly put the nam pla to the back of the shelf, in the light of the morning's revelations. Had she used it, she would have had no compunction pleading ignorance, if it had even got as far as court. How could she have been expected to know that nam pla was Thai for fish sauce, especially when the writing on the bottle was in indecipherable hieroglyphics, bought from an exotic food emporium? She would have talked her way out of it, feigned distress, joined in the frantic search for Justine's adrenalin pen, stowed in the Fendi baguette bag that would have come to light, tragically too late, under one of the enormous cushions in the sitting room.

Instead, she deftly chopped two handfuls of fresh coriander with her mezzaluna and brought the dish through into the garden room where she'd laid the tiny table with earthenware bowls.

To her surprise, Justine dug into the curry with relish.

"I've been absolutely starving, ever since I found out. This is delicious.'"

"Maybe we could get mum to do this for the christening."

"Michael!" Justine shot him an exasperated glance, then rolled her eyes at Rachel. "He's impossible. He's so excited. He's got everything planned."

"I'd be delighted to cater the christening," said Rachel. "If that's what you decide you want."

She glanced at Justine digging the serving spoon into the bowl of sticky, fragrant Thai rice in an uncharacteristic display of greed. Maybe motherhood would mellow her. Maybe she would learn not to be so self-centred, self-absorbed, self-obsessed. Maybe she would pick up her child, smother it in kisses of delight, revel in its chubby charms. Rachel suspected not. Justine wasn't the type for finger-paints and gingerbreadmen. She'd have Michael running round Sainsbury's on a Saturday morning, with the children in tow, while she had her roots done. And Michael, good-natured, anything-for-a-quiet-life Michael, would do her bidding.

Nevertheless, thought Rachel, she had to give Justine the chance. And if not, there was always that secret ingredient, stashed away on the shelf, ready for use another day.

Thai Chicken Curry

Serves 4

Ingredients

1 onion
2 cloves garlic
2 green chilllies
1 knob of ginger
juice and zest of a lime
1 tbspn curry paste [I use Madras]
large bunch coriander [keep some aside for garnish]
2 tbsp nam pla! [soy sauce will suffice]
Also
4 skinless chicken fillets, sliced to your liking
1 tin coconut milk
Optional Extra
2 sweet potatoes, diced
1 packet green beans

Method

Roughly chop onion, garlic, chillies and ginger then put all the sauce ingredients into a blender until emulsified.

Brown the chicken pieces in a wok (and the sweet potato if using) then pour over the sauce and add green beans if using. Leave to simmer gently until sauce is slightly thickened and reduced, and the vegetables are cooked through. Add the tin of coconut milk and gently heat through. Throw in another handful of fresh coriander and a squeeze of lime juice before serving on a bed of Thai rice.

The Dinner Service

by Betka Zamoyska

Ella was bubbling with excitement, the kind of excitement you only feel when you are seventeen and have just arrived at your personal Mecca. All her schooldays, she had announced to anyone who would listen that she would go to Cambridge. She used to picture herself floating down the river, like Helena Bonham Carter in a James Ivory film, trailing one hand through the water, surrounded by admiring undergraduates in punts. As the 'A' levels grew closer, she became more circumspect about her future plans. Her local comprehensive was not known for sending students to Oxbridge, the girls mostly went to nearby Southampton university, art college or were signed up for some sort of local training scheme. Ella's friends were amazed when she got a place. She was not considered to be particularly outstanding, except in English, and her best-known talent was for making the funny part in the school play overshadow the lead. Small-boned, with light, mousy hair, cut in a page-boy, and large grey-blue eyes, she looked like an inquisitive owl, but she had the kind of face that people watched; it lit up when she talked.

She had only been in possession of her room in college for a few weeks. She already had several good friends at college but her most exciting discovery was Marcus, whom she had met during Freshers' Week, when students are encouraged to meet those from other colleges. To Ella he seemed straight out of her favourite kind of costume drama – a tall, laid-back, public school boy, with curls that clung to his tattered shirt collars like ivy. They had hit it off over their plastic mugs of coffee and agreed to study Milton's *Comus* together for their first paper. Now Ella had persuaded him to come to her room for a working supper. This was her first 'at home' and she was determined to make it a memorable occasion. After giving the matter some thought, she decided to cook him a Polish dish called 'Bigos' or 'Hunter's Stew', which she had learnt from her grandmother. She thought that Marcus, with his olive skin and dark hair, must be partly Italian and she felt this would emphasise her European roots. Bigos had the advantage of being quite cheap, filling and exotic at the same time. It was designed to keep the Polish hunter warm in the Carpathians as he stalked bears or wild boar. The local deli stocked quite a lot of Polish food, including sauerkraut and Polish sausage, the two main ingredients. A friend had lent her a large saucepan and, as the stew gurgled away in the communal student kitchen, giving out its familiar smells, Ella felt a little homesick but a more practical problem soon drove such thoughts from her mind. She had been so intent on cooking the stew, she had overlooked the important matter of cutlery and crockery. She did not even have a paper plate or plastic knife stashed away in case of emergencies. So far, she had only eaten at the student canteen and had not given a thought to domestic matters. She searched her room in the vague hope that the previous inhabitant could have left something behind but all she found was one plastic mug, caked in toothpaste. She put it in her basin to soak in hot water and decided to check out the communal kitchen, in the hopes that she could find the odd plate or fork that a student had smuggled out of the canteen for a take-away.

To Ella's amazement, the cupboard in their students' kitchen was full to bursting point with an expensive, china dinner service, gold-rimmed, with a dark green, ivy leaf motif. There were at least twelve matching plates with twelve side plates in the same pattern. She pulled at the drawer beneath the sink; it shot out, almost knocking her backwards. Inside was a polished, mahogany box. Lined up in its green-baize slots, like small soldiers, were knives and forks, with elegant ivory handles and some silver spoons, ranging from serving spoons to delicate teaspoons. Ella was still staring at her discovery when she heard a shy cough close behind her.

"Who on earth could have put all this in here?"

"Do you think I'm a complete idiot? I mean, I only put it there because I've no room for it all in my room."

Ella looked at the awkward, plump student, with frizzy, reddish-brown hair, that sprang out around her head in an uneven halo. She wondered why she had never seen her before. She did not want to look like a snooper so she held out her hand and introduced herself.

"I'm Ella, I'm two doors down on the right."

"I'm Rebecca Goldstein. My room's at the far end of the passage."

Rebecca studied physics and she must, thought Ella, spend all her time in labs.

"You really shouldn't leave this stuff here," Ella warned her. "It's bound to get nicked. Couldn't you fit it in under your bed?"

"I'm crammed to the gills with stuff mummy insisted I would need. I don't have any use for most of it – I don't know many people here and so far no-one's been to visit. Physics is a really demanding subject, there isn't much time… I don't suppose you'd like to keep a bit of it would you, just for this term? You could use it, of course, as long as you were careful."

It was an unforeseen solution to Ella's predicament but the plates looked so imposing – the sort you dined off with elderly aunts – that she hesitated before giving a reply. Rebecca pulled half a dozen of the big dinner plates and a handful of the side plates out of the cupboard and had piled them up on the sideboard.

"Why don't we split them and have half each? You can always borrow more if you need them for a party."

A deal was struck and Rebecca looked exceptionally pleased with their arrangement. The embarrassing plates, forced on her by her mother, had at least brought a friend into her lonely existence.

Ella was already picturing Marcus's look of surprise. She cleared her desk, laid out two dinner plates, two side plates, the plastic mug and some of the silver crockery that Rebecca had leant to her for the evening. She was a mug short but she did not want to ask Rebecca for anything more. She suspected that Rebecca, if asked, might well come up with a collection of glasses.

Marcus arrived nearly an hour late but Ella was pleased to have had the time to tidy up the room and bigos is one of those dishes that improves with over-cooking. She had decorated the desk/dinner table with some ivy she had picked off the college walls to match the crockery. She had asked Rebecca if she would like to join them (she knew this would irritate Marcus, but after so much generosity she felt this was the least she could do).

Fortunately Rebecca was unable to come, she had to pack for her brother's Bar Mitzvah.

"Are your parents coming to collect you?"

"No, they're sending their driver." Rebecca looked more awkward than ever and scuttled down the passage.

"What on earth?" Marcus had thrown the door open wide to announce his arrival. Her did not seem to be aware that he was late. "I didn't realise you were a budding Delia Smith where the hell did you get those plates?"

Ella hurried down the corridor to get her bigos before the kitchen filled up with students reheating their takeaways or frozen pizzas from the local supermarket. She waved a hand at the far end of the desk and tried to do a small curtsey but the loose end of her jeans got stuck in her gym shoes.

"Un tout petit peu de bigos, signor?"

She ladled the steaming stew on to Marcus's plate with one of Rebecca's silver spoons and told Marcus about her new benefactor.

"She must be Sol Goldstein's daughter…phew, this stew's hot. What's it got in it?"

"Lots of delicious Polish ingredients, my grandmother's speciality. Who's Sol Goldstein?"

"A very big bigwig in the city. Looks like Wedgewood," turning over a plate he examined its markings, "yes, it is. Not surprising. They're seriously loaded. What's Rebecca like?"

Ella tried to give a description that was truthful but would dampen his enthusiasm then switched the conversation to *Comus*. After all, it was meant to be a working supper.

"Did you know that Milton's other work, *Paradise Lost,* is full of phallic symbols? Pity we're stuck with *Comus*."

Ella laughed. They were back on form. To accompany the bigos, Marcus had brought a bottle of Hungarian red wine, which they shared in the tooth mug. They read the seduction scene in *Comus* and Ella wished it could have been for real but Marcus stretched out his long legs and yawned: "I'm too pissed to do any more tonight. We shouldn't have finished off the wine. Let's come back to it next week."

He gave her an all-embracing hug and strolled off down the corridor, she could hear his gym shoes squeaking against the polished wooden floor. At the swing doors, he turned and blew her a kiss. Ella knew there was already a line of eager girls queuing up for him. She would have to play it slow, but the evening had undoubtedly been a success.

Two days later there was a knock on her door. It was Rebecca.

"Come in," said Ella. "How was the celebration?" She could not remember exactly what Rebecca had called it and had no idea what it was.

"The Bar Mitzvah went really well…my brother's speech was so good. he's only fourteen but he suddenly looked so…"

She looked up and saw Ella's puzzled frown.

"Of course, you probably don't know, it's a sort of coming-of-age celebration – just an excuse, really, for a family party, but my family take it pretty seriously."

"Are you sort of religious Jewish?" Ella did not want to hurt Rebecca's feelings but she felt out of her depth.

"My family are very Orthodox so, yes, I suppose we are. It's a bit of a special thing. I'm proud to be Jewish but you can be overwhelmed by all the family bit. you know. It's not just the living family, we're very aware of all our ancestors. sometimes you don't like the thought they're all there looking down on you.."

Ella thought of her strong-minded Polish grandmother and nodded. She made some coffee. She had now bought two mugs of her own, so Rebecca would not feel that she was a complete scrounger. Ella was finding it hard to cope on her grant and her mother could not afford to give her much more. She had already given Ella money for books and had paid for her new laptop but being a student, as Ella had discovered, was an expensive business.

"Did you have a good dinner with your friend?" Rebecca was asking, wishing that she could have a boyfriend who did not have to be vetted by her family.

"Yes," said Ella. "I gave him this Polish stew."

Rebecca looked troubled.

"What was in it?"

Rebecca turned pale when Ella mentioned the Polish sausage.

"It wasn't pork sausage was it? We're not allowed pork – it would mean I could never use those plates again."

There was a long pause. Ella thought in dismay of the replacement value of the Wedgewood and the silverware.

"I…I will have to ask Marcus," Ella stuttered. She could think of no way out of her predicament and was stalling for time. What would she tell her mother? Her student debts had already started mounting.

Rebecca stood up and thanked for the coffee. She could see the pained expression in Ella's eyes. The tribes of her ancestors were bearing down on her, as they had so often in the past, but this time she felt a sudden surge of independence.

"I saw you cooking in the kitchen. That stew was definitely beef."

Ella's eyes widened and she opened her mouth for the Catholic confession she knew that she should make…

"Beef," said Rebecca firmly with a confident smile. "Let's never talk about it again."

Ella blushed with both relief and confusion. Now she was the one who felt shy. They stood facing each other and shook hands solemnly, like two Indian chieftains making a secret pact.

The friendship continued to blossom between Ella and Rebecca. To Ella, Rebecca was from a different, exotic world. She learnt about the Jewish festivals, Rosh Hashanah, the Jewish New Year, and Yom Kippur – the day of Atonement, and how Rebecca's brothers, sisters, aunts and cousins got together for these occasions. It reminded her a little of her Catholic grandmother's descriptions of family get-togethers in Poland for feast days and saints' days. Her grandmother was now the only survivor of the older generation and Ella was an only child.

When Rebecca returned from the lab, they would take walks along the Cam in the early evening and watch the water turn from a brilliant orange in the setting sun to its usual murky brown, as night drew near. They talked about their families, their ambitions, their secret hopes and fears. Rebecca admired Ella's way of dressing, which was artistic and eccentric at the same time. Ella wore enormous floppy hats; she embroidered her jeans with her own designs and made jewellery from odds and ends she found in flea markets. Rebecca grew her reddish brown hair so that it was no longer frizzy but hung down her back in Titian waves. She took to wearing flowing dresses and their long walks improved her dumpy figure.

"All I need now," Rebecca joked with Ella, "is a Jewish boyfriend. I want him to be Jewish but I don't want him to be chosen by my dad."

"Is there anyone at the synagogue?"

"No," said Rebecca firmly, "they're too like my dad. I want someone freer than that, more fun."

Ella's own love life seemed to have dwindled. Her weekly sessions with Marcus had come to an abrupt end. Marcus' debts had surpassed Ella's and he had now taken on the job of escorting tourists round Cambridge which took up most of his spare time. *Comus* he told Ella firmly would have to wait until he was out of the wood financially.

One evening, when Ella went to find Rebecca for their usual walk, there was no reply when she knocked on her door. She walked over to the labs, curious to see what the science students got up to, but the labs were deserted. Ella wondered if they were all at some special lecture and decided to take their usual walk along the river alone. It was now late autumn; there were less tourists and the busy river traffic had died down. Deep in thought, she walked further along than usual and noticed ahead of her there was a large, weeping willow. Its branches reached down into the river, as though the two could not bear to be parted. Through the leaves, she could just make out a couple, sitting underneath, near the trunk. Light filtered through the leaves on to their backs. As Ella grew closer she noticed that they were sitting on a rug and, on the girl's right, there was a large, wicker picnic basket. The sunset was at its most brilliant. The water was aflame. The girl suddenly leant forward and lifted a plate out of the basket. The setting sun caught its rim and it shone out in glints of gold. Then Ella recognised Marcus's dark curls leaning possessively towards Rebecca's wavy locks that reflected the fiery, orange rays of the sun.

She halted abruptly in her tracks, uncertain what to do, then, blinded by tears, made her way back along the river. She felt empty with her double loss; her heart was pounding in a mounting panic. Like a sleepwalker, she returned to her room and pulled her half of the dinner service from under her bed. With an armful of plates, stacked up to her chin, she staggered down the corridor and stopped at the door of her former friend's room. The plates dropped, with a loud crash on the wooden floor, and splintered into a thousand jagged pieces.

Polish Sausage Stew

Serves 6

Ingredients

1 can condensed cream of celery soup, undiluted
⅓ cup light brown sugar, packed
1 can or bag (24 oz) sauerkraut, drained and rinsed
1½lb Polish pork sausage, cut in 2" pieces
4 medium potatoes, peeled and cubed
1 cup chopped onion
1 cup shredded mild Cheddar or Jack cheese

Method

In crockpot, combine the soup, sugar, and sauerkraut. Stir in sausage, potato, and onion. Cover and cook on LOW for 8 hours. Skim off excess fat, stir in cheese. Spoon into serving bowls and top with additional shredded cheese.

Tea And Sympathy
by Adele Parks

"So why here?" I ask as I plonk myself down, reach for a Rusk and hand it to Charlie, in the vain hope that it will keep him quiet at least long enough for Angie to answer the question.

I briefly worry about the sugar content of the snack, as I sip on the cappuccino that Angie has already, thoughtfully, ordered. But the concern is mild compared to whether I'm stimulating my child enough to unleash all his potential, whether he'll ever make it to the top of the waiting list for my preferred school and whether I should have him inoculated in one fell swoop or mess around with three separate injections. Today's concerns. All of which are forgotten in light of Angie's, my best friend forever, extraordinary behavior.

This morning, she called me and insisted on a change of venue. It should be no big deal; we're only talking coffee shops. We meet weekly, our criteria isn't demanding. We simply need somewhere that won't actively loath us for having children, serves warmish beverages and allows us to talk about the joyful insanity that is childbearing. The extraordinary thing is Angie called at 8.30am this morning and demanded that I got to her appointed cafe as soon as possible. 'It opens at nine,' she insisted. I told her I'd do my best to get there near ten. I used to be punctual, now I'm hap-hazard. I had planned on doing some cooking before I met Angie – Organic chicken and vegetable stew for Charlie. I planned on freezing several tiny portions because having something wholesome in the freezer takes away potential stress at tea time. But Angie, normally reserved and accommodating, wouldn't hear of it. She actually commanded that I got to this particular cafe, ASAP.

I look around. The cafe is on Highgate high street, it's quaint but not prepossessing. I wonder if they serve good cakes.

"So why here?"

As she tells me (no eye contact, fiddling with a tissue, beads of sweat on her upper lip), I think that it is too beautiful a day to receive news like this. The sun is shinning and I'm dressed in just a t-shirt, no coat, although it's only April. This time last year we were damp proofing the house and still wearing thermals.

"You must be mistaken, David is away on business," I say, weakly.

It turns out that my best saw my husband in a restaurant last night, one local to here. He was holding another woman's hand. He helped her into her coat as they left the restaurant together.

"It was him," replies Angie, quietly but firmly.

Angie looks terrible. There are dark shadows under her eyes and I notice for the first time that she has very deep crows feet. She is thirty-four, the same age as me. She looks older. Her ten month old daughter has never slept a night through since she was born. Angie has always envied the fact that Charlie is a good sleeper. I sigh and wonder whether her baby was responsible for her sleepless night last night, or was it my husband's infidelity? Angie also envies the facts that I am now thinner than I was before I got pregnant, and the house David and I bought in 1998 has just sold making a massive one hundred and eighty per cent profit. She never got on the property ladder and so she and her husband Robert throw huge sums of money at a landlord every month.

I feel sick.

Angie moves her coffee cup and nudges aside the half eaten muffins and soggy paper napkins that she's used to mop the various spillages that are part and parcel of the coffee-morning-with-children experience. The debris suggests Angie has been waiting for me for some time. She discreetly lays her hand on top of mine, and squeezes tightly. Her hand is clammy. She's plainly extremely nervous. I bet she wishes that she and Robert hadn't chosen that particular little Italian last night. I could almost feel sorry for her, except I feel too sorry for myself to spare the emotion on anyone else.

"I've... we've," she corrects, "we've suspected for a while."

I assume the 'we' she is referring to is her and dull Robert (Angie married the dull one, I married the fun one). But the 'we' might be any number of my friends, it might be all of North London. I don't know and I don't want to know. "There's been talk, rumours."

I want to tell her that there are always rumours. Our hands are always full with loads of dirty washing, babies and saucepans but our minds are empty except for gossip and speculation. Except, I know that I'm not being fair.

"I followed him. They went into that house, over there."

Angie points across the road to a terraced cottage, the type that are extremely prestigious to own and expensive to rent, it is clear that David's mistress is wealthy. And her windows are clean. Both facts annoy me intensely. I stare at the door that Angie is pointing at. It's a cold blue colour. The brass knocker is huge, vulgar. The pretty window boxes – full of fashionable black tulips – enrage me.

"I thought perhaps the woman was his sister, but…"

She knows David doesn't have a sister, so the conversation trails away. After a moment she finds inspiration enough to add, "Or maybe just a good friend."

I could declare that to be the case. Angie would believe me or at least pretend to. And that would be enough. If Angie could pretend this conversation hadn't taken place, then I could too.

Easily.

Because, I am good at pretending. I pretend to believe David when he rings me to say he has to work late, again. I pretend I believe him when I ask who he was talking to on the phone and he says it was a wrong number. I pretended to believe him when he told me that it was no longer company policy to take wives to the Christmas party. I've pretended so well that I had myself convinced.

It's as if Angie knows this, because she adds, "he's still in there. His car is parked around the corner. I thought you'd need to see for yourself."

I can't speak. If I open my mouth I'll howl. I look at her, and with difficulty, she meets my gaze.

"It's probably just sex, if they have, you know, had sex... that's all there will be to it." She sighs, recognizing the inadequacy of her flimsy excuses for my husband. "Did I do the right thing by telling you?" she asks again.

She's really asking do I hate her or him? Angie has baby spew on her cardigan. Her daughter is a sicky baby, she can't keep anything down. Charlie's a very neat baby. It is good luck, not good management, if you end up with a baby that doesn't puke up everything you force down. Angie has never believed that. She thinks I have magic formula which helps me be a more pristine mum and envied me for that.

I nod, as I still can't trust myself to speak.

"So what are you going to do now?" her face is contorted with the peculiar cocktail of relief and concern, it's devoid of envy.

I gather up the baby paraphernalia. His comfort blanket, which is as filthy as it is loved, his beaker, the nappy bag, his dummy. I carefully put these essentials away and then gently cajole Charles into his buggy.

As I pass out through the cafe door, it is as though I have two choices. I could go home and make casserole or...

I lift the vulgar knocker and rap it hard against the blue paintwork of David's mistress's door, the pretending has to stop: his and mine. I'm going to make more than stew this morning.

Chicken Stew

Makes 12 baby portions

Ingredients

½ small onion, finely chopped
15g butter
100g chicken breast, cut into chunks
1 medium carrot, trimmed and sliced
275g sweet potato peeled and chopped
300ml chicken stock

Method

Sauté the onion in the butter until softened. Add the chicken breast and sauté for 3-4 minutes. Add the vegetables, pour over the stock, bring to the boil and simmer, covered, for about 30mins or until the chicken is cooked through and the vegetables are tender. Puree in a blender to the desired consistency.

First, Catch Your Fish
by Penny Feeny

Tony was the sort of person who put his name down for an allotment. He was not the sort of person to walk out on a marriage. On a mild September morning Fran sat in shock at the kitchen table. Two letters lay in front of her. One, from the council, announced with pleasure that she and her husband had reached the top of the waiting list for an allotment. The second was from said husband, requesting 'space'. Sensing distress, the cat wound its tail around her legs. In the corner, five year old Molly, perplexed by her father's absence and her mother's shaking shoulders, quietly turned the pages of her book of fairytales.

<u>Jack and the Beanstalk</u>
Fran took Molly to visit the allotment. She'd never done any gardening and doubted she'd have much use for it. On the other hand, the notion of denying Tony even this small segment of 'space' conjured a sensation of sweet revenge. He'd already moved into a flat the other side of town, poky, she hoped, and rat-infested.

Molly was enchanted by everything she saw – from the functional metal lock-up – 'Oh, mummy, a little house!' to the fierce tangle of blackberries on which she feasted. Fran walked up and down the path between her allotment and the next and wondered if anything else was edible.

The adjoining plot was a magnificent tapestry of geometry and colour. There were big bright blocks of dahlias and chrysanthemums, a crimson line of beetroot, a golden clump of sweetcorn, and a vivid green ladder of runner beans climbing skywards. An elderly man was digging over a trench of bare earth.

"Excuse me," ventured Fran.

He unbent, stiffly. "Yes?"

"I wondered if you could tell me what's growing here."

"You new to this game?"

"Yes." Clearly she was a novice. She had no Wellington boots, no thermos of tea, no tools, for God's sake. And she was several decades younger than any other gardeners she could see. Perhaps her prospects here were limited after all. What use was getting her hands dirty on a Saturday afternoon if Tony didn't know what he was missing?

"It's all weeds," said the old man with satisfaction.

"I thought that might be spinach over there."

"Oh no. Docks." He paused. "You'll want to root them brambles out an' all."

"Couldn't I turn them into jam?"

"Aye, an' you could make nettle wine while you're about it."

Fran buried her face in her hands. "Oh God," she wailed. "I don't know where to start."

Molly bounded over and clasped her mother's legs, leaving a pattern of blackberry stains. The old man introduced himself as Jack and said soothingly, "Nowt to get in a tizz about. This time of year, everything's dying down anyhow. You want to drop by over the next few weeks and I'll give you a hand."

By the spring Fran felt a little more in control. Christmas had been difficult, but Christmas was over. Spring gave her new strength and new purpose. Under Jack's guidance she planted peas, lettuces, beans, leeks and tomatoes. Then he dropped his bombshell.

"Me, I'm just doing potatoes this year," he said. "I'll get my grandson to come down and earth them up. Got to go into hospital for a few weeks. They're giving me a new hip."

"Oh, I'm sorry."

"What's to be sorry? The old one's been plaguing me something fearful. I'll be glad of a new one."

What she meant, but couldn't say, was that just as she'd started to feel optimistic, she found herself stranded again.

<u>The Elves and the Shoemaker</u>

For over a month Fran avoided her troublesome patch of earth entirely. She wandered instead through shopping malls and planned recipes for dinner parties she never gave.

"How are the green fingers?" asked Tony when he dropped Molly off one evening. His knowing smirk infuriated her. On

Sunday morning she stormed over to the allotment, intending to grub up weeds until her back ached. She would prove she could control her crops even if she could control nothing else in her life. Within weeks she'd be podding her own peas, caramelising her own onions and stuffing her own courgettes.

Molly ran ahead – and then stopped abruptly, as if teetering on the edge of a cliff.

"Mummy, mummy, come quick!"

"What is it, darling?"

Molly's eyes were wide and shining. "I think it's magic."

In between rows of fresh green seedlings, the earth was newly churned, dark and moist as chocolate cake. Bamboo canes supported fledgling beans; feathery carrot fronds contrasted with the stiff spikes of onion and leek. Fran swivelled her head wildly. "Jack must be back," she declared and went to confer with one of the other old men on site. But nobody had seen Jack. As far as they knew he was still hobbling on crutches, complaining at the inferior quality of shop-bought vegetables. They'd assumed she'd been coming along herself at odd hours. As if I had the energy, she thought ruefully, let alone the inclination.

"It has to be a mistake," she said to Molly. "Someone's got the plots mixed up. We'll come back next week and sort it out."

Next week the patch was again immaculate. The produce had grown and prospered; weeds had been eliminated. Fran was as disturbed as if she were the target of an extended practical joke. It crossed her mind that Tony was taunting her, secretly taking over the land he'd always intended for himself. Unfortunately she couldn't accuse him without confessing her own incompetence.

"Molly," she began, "Has Daddy ever said anything about working here?"

Molly was kneeling, building a wigwam of little sticks. She looked up. "Oh but I know who's doing it," she said brightly.

"So he is?"

She shook her head. "Not Daddy, no. It's elves."

"It's what?"

"You know mummy, the elves and the shoemaker. The elves come and work all night and in the morning there are beautiful new shoes on the bench and the shoemaker sells them and buys more leather and they make more shoes. Only he never sees them and when they've made him rich they go away and don't come back."

"Molly, it isn't elves."

The stubborn set of her shoulders said she was insistent.

<u>The Pied Piper</u>

The strawberries were the first fruits to ripen. Molly begged to go after school to pick them. She'd crouch among the plants – each one lovingly surrounded with a collar of clean straw – popping juicy berries into her mouth. Fran, having nothing else to do, sat in a deckchair with the newspaper – like one of the old men herself, she thought grimly. She was still hoping to catch Tony red-handed. She now wondered if he were trying to make amends, to sweeten her up for a reconciliation. She'd turn him down of course.

It was a bright evening, the sun still high. The newsprint flickered and blurred. She'd left her sunglasses in the car and called to let Molly know she was going to fetch them. The trip, along the hedge, out into the cul-de-sac, locating the glasses in the glove box and exchanging a few words with a neighbour, took about five minutes. When she got back her paper was fluttering limply on the seat of her chair and Molly had disappeared.

Fran willed herself not to panic. Probably she'd gone to wash her hands at the stand-pipe, or perhaps she was chasing a butterfly in the heedless way children do. Then she noticed the door of Jack's lock-up was slightly ajar. With relief she picked her way along the grass path, preparing to scold Molly for running off and to welcome Jack's return at the same time. In the gloom she could see two shapes squatting on their haunches. She was surprised to find Jack so agile already and then realised in an instant this man was a stranger. A stranger holding hands with her daughter.

"Molly!" she screeched.

Molly bounced upwards, beaming. The man also stood and turned. It was too dark to see his face, but she was certain he was unfamiliar. "Who are you?" she demanded.

In curiously accented English, he said. "I'm Jack's grandson."

"Really?"

He seemed amused. "Yes. Really."

Fran couldn't say why she'd expected the grandson to be a teenager helping out for a bit of extra pocket money – Jack was well into his seventies. As the three of them stepped outside into the light, she saw a young man, near her own age, with eyes as dark as treacle.

Molly was tugging her skirt. "It's him, mummy. He's the one."

"What one?"

"He's the elf.""

"The what!?"

"My grandfather," he explained, "Told me you may need some help." He smiled modestly. "I do what I can."

Fran didn't know whether to be angry or grateful. "But why didn't you tell me what you were doing – leave a note or something?"

"I think for many weeks you aren't here. I supposed you are away."

Fran was puzzled. Unlike Molly, she found it hard to accept that a grown man could descend apparently from nowhere and perform magic.

"You aren't local, are you?" she said accusingly, recalling Jack's slow Yorkshire vowels.

"I am Catalan. My name is Xavier."

It appeared Jack's daughter had married a Spaniard and moved to Tarragona. Xavier was involved in the family business, exporting wines and oils. He was combining family duties with investigating new markets. He worked hard, he didn't meet many people, he found growing things relaxing.

"I should thank you,' said Fran, ashamed of her suspicions. "I'd never have managed all this on my own. Though I'd meant to prove I could."

Xavier plucked a broad bean from a row beside them. He ran his thumbnail along the edge of the pod and opened it to expose the pale tender beans like pearls in their velvety beds. "These are now ready," he said. "Also the peas. You should eat."

"You've done all the work," said Fran. "You should have first pick of the crop."

"They are most delicious," said Xavier, rolling a bean on his tongue and crunching it between his teeth, "If they are softened for moments only in the best olive oil."

"Well then," said Fran boldly. "Why don't I cook some for you. Why don't you come to dinner?"

Pussycat, Pussycat

Molly was furious Xavier was coming for a meal on a night when she would be staying with her father. "There'll be other times," Fran assured her, although she had no idea how the evening would develop. She knew only that if she were going to make a fool of herself she'd prefer to do so without Molly's help.

She'd spent hours making a hollandaise sauce to go with the salmon she was planning to grill. She wanted Xavier to arrive and find everything perfectly organised, from the Sweet William on the table to the new potatoes scraped and ready to boil. She wanted to coil her hair into a chignon and try out a new lipstick. But he arrived early and she answered the door with her hands dripping wet, convinced she must smell of fish.

He'd brought two bottles of white wine. "Is better if we work together, no?" he said. He cast an admiring glance at the salmon and then spotted the pile of peas and beans awaiting podding. He scooped up a handful and began shelling them.

Fran, more accustomed to tearing open a frozen pack with her teeth, tried to match his pace. The rhythm of their movements, the close proximity of a male body after so many months drew her in. Concentrating on the pattern of their hands working together, she scarcely noticed the sudden movement behind her. If she had turned her head more swiftly she'd have seen the salmon appear to leap into the air. In practice she heard the light thud of four paws landing gracefully and the click of the cat-flap swinging shut. By the time she pushed back her chair and jumped to her feet, neither cat nor fish were anywhere to be seen.

Clearly this was the stuff of comedy. On Xavier's face amusement had already replaced surprise. But Fran was devastated. At a point where her hopes had risen far higher than was wise, she suddenly saw how absurd her optimism had been. Against all her good intentions, she burst into tears. Xavier, startled by her reaction, put his arms around her. "Is not so terrible," he said.

"I know!" she wept. "I know I'm being stupid but I can't help it…I'm going to kill that bloody cat."

His embrace tightened. He dipped his face; his mouth closed on hers. He tasted of wine, of fruit; his skin had the warmth and colour of honey. Fran, not wanting to break the seal of their kiss by drawing breath, felt her own flesh liquefy. She was overcome by the force of her body's reaction. Glancing down at her bare arm, she expected blisters to break out where his grip had scorched her skin. She made herself take a step back.

"I didn't realise I was so…hungry," she said.

Xavier looked delighted. He traced his finger from the tip of her chin, down her throat, between her breasts and along the curve of her hip. "So now we cook the dinner together, no?"

In fact he was the one who dressed the potatoes in the glossy hollandaise, who sliced transparent circles of white onion to mix with the broad beans. Fran moved shakily about the room finding plates and cutlery, adjusting the slatted blind against the probing rays of the sun. Every time their paths crossed she was jolted anew by the heat of contact.

"This," said Xavier, when they finally sat down, "will be a most memorable last meal."

The flush of colour drained from Fran's face. "Last meal?"

"Tomorrow," he smiled, "I must go home."

"I see."

A long account followed: of Jack's improved mobility, of the progress made with distributors, of the need to attend to the vineyards, his hopes for the harvest. But Fran wasn't really paying attention. Somewhere in her brain, another door slammed shut.

<u>Queen of Hearts</u>

Tony called round with a bunch of red roses interspersed with frothy gypsophilia.

"Molly said something about a Spaniard."

"Really? Are you sure she didn't mention an elf? Or the pied piper of Hamelin?"

"Elves…" said Tony slowly. "Now you come to mention it."

"She's always had a vigorous imagination."

He held out the flowers. "Apparently I forgot your birthday."

Over thirty was over the hill. When Molly found her crying on her birthday, she'd used the excuse of Tony's appalling memory. She took the roses graciously; it was not his sort of gesture. "Thank you. Flowers are always appreciated."

"I was wondering…" By now he was leaning against the kitchen counter, watching her fill a vase with water.

"Yes?"

"If you need any help on the allotment." He flexed his arm muscles. "I wouldn't mind a bit of fresh air and exercise and it must be hard work for you."

"No, I'm fine. It's all harvesting at this time of year anyhow. I enjoy it."

She could see he was casting around for excuses to stay but she didn't encourage him. There was a cornucopia of tomatoes to pick and she wanted to try slow-roasting and preserving them with oregano and olive oil. Sometimes she imagined Xavier returning. She imagined him bending to wrap himself around her as she stooped to pull carrots or beets, the warmth of his breath on her neck. But it would never happen. Jack's hip was just fine and dandy now; he was quite able to do his own digging. If she ever saw Xavier again it would be as a businessman in suit and tie, making a brief courtesy call. She should stop day-dreaming.

On an Indian summer Saturday, Molly wanted to have a teddy bears' picnic. She spread a tablecloth in front of the Wendy house, as she called the lock-up, and set out a bottle of lemonade and a plate of jam tarts. She'd rolled the pastry herself so the tarts were oddly-sized and misshapen, but this year's strawberry jam glowed a satisfactory ruby red.

A barricade of runner beans hid the tea party from Fran's view. She was searching under the leaves when Molly's squeal pierced her. She dropped her basket and raced towards the wail. Molly had been distributing tarts to her teddies. "Two's been stolen!" she sobbed.

"Darling, you probably counted wrong."

"No," she insisted. "I counted right. One, two, three, four, five, six, seven and one for me." Her sorrow was heart-rending. Fran sank down to her knees and gently wiped away her tears with her thumb. A shadow slanted across the sad little grouping.

"I'm sorry," said the shadow and held out his hands. On each palm lay a jam tart. "They looked so delicious," he said. "And I couldn't see you, to ask permission."

"I was getting water." Molly had brightened considerably. "It's OK . You can eat them."

Xavier turned to Fran who'd not said a word. She'd straightened up and was standing very still, wary of breathing out.

"I have brought you a present," he said.

"I didn't know if you'd be coming back."

"We're opening new premises here. I have to oversee."

He opened a large bag and pulled out an oblong package. Unlikely to be jewellery, thought Fran. The package was hard and had a curiously pungent smell. Not clothes or perfume either. Possibly something made of leather, although the shape was puzzling.

"Open it," said Xavier eagerly.

She found herself holding a stiff flat object encrusted with salt.

"What is it, mummy?"

"The finest bacalau," said Xavier. "But your cat will not like."

Fran turned the salt cod over; she didn't know what to say. Xavier seized her wrists in his hands. He was grinning. "I know a very good recipe," he said. "You cook with onions, potatoes, cream, a little nutmeg, a little pepper. It becomes very rich and full of flavour. I will show you. But first…"

"First?"

"First you must soak the fish. For two, three days, maybe more. This dish takes a very long time..."

Xavier's Baked Bacalao

Serves 2

Ingredients

400g dried salt cod
2 medium onions
2 large potatoes
Sauce
20g butter
1 tbsp flour
300ml milk/single cream
2 egg yolks
2 tsp lemon juice
nutmeg and black pepper

Method

Soak the salt cod in several changes of cold water for at least two days. Poach the cod in boiling water for 10 minutes, skin and flake into chunks.

Chop the onions finely and fry very slowly and gently until they melt.

Meanwhile slice the potatoes into discs and parboil.

Make a thin white sauce by combining butter, flour, milk and/or cream. Add grated nutmeg and black pepper. Beat egg yolks and lemon juice together. Pour on the hot white sauce and mix.

Layer the cooked onions in an ovenproof dish. Add the chunks of cod and finish with the potatoes.

Pour the sauce over the potatoes and bake the dish in a moderate oven for 25-30 minutes

Weather Change
by Rose Bray

As they turned the corner of the street, the wind and rain hit them with full force. Lisa's flimsy umbrella blew inside out and was wrenched out of her hand.

"Oh let the damn thing go," she muttered. She felt so miserable that she couldn't care less about it. But no, he had to go chasing after it, as it went twisting and turning down the street to end up in the gutter.

Tom retrieved it and brought it back triumphantly. He closed it and then opened it up again, looking ruefully at the crooked frame. "One of the spars is broken, I'll try to mend it when we get home."

"For heaven's sake, Tom, chuck it in that rubbish bin. It's had it!" Irritation made her speak more sharply than she had intended. She'd had enough. Three days camping in non-stop rain on a misty headland had made her want to abandon this holiday.

The rain was beating down, chilling her scalp. Within a few minutes, her short hair was plastered to her head like a scull cap. Icy fingers of water ran down her hair and edged their way between her collar and warm skin.

"Won't be long before we're there, Lisa." He gave her shoulder a squeeze. "See there's the Star of India over there on the corner. Don't the lights look lovely reflecting on the wet road?" Why did he always have to look on the bright side of everything? She didn't want her spirits lifting at the moment. It did look like an exotic place shining out amongst the stone buildings and closed shops, but she wasn't going to agree with him.

"Look at this skirt. It's soaked!" The folds of the fabric clung to her legs unpleasantly. She'd made the effort to get out of her jeans for the evening to please him, but nothing was going well.

"You'll be all right when we get inside," he soothed.

It's OK for him, she thought. He's like a great bear with an impervious skin, and that mop of frizzy brown hair just throws off the rain.

Right now, we should be walking along a beautiful sandy beach on a Greek island, just as the heat goes out of the sun. Instead, what are we doing? Trying to keep dry in a tent!

Why had she let him talk her into this situation? But of course she knew why. When they were planning their holidays in May, England was enjoying a heat wave. They'd sat in the garden with cold drinks in their hands, trying to decide where to go.

"Let's go to Samos," she'd said waving the brochure with its blue seas and dazzling white houses in front of him. She'd wanted this holiday to be special.

"Or we could go camping in England, on the coast, somewhere unspoilt," Tom said. "No airport queues. No traffic or stress." She knew he pictured himself as a boy again, running across fields, building makeshift bridges over streams, leaping from rock to rock on the beach.

Lisa wasn't so sure, never having camped before in her life. She was a 'daily shower and shampoo' sort of person. She imagined herself strolling along some foreign shoreline in a short skirt which would show off her long legs and fantastic tan.

"With the money we save we could have central heating put in next winter." He'd touched her weak spot. They were doing up an old place that was so cold, last year, that they'd had to go to bed early to keep warm. She smiled, well, at least that was one excuse. After a bottle of white wine, and the thought of a warm winter in the flat, he'd convinced her.

Now look where she was. A whole week with rain and mud. She didn't get much holiday as it was. "Well, I've had enough! It's home for us tomorrow unless some miracle happens and the weather turns fine."

"Let's try one more day," he said, not very hopefully.

"No chance. I'd rather be home."

As they crossed the road, Lisa had to admit to herself that it looked an attractive restaurant. Tom held open the door for her and a rush of warm air welcomed them in. She delighted in the rich aroma of spices, cardamom, cumin, ginger and roasted garlic.

The waiter, complete with waistcoat and black bow-tie, greeted them with a broad smile. He took their wet anoraks and hung them on coat hangers as carefully as if they'd been bought at Harrods. "Please wait," he said. He reappeared a minute later with a fluffy white towel and indicated that it was for Lisa's hair. Things were looking up.

"Well, this is different," she said turning to Tom. "I've never had service like this before." She towelled her hair vigorously. "People pay a lot of money for a style like this," she quipped.

They were shown to a table in a corner. Lisa looked round appreciatively. Each table had a dark red cloth which reached almost to the floor, with a white cloth placed diagonally across it. Every table had a candle in a glass holder and fresh red carnations. Always a good sign, when the flowers are fresh, she thought. The room was full of diners and, as a background to their chatter, was the sound of Indian sitar music with its strange but not unpleasant rhythms.

A salver with a pile of poppadums was placed before them and they started to eat hungrily. The poppadums were light and crisp, crackling in their fingers, exploding in their mouths.

Lisa began to relax. Tom leaned across and touched her cheek. "You look so beautiful in the candlelight," he smiled, "with your spiky hair and your glowing cheeks. "

Suddenly, she knew that she did. All that fresh air (correction, all that wet fresh air) had given her cheeks colour. And an appetite. She'd never felt so hungry! Their roghan josh and pasanda arrived with naan peshwari bread and rice.

"Good heavens. We'll never manage all this," they laughed as the waiter put the dishes in front of them.

But they did. The warmth of the food and hot spices coursed round their bodies, driving out the coldness that had settled in their bones during the day. They smiled at each other. Tom reached across and held her hand, then he kissed the palm sensuously. "I've made enquiries into The George and Dragon for bed and breakfast tonight. En suite – with a big deep bath with lashings of hot water, it's just across the way. Do you fancy staying there?"

"Oh you wonderful man! I would love it! You know I would." The thought of a hot bath, clean sheets and a proper bed almost made her cry. She wanted to hug him there and then, but he was a shy man. "But I haven't brought my pyjamas, Tom," she teased.

"Do you think you can manage without them for one night?"

"Well, I shall have to, won't I?" she laughed happily.

As they strolled across the road, they could see a few stars. The rain had stopped, leaving the town with a new, fresh feeling.

Maybe the sun would shine tomorrow. Somehow, she felt it just might.

Roghan Josh

Ingredients

450g lean boneless lamb cut into bite sized pieces
2.5cm green root ginger (peeled and chopped)
3 cloves of garlic
50g natural yoghurt like natural Yeo Valley
1 level tsp of chilli powder
1 tsp of salt
50g of unsalted butter
2 medium-sized onions (finely chopped)
1½ tsp turmeric powder
1 tsp ground coriander
½ tsp cumin seeds
4 small cardamoms
110g peeled tomatoes
1½ tsp of garam masala
freshly milled black pepper
25g of ground almonds
fresh coriander to garnish

Method

Place all the cubes of lamb into a bowl.
Mix the ginger, garlic, yoghurt, chilli powder together and add to the meat. Coat the meat on all sides. Cover, then leave in the fridge for 3 hours or overnight. Melt the butter and fry the onions until evenly browned. Add turmeric, coriander, cardamom and cumin seeds. Fry for one minute, then add peeled tomatoes and simmer for 2 to 3 minutes. Put the lamb with its marinade into the pan and stir constantly for 5 minutes before adding the garam masala and 275ml of cold water. Bring everything to the boil and reduce to the lowest heat you can get. for about 1hour or until the meat is tender. When cooked stir in the ground almonds and garnish with coriander leaves.

Desserts

Too Many Cookbooks Spoil The Troth

by Dawn Hudd

Greek tomato salad to start, followed by grilled mackerel with sweet and sour cabbage. Jenny flinched at the feel of the mackerel skin, but it had to be washed, dried, sprinkled with lemon juice and left to stand. Thank goodness feta cheese was easy to come by these days. The salad was waiting in the fridge, with just the dressing to be poured over it just before she served it. All she had to do was wait for Tom to come home and then she could grill the fish. It had to be fresh and perfect.

This new cookbook was fine except for one thing, she thought. It took an extra ten minutes to work out how long each recipe would take to prepare and cook. Jenny shuffled through the pages at the front of the book and noted down the publisher's address. She made a note to write to them and suggest that they put timings in the next edition. Maybe the new Jamie Oliver she'd ordered would be better.

Right from the beginning, from the moment she'd accepted Tom's marriage proposal, they had agreed that theirs would be a traditional, old-fashioned marriage. Tom, who had a good job and great prospects, would be the breadwinner, and Jenny would be the homemaker. The housewife. She rolled the word around her tongue and savoured it. None of this politically correct domestic-engineer nonsense for her. Housewife – and by golly she was going to be good at it.

Jenny looked around her pristine semi. Not a book or an ornament out of place. Of course, she mused, it would be different when the first baby came along, but until then Tom would have a wonderful home to come back to every night. And good home-cooked fresh food prepared with love.

"Was it like this for you, Mum?" Jenny sat in her parents' perfect living room, sipping tea from bone china tea cups, fairy cakes delicately placed on matching plates. “Did you find it hard to keep home when you first got married?”

“Goodness. No, my dear. I’m a natural housewife. I’m afraid you take after your father.” Mrs Lewis glanced out of the window to where Jenny’s father was digging the potato plot. “You just have to try that bit harder.” She picked up her linen napkin and dabbed daintily at the corner of her mouth.

“But Tom doesn’t seem to appreciate how difficult it is for me.” Jenny was near to tears. “Last night he didn’t even comment on the meal I prepared for him, and it took me hours.”

“Well there’s your mistake.”

“I don’t follow you, Mum.”

“You see, darling, you shouldn’t be expecting him to show gratitude all the time. He’s a man. They expect perfection in their lives as a right, even when they’re so failing in themselves.” She sighed and looked again towards Mr Lewis in the vegetable garden. “Even your father isn’t perfect, you know.”

“Mother! I’ve never heard you talk like that before.”

“Between you and me, sweetheart, since he retired he’s spent more and more time in the garden than ever. And the mud he brings into the house, you wouldn’t believe.” She made a mock gesture of shock. “Keep your house your own and make sure your husband knows his place. That way you’ll both know where you stand.”

Next day she took lunch with her old school friend, Olivia.

“I don’t know why you’re asking my advice, Jen. I can’t keep hold of a man for more than six weeks, tops. At least you married yours.”

“Yes. But last night he hardly touched the Salmon Louise I prepared for him, and I had to throw away the champagne sorbet. He said he was full.”

“Salmon Louise? What’s that when it’s at home? Oh, Jen. Don’t you think you might be trying just a bit too hard? Maybe he’d just like to come home and cuddle up to you on the sofa.’ Olivia picked at her salad with her fork. ‘Why don’t you just order a takeaway instead of spending hours creating gourmet food and washing up?”

“But I’m at home all day, Liv. We agreed that it was my job to do the cooking and cleaning. He *should* have good home-cooked food to come home to. And a tidy house.”

"Tidy! Your house is like a show home. Do you still make him take his shoes off at the front door?"

"Of course." Jenny looked indignant. "The carpet's almost brand new."

"Yes. And cream," added Olivia. "What on earth made you choose that colour? Not very practical for when the sprogs start to arrive."

"If they ever do."

Olivia reached across and touched Jenny's arm. "Oh, Jen. You haven't been trying very long. These things take time."

"It happened easily enough for you."

"And look where it got me. A single mum at twenty-seven, slogging my guts out to keep a roof over our heads. You're very lucky. You have a man who loves you, a wonderful home, and soon you'll have a perfect family to go with it, I'm sure.'

"I doubt it. Things aren't very good in *that* department at the moment, either. All he wants to do these days is sleep – and I mean go to sleep."

"I'm sure it's just a blip. You two were made for each other. Look, I have to dash. Two more hours at work and I can pick Amelia up from nursery. You and Tom should come over at the weekend. See a bit of real parenting in action. You never know, it might help.' Olivia kissed her friend's cheek affectionately, pressing a ten pound note into her hand. "For my share of the lunch. Ring me."

Jenny watched her leave, full of admiration for the way Olivia managed to cope with her rich and complicated life.

Jenny knocked on the door.

"Oh, hi sis. I wasn't expecting you today. I thought you two lovebirds would want to spend your first anniversary together. Oh, what's wrong?" Sandy looked at Jenny's tear-stained face and led her into the kitchen. She moved a pile of children's paintings from a chair and sat Jenny down. "Now. Tell Big Sister all about it."

"I don't think he loves me any more," wailed Jenny. "'Last night he was late home, and he didn't ring me. He said he couldn't get a signal on his mobile, and he was stuck in traffic. Dinner was ruined. I said I'd make something else and he said he'd get fish and chips. We had an almighty row, and he slept on the settee last night, and…"

Jenny paused for breath and Sandy took the opportunity. “Whoa, there. Aren’t you jumping the gun a bit? Everybody has arguments. Kissing and making up is what it’s all about. He was probably a bit uptight about being late and ruining your lovely food. After all, you do try really hard.” Jenny didn’t notice the wry expression on her sister’s face.

“But it was my fault.”

“What do you mean? He was the one who was late, wasn’t he?”

Jenny lifted her head, her eyes puffy from all the crying, and told her. “When he said he’d get chips I said wasn’t my cooking good enough for him. Then he said I should stop being so neurotic, and why didn’t I get myself a job or something, anything, instead of fussing over the house and everything. It was horrible.”

Sandy covered Jenny’s hand with hers and looked straight at her sister. “Maybe he has a point? You are a bit preoccupied with the house and cooking. Maybe a part-time job, until you do, you know, have a family.”

“But we agreed, me and Tom. I’d stay at home and he’d go to work. That way, when we did have a family, we wouldn’t miss my income because I wouldn’t have one. We would have a lovely home and…and…” Jenny was crying even harder now.

“‘And what?”

“And now it’s too late.”

“What’s too late? You’ve only had a tiff, for goodness sake. Buy a bottle of wine on the way home, light a few candles and it’ll be fine.”

“No it won’t,” sniffed Jenny. “He’s going to leave me, I know he is. There won’t be any babies. He hasn’t been near me for weeks. He leaves half his dinner most nights. Sandy, I’ve made such a mess of things.” Jenny got up to leave.

“Sit down,” said Sandy, sharply. ‘I think you need to hear a few things if you want to get your marriage back on track.’

Shocked, Jenny did as she was told.

“Jenny? Jen? I’m home. Where are you?” The rooms were dark, the curtains drawn. “Look, I’m sorry about last night. I shouldn’t have said those dreadful things. Can you forgive me?” He spoke into the void. There was no answer.

He put down the bunch of yellow roses and the bottle of champagne he'd brought in and sniffed the air. There was something wrong, something he couldn't quite place. No smells! Nothing cooking, and the table hadn't been set. With panic rising he raced through the rooms, calling her. Then he heard it. From upstairs came the sound of music. Taking the stairs two at a time he followed the sound – to the bedroom. He pushed open the door.

"Jen?" She was sat on the edge of the bed. "Are you ill? What's wrong?"

"No. I'm not ill. I've been thinking. I'm sorry, I didn't realise the time. I haven't cooked any dinner. I was wondering, as it's our anniversary, whether we could go out for a meal. If you're not too mad at me?"

Tom leant down and kissed the tip of her nose. "Mad at you? I love you. I couldn't stay mad at you for long."

"There's a new restaurant in the high street. I thought we could go there?"

"I've got a better idea,' said Tom. "How about we just have a rummage in the cupboard? I noticed a bottle of red on the kitchen table."

"But there's only a couple of tins of beans in the cupboard – the ones I keep in for Sandy's boys."

"Can I let you into a little secret?" Tom sat down on the bed beside her. "I love beans on toast.'"

"But I thought…"

"And I love sausage and chips," he continued, "and Indian take-aways, and pizza. In fact, I love junk food almost as much as I love your gourmet cooking. It's about time you stopped listening to your mother and started listening to your husband. We have to find what works for us, not what works for her."

Jenny thought back to her Dad, beavering away in the garden in all weathers. "Or doesn't work for her. Oh, Tom. I've been so silly."

"Champagne really goes well with beans, doesn't it," giggled Jenny, an hour later as they sat at the kitchen table.

Tom moved round and refilled her glass. He bent down and whispered into her ear, "I can think of something else it goes really well with.' He took her hand and led her upstairs. "It's time for dessert, and I don't mean lemon mousse."

Revenge Tastes So Sweet

by Kelly Rose Bradford

"Do you have anything for…" The blonde at the counter lowered her voice and looked self-consciously around her. "Constipation?" she whispered.

I nodded sympathetically and reached for a packet from the shelf behind me.

"This should do the trick," I smiled, "That's two twenty please."

"Oh, and can I put this in as well please?" She handed me a prescription and I gave it a cursory glance.

Shannon Wallace.

I felt a little chill run down my spine and my Shredded Wheat perform a jig in my tummy.

"I'll, er, just check with the Pharmacist," I stuttered.

I'd seen Shannon Wallace's name written down before. The first time it was on a cigarette paper folded up in Jake's back pocket. I'd fished it out before putting his jeans through the wash.

"Met her in the pub last night – wants a quote for new windows," he'd shrugged, not meeting my eye as he shovelled his chips in his mouth.

Then I'd seen it again, this time on a 'while you were out' slip on the dashboard of his van. It just said 'Shannon called' this time. No surname, and the message had been taken by the receptionist at the building firm where he worked. He had shrugged it off again. "Be about her windows again, I suppose, I'd best give her a call." Then I'd seen it flash up on his mobile phone screen one morning a few weeks back. He was supposed to have been at work but the van had needed a wheel changing and whilst he was on the drive doing it, his phone had trilled out from the kitchen table. He had the audacity to have the ringer programmed to 'Sex Bomb'.

"Don't answer it!" he'd shouted, all of a fluster, "It'll be work…checking up on me." But I'd already seen the 'Shannon' flash up on the display.

Of course I'd had it out with him, but he denied there was anything going on and Shannon was no more than a customer. "She must be pushing fifty, for gawd's sake," he'd insisted, "Face like a bag of nails. Good grief, Fiona, if only you could see her, you'd realise how stupid you're being."

The pharmacist approved Shannon's prescription request and I walked slowly back to the counter to give her the receipt. Fifty indeed. The prescription gave her date of birth – 1980! Her straight blonde hair hung centre parted down past her shoulders like a pair of satin curtains, her full lips glossed into a pink pout. Her cleavage heaved up around her neck and a golden S on a chain snaked its way between her breasts. I hated her.

"That'll be six pounds forty please," I said, giving her ticket.

"Er, no," she replied, "It's, er, the Pill. I don't have to pay for it." I glanced at the prescription again and realised my mistake. A ball of rage engulfed my stomach. The Contraceptive Pill!

"It'll be about ten minutes." I finally said, "Will you wait?"

She glanced at her watch and shook her head.

"No, I need to pop to the supermarket." Her mouth relaxed into a soft smile, "My man is coming over for a romantic dinner tonight – I'm going to do the works – three course meal, champagne, the lot."

"Best get some oysters then," I suggested helpfully, "They're an aphrodisiac, so they say."

"Yeah?" She looked smug, "Not that my Jay needs an aphrodisiac, but yeah, oysters sound good."

"Strawberries and cream for dessert?" I asked bitterly, knowing that 'Jay' hated them.

"He's bringing dessert," she sighed dreamily. I almost felt sorry for her. Poor deluded fool. That'll soon change.

"It's a bit naughty really," she said, with a wicked grin, "He's married – told his wife he's going to visit his friend in hospital!"

"That is very naughty." I agreed.

Poor Trevor had broken his foot when Larry had run over it with the tipper truck apparently. Jake was full of concern.

"I know it sounds soft, love, but I've even got him some flowers. You know how Trevor loves his garden!"

"I'm sure he'll appreciate it," I said, "And the red ribbon too."

Jake blushed a little and shoved the dozen red roses into a carrier bag.

"And I'm sure he'll be pleased to see you've made such an effort with a suit – and aftershave. You're such a good friend, Jake." I gave him a kiss on his clean shaven cheek. He looked a little taken a back. "Give him my best, won't you?"

Jake nodded and picked up his car keys.

"Oh, before you go, look, I've made him a lovely chocolate pudding – you know what hospital grub is like."

I took a huge bowl from the fridge.

"Thanks, love," Jake said with genuine gratitude in his voice. No doubt I'd saved him from having to buy a frozen dessert from the garage en route to Shannon's.

"Might be a bit late, you know, if I pop for a quick one with the boys afterwards."

"You take as long as you like."

I waved him goodbye from the porch and climbed the stairs to the bedroom where I began packing my bags. Shannon was welcome to Jake. I'd had enough. I hoped they enjoyed their romantic meal together. She obviously didn't know that Jake was allergic to seafood, so I couldn't see the oysters going down too well. At least they had my lovely dessert to indulge in.

Oh yes, Shannon, I have something for constipation all right. A gorgeous chocolate pudding, lightly laced with my own special ingredient. Good job I get a staff discount – those boxes of laxatives don't come cheap.

Chocolate Cake

Ingredients

125g/4½oz plain flour
120g/4¼oz caster sugar
3 tsp baking powder
4 tbsp cocoa powder
250ml/8¾fl oz milk
85g/3oz unsalted butter
2 eggs, lightly beaten
1 tsp vanilla extract

Method

Preheat the oven to 180ºC/350ºF/Gas 4 and sift the flour, salt, sugar, baking powder and cocoa powder together, then beat in the butter, milk, egg and vanilla extract. When well combined, divide between four greased pudding moulds. Pour boiling water over the puddings then bake in the oven for 20-25 minutes. Serve with crème fraîche or double cream

Brief Encounter
by Jill Steeples

In my kitten heels and polka-dot skirt, I'm doing a sixty metre sprint to catch the 17.34 from London Euston and today, like most days, I make it to platform nine, with only seconds to spare. But by the time I reach the ticket barrier it seems that neither I, nor the train, will be going anywhere fast.

"Sorry love," says the guard in a wearily resigned fashion, that suggests it's not the first time he's trotted out the words, "points failure at Watford Junction. It'll be another forty minutes before the next train leaves."

Despite the temptation, I refrain from stamping my foot in frustration and sobbing pathetically into the arms of the unsuspecting railway worker. Instead, I curse inwardly, raging against my much-loathed job in the city and its equally loathed journey. A light bulb flashing moment, if ever there was one, I reflect, vowing there and then to spend the next weekend scouring the newspapers to find a job closer to home.

For the time being, only a cup of coffee and sugar-fix will do, so I wander up on to the concourse and head into the first café that I find. The place is heaving with disgruntled commuters, I wait my turn and order a cappuccino, picking up a blatantly seductive packet of Heavenly Cookies. To hell with the diet! Juggling my tray, handbag and newspaper I head towards the only vacant seat at the far end of the café.

"Do you mind if I sit here?" I ask the man sat opposite, whose belongings are spread haphazardly across the table.

"Sure," he says, looking up to meet my eyes, making a half-hearted attempt at clearing some space.

I recognise him as a 17.34 regular. Thirty-ish with dark, closely cut hair, come-to-bed eyes and a bone structure to die for, it'd be hard for any girl not to notice this guy in the crowd. And, at such close proximity, I find myself checking out the third finger of his left hand. My heart does a little leap of triumph when I find it tantalisingly bare.

Sadly though, I don't think my presence has even registered in his stratosphere, as he's turned his attention straight back to his book without so much as a friendly smile in my direction.

I stir my coffee and reach for my packet of cookies, which has edged its way under his papers. As my newly manicured nails settle on the distinctive red packaging, I notice his dark eyes flash from his book onto my hands. Slowly now, aware of his full-on attention, I take a cookie from its cellophane wrapping. He puts down his book and turns the intensity of his gaze onto my eyes, watching intently as my lips settle around the crumbling contours of my snack. And, quite why I cannot understand, but the atmosphere between us now is electric and Mr Gorgeous cannot take his eyes off me as I nibble seductively at one cookie after another. Feigning indifference to his scrutiny, my tongue traces the outer corners of my mouth in search of stray crumbs. I'm just about to lay claim to the final cookie when his strong hand comes down firmly on mine, and gently he removes my hand and picks up the remaining one for himself.

Now it's my turn to watch in amazement as, audaciously, he savours the last few delicious mouthfuls of my chocolate biscuit! I'm speechless, but only too aware that at a moment like this, there's no need for words. We're talking our own language, the language of love. The intensity between us speaks volumes.

I laugh coquettishly in an attempt to draw him into conversation, but before I get the chance, he's standing up, gathering together his papers and with a final lingering look, he leaves me, feeling bemused and deflated, alone at the table

"Er, excuse me," I say meekly, to his departing figure, but it's too late, he's already out the door and on his way to the train.

"Train!" I shriek, suddenly remembering what I'm doing there. Hurriedly, I pick up my handbag and make a mad dash for Platform nine.

I scan the carriages for Mr Gorgeous, hopeful that I'll find him sitting waiting for me, but I can't see him anywhere and it's with some disappointment that I climb into the last carriage, settling myself into a window seat.

It's then as I'm fumbling around in my handbag that I let out the heartfelt scream.

"Aarrgghh!" The other passengers turn to look at me in concern.

"Oh my God!" I gasp, clasping my head in my hands in horror. Everyone's staring at me expectantly.

"My cookies!" I say, by way of explanation, wrenching the unopened packet from my handbag and holding it aloft.

In the weeks that follow, I do my utmost to miss the 17.34, electing instead to work late to avoid the humiliation of bumping into that man. And, with time, I'm able to put the whole embarrassing incident out of my mind, as I focus on the more important task of finding a new job, closer to home.

So that's what I'm doing here now, sitting in this plush reception area of a purpose-built office block, only a stone's throw away from my road. And the job, as a marketing research assistant for a company re-locating from London, has my name written all over it. It'll mean a salary cut, but with the money I save on travelling it'll make it more than worthwhile. Perhaps, on reflection, it does seem a little too good to be true.

"You can go in now, Miss Jewell," says the young receptionist. "Mr Phillip's office is the first door on the right."

Confidently, I walk into the office, but as soon as I see the suited figure behind the desk, my heart plummets to the ground. It's him. Mr Gorgeous. Mr Stuff-my-face-with-chocolate. If he didn't recognise me before, in the coffee bar, he certainly does now and he does a delightful double take as he clocks the discomfort on my face.

"Ah, Carly Jewell, haven't we met before?" His eyes, I swear, are dancing with delight.

"Not sure," I mutter, lamely.

He picks up my CV, turning it over in his hands.

"Would you like a coffee?" he asks.

"No, thank you," I say, eager now to get this whole thing over with as quickly as possible.

"How about a biscuit?" he suggests, pushing a plateful of chocolate digestives my way.

'No, thank you,' I croak again.

"Well, I hope you don't mind if I do?" he says, with a devilish grin. Slowly, he takes a biscuit from the plate, places his lips around its smooth contours, hesitates a moment before biting into its crispiness. He looks at me with a look I've seen before, a look I realise I shouldn't even attempt to make sense of.

I don't remember much after that as the rest of the interview descended into a hazy blur. I think he may have asked some intelligent questions and I gave him some answers, but intelligent? I don't think so.

Really though, it wasn't too bad because by that stage, I'd had a change of heart over the job, so I wasn't too disappointed when, a few days later, I received a letter informing me that I wouldn't be asked back for a second interview.

I'll start looking again tomorrow. But for tonight I've got other more important things on my mind. Darryl Phillip might not make ideal boss material, but when he asked me out for dinner, saying I looked like a woman with a healthy appetite, I felt, in the circumstances, I could hardly refuse…

Heavenly Cookies

(makes 35-40)

Ingredients

4oz butter at room temperature, plus a little extra to grease
2½ oz caster sugar
1½ oz soft brown sugar
1 medium egg
6oz self-raising flour
4oz plain chocolate drops
3oz white chocolate drops

Method

Preheat oven to 190°C/375°F/gas mark 5)
Grease three baking sheets with a little butter
Beat together the butter, sugar and the egg until the mixture is light and fluffy.
Thoroughly mix in the flour and chocolate drops.
Place teaspoonfuls of the mixture 1½" apart on the baking sheets.
Bake for 10 minutes until golden brown.
Cool cookies on racks.
Store in airtight container.

Walking Into It

by Wendy Turner

It started out as a pleasant afternoon stroll. Caroline was looking forward to a whole afternoon with David, their first bit of time alone. They had met some months ago at Sylph-vestors, the local slimming club. Caroline had weighed in at seventeen stone and David at eighteen stones four pounds. For four months they had counted calories, studied fat units, absorbed riveting information about proteins and carbohydrates, all the time eyeing each other across a crowded, bulky room.

The cliff-top walk was beautiful with weak sunlight flashing between misty patches of light. A fresh breeze accompanied them and gulls shrieked far overhead. After an hour or so, a rest was in order. David creaked to a halt, helpfully held Caroline's hand while she settled herself, and lowered his bulk onto the flattish surface of a nearby rock. Gratefully, he slipped off his rucksack and swung it onto the grass.

"What a lovely place to stop," said Caroline, removing her sunglasses. "Look at that gorgeous view, beach for miles."

"I am looking at a gorgeous view," David smiled, making her blush. "And the beach is lovely too. But, I must admit, I'm famished. What did we pack in the end?"

The packed lunch had been a bit of a tussle. They hadn't wanted to squander too many points so had agreed to keep it simple. Caroline had made lettuce and cucumber sandwiches with low-cal Nimble and a flask of Good For You Cuppa Minestrone Soup. David had undertaken to provide dessert, which consisted of one Weight Watchers fairy cake each, two apples and a banana to share. That would allow them grilled cod and broccoli later. The sandwiches and soup disappeared like magic and they lingered over the fruit, cutting it up into tiny pieces to make it last longer.

"Delicious," David murmured, thinking that it hadn't even touched the sides. What he'd give for a pint and a steak pie.

"Wasn't it nice. I'm glad you enjoyed it," said Caroline, with visions of the thick-cut toasted sandwiches she used to have, dripping with melted cheese and mayonnaise.

They packed the picnic things away and staggered to their feet. "Nice cup of tea when we get back." David said. Caroline smiled in return, thinking that she could demolish a church bazaar pot all by herself. She pulled her cardigan from her bag and threw it around her shoulders. The mist had come down a bit and she shivered as a band of cold air hit them.

"Not cold then, are you?" David risked putting an arm around her.

"Oh no, not really," she said. "Well, perhaps just a little bit."

They continued around the coast in pleasant, quiet friendship, admiring the lacy sea and the blue haze. It did cross David's mind that he hadn't a clue where they were, but it was such a delightful afternoon he really wasn't worried. They could always go back the way they'd come.

After a while, banks of grey fog began rolling in. The sun and sea disappeared and the birds' chatter, out of sight, sounded ghostly. Caroline was uncomfortably aware that they were walking near the cliff edge, which was also rapidly fading from view.

"Do you think we're going the right way?" she asked, hiding a twinge of anxiety.

"I think so love. We've probably come round in a huge circle. Let's turn left away from the cliff." But what if it's the wrong way? said a little voice in his head. You could both lose your footing over the edge. He shuddered. It didn't bear thinking about. But what if they couldn't find the way back? Could they last all night up here? Exciting as it would be to cuddle up, they might die from hypothermia.

After another hour of wandering, David called a halt.

"We'll have to stop for a minute, love," he said. "I'm done in. Have we got any soup left?" It felt like a week since he'd eaten.

Caroline was only too glad to stop. They'd pulled on their waterproofs but her hair was soaking and she wore only sandals. Between them they produced a few drops of minestrone soup, a nimble crust and a packet of peppermints that David had on him. They shared them in abject misery.

"Don't worry too much, love," David said. "This is England, you know, not the Scottish Highlands. We're bound to find something if we keep going."

"But it's getting dark, and my feet are freezing. We might wander around all night."

"Come on." He pulled her up. "Let's get cracking. The sooner we start, the sooner we'll be home." She smiled a weak smile. Not that he could see it in the murk.

They trudged on for a while until they spotted a far-off light. "Looks like a farmhouse. We're in luck love," David said, hoping so with all his heart. He knocked anxiously at the door. It was opened by a large woman in a clean apron, who listened to their tale of woe sympathetically. "Come on in," she said. "You must be tired out."

She said her name was Mabel and led them into a warm kitchen with a roaring fire. Huge hams hung on hooks from the ceiling and trays of eggs were stacked up on the floor. The wonderful aroma of baking bread and hot coffee wafted around. They collapsed at the huge refectory table, Caroline holding out her squelchy feet to the fire. "You've saved my life," she murmured. "You're so kind," said David, overwhelmed with relief.

"Now you two just warm yourselves up while I get you a nice meal," Mabel said, bustling about. David squeezed Caroline's hand. "Told you it'd be OK," he said.

Mabel returned with two massive trenchers. On each were four huge slices of thick cut ham with a breaded crust, a hand of sizzling outsized sausages dripping with gravy and mustard, half a cold chicken and a mountain of fried potatoes. She produced a whole cottage loaf, which she whacked into wedges with a cleaver, and a tub of home-churned butter. "Eat up, my dears", she said, pouring out two tankards of home-brewed beer. "I'll leave you to it."

They stared at the enormous plates of food, and then at each other. Their faces lit up like children at Christmas. David raised his glass.

"To you, my partner in adventure. May it be the first of many."

"Well, perhaps not too many quite like this," she said. "But yes, to a long and happy partnership."

The meal vanished within five minutes. Caroline would never have imagined that she could have seen that lot off. David sat back happier than at any time during the last four months. Mabel reappeared with a lace-covered tray, a coffee pot, brown sugar and a pint jug of cream.

"That was just great," they both breathed, with huge sighs of contentment. "What a wonderful meal and not a cucumber or poppy seed in sight."

"Oh yes there is," Mabel said. "You must try this poppy seed cheesecake" Caroline and David nodded happily in agreement. "And I'll pour," she continued. "Anyone for sugar?"

"No, not for us, thanks, my dear. " David replied. "We're dieting."

Poppy Seed Cheesecake With Vodka Raisins

Serves 8-10

Ingredients

Filling
50g/2oz sultanas
4 tbsp lemon or other vodka
700g/1½lb cream cheese
225g/8oz caster sugar
2 medium eggs
350ml/12fl oz whipping cream
40g/1½oz sifted plain flour
1½ tsp vanilla essence
1-2 tbsp poppy seeds
Base:
25g/1oz softened unsalted butter
25g/1oz fresh white breadcrumbs
1 tsp caster sugar

Method

Put sultanas in bowl, pour over vodka and leave to soak overnight
Preheat oven to 190ºC/375ºF/Gas Mark 5.
To prepare the base: grease a 20cm/8in spring form cake tin with the butter. Mix breadcrumbs and sugar and press to sides and base of tin.
To make filling: blend cream cheese and sugar in food processor. Add the eggs and cream, and fold in the flour and vanilla essence. Mix in sultanas and any residual liquor. Spoon mixture carefully into the tin. Dust the surface with poppyseeds and cook for 45mins until puffy around edges and just set - cheesecake should wobble if moved.
Turn off the oven, keep door ajar and leave cheesecake in the oven to rest for 1 hour. Remove and cool completely. The cheesecake is at its best a day after cooking, at room temperature. If chilled, bring back to room temperature 30 minutes before serving.

Picking Cherries

by Sue Johnson

Britty looked the same as she always did. Red lipstick instead of red hair ribbons. A little heavier. Still the same lazy smile and the mischievous twinkle in her dark eyes. She was selling make-up on a stall in the market. She winked and offered me a squirt of 'Romance' perfume.

"That'll bring you luck. Looks as if you need it. The one you've got isn't worth wasting time on."

"How do you know?"

"I know what I know."

The same old Britty response that used to drive the teachers mad.

I hadn't seen her for years. Her family were travellers and they came every year for the fruit picking. Britty spent every summer at our school.

"We're not gypsies exactly," she said. "We just haven't found a place to settle yet."

I remembered those words as I looked at Britty. I pointed to the stall.

"Does this mean you've settled down?"

She looked at me and laughed.

"What d'you think? I've come back to get married. Remember old times. I'm just looking after the stall to help somebody out. A bit of this and that like I've always done."

"Do you still tell fortunes?"

I remembered how our teacher, Miss Reynolds, didn't like Britty telling fortunes. She said it was dangerous. She told the class not to believe the stories Britty told about her travels.

I loved the stories. I wanted to be like Britty, sleeping under the stars on warm nights and cooking on a camp fire.

Britty wore brightly patterned dresses to school. Her gold earrings gleamed against her dark skin. I was fed up with my blue check school dress.

"Why can't I have red hair ribbons like Britty?" I asked my mother.

"They're common," she said.

Today Britty takes my hand and traces the lines.

"You'll marry a dark-eyed man and have five children," she said.

I snatched my hand away.

"That's just where you're wrong. I'm marrying John and he doesn't want children."

"Then you'll be unhappy." Britty wore her smug, always right expression.

"Are you marrying to please yourself or to make your parents proud of you?"

"Why would I worry about what they think?"

"You do. You're still the same. I know what I know."

I remembered Britty's last day at our school. The day her father talked about taking the family on a trip around the world.

Miss Reynolds' face was a delicate shade of purple.

"It's bad for her education to be continually taken out of school like this. No wonder she never learns anything useful."

"What's she going to learn here that she can't learn out in the world?" asked Britty's father.

That was the day that we learned about clouds. I was disappointed to learn they weren't floating palaces for sky princesses. Miss Reynolds made me stand in the corner for being stupid.

She still hadn't forgiven me when it was time for games. She left me standing in the corner.

Britty tugged my arm. We crept out of school and along the lane towards the orchard. Butterflies and bees cruised lazily in the hedgerows. The sun was warm on my skin. We climbed the gate into the field and ran across it to the stream. We took off our shoes and socks and paddled. We shook out our ponytails and made garlands of wild flowers.

Next, we went into the orchard.

"My Mum and Dad are picking cherries," said Britty. "Nobody'll mind what we do."

The cherries hung like rubies on the trees. The grass under the trees was cool on our bare legs. We made a den and watched the men and women picking cherries. A fiddler played and we heard fragments of a song.

Britty and I ate cherries until we were full. We hung pairs of them over our ears.

We made daisy chains to decorate our den. Then we fell asleep in the drowsy heat.

We didn't wake up until we were disturbed by loud voices and flashlights. The night was velvet dark and the stars were out.

My parents were angry with me. The next day Britty was gone and I didn't have a chance to say goodbye.

Now we laugh about old times. Nothing's changed between us. It could've been yesterday.

"Maybe we could have a double wedding? Next month in the orchard when the cherries are out."

I try to tell Britty about John. The open air life isn't his scene. He likes things organised and computerised. Yesterday we had a row about me wanting to work at the garden centre instead of in an office. I half close my eyes as I remember his nagging voice.

"Why're you being so unreasonable when you know we need the money?"

"I'm not being unreasonable. I want to work with plants. I'm not bothered about having a flash wedding or a posh house."

"Well I am. People expect it of someone in my position."

"So a wife working in a garden centre isn't good enough for you?"

"It'd be less of an embarrassment if you did nothing at all."

"So now I'm an embarrassment?"

He stormed out. Two hours later he phoned to say the engagement was off unless I was prepared to be sensible.

I thought about this as Britty and I sat over a pot of tea in the market café.

"I've been trying to force myself into the wrong mould."

"I could've told you that."

"Don't tell me. You know what you know."

"What're you going to do?"

"Did you say something about a dark-eyed man?"

She nodded.

"When do I get to meet him?"

"No time like the present."

I knew I wouldn't phone John and apologise.

We walk back to Britty's stall. She invites me to choose a lipstick. I pick one called 'Cherry Blush.'

I feel lighter now I've made my decision. Tonight I'll dance under the stars. Britty says there'll be a special day for me soon. Maybe we'll have a double wedding after all.

Cherry Almond Tart

Ingredients

For the pastry:
150g self raising flour
100g margarine
1 tsp brown sugar
a little water to mix
For the filling
small tin of cherry pie filling
100g margarine
100g caster sugar
100g self raising flour
2 eggs
1 tbs ground almonds
flaked almonds and icing sugar to decorate

Method

Make the pastry and line an 8" flan dish.
Spread cherry pie filling onto the raw pastry.
Beat margarine and caster sugar together until white and fluffy.
Add eggs. Fold in flour and ground almonds.
Spread over the cherries. Press in flaked almonds.
Bake in a medium oven (180ºC/350ºF/Gas Mark 4) until the top is golden.
Allow to cool slightly. Sprinkle with icing sugar and serve with whipped cream.

Party Peace
by Sue Houghton

Life should come with an 'undo' button. You know, like on my computer. One click and voila, I could've miraculously backtracked and erased my last action. But it doesn't, so there was no chance of editing, erasing or reversing what popped out of my mouth.

"What did you call me, Patricia?" Tara's voice was so shrill that bats must have been stirring in Pumfrey Manor's bell tower. "Fat? How dare you?"

"No, you misunderstood. I said you needed to be skinny to get away with wearing horizontal stripes." Particularly if it's in acid orange Lycra.

"But I've bought it to wear for Ben's party. It cost a small fortune," she enlightened me. "And I don't remember asking your opinion anyway."

She doesn't mean to sound harsh. I have a soft spot for Tara. And whether she likes it or not, she'll get the benefit of my advice if I think she needs it.

There was a time when she always asked my opinion. She treated me more like a friend than an employee. But it all changed when her husband, Sir Humphrey Pumfrey, walked out, leaving her and Ben in this big old house. Despite its grand name, Pumfrey Manor is modest as manors go. Just takes a cook and a gardener to keep it shipshape. Plus me of course.

Anyway, the dress, if it made her happy to wear something that made her look like an angry bee to her son's fifth birthday party, who was I to criticise?

After all, I'm only her personal assistant, hired to organise her busy schedule, sort her mail and fill her social diary.

"You did remember to book Figaro's for the party, didn't you?" she said, staring fondly at her husband's photo, which she still keeps on the mantelpiece.

"Yes, but are you sure you really want to go there?"

Figaro's is the posh restaurant in the high street. It's where her husband took her to break the news that he was running away to join his offshore account, accompanied by his secretary.

I'm sure Lady T still thinks he'll come back, even though everyone else was glad to see the back of him. He wasn't a very likeable sort of person. The only good deed he ever did was to make sure Tara and Ben were left financially sound after he scarpered.

As for Figaro's, any other woman would avoid going back there. Unhappy memories and all that, but not Lady T. I think she was trying to say to the world that her life's as it always was. But I know it isn't. Poor Lady T. She should be awarded an MBE for her services to the stiff upper lip.

"I suppose you think I should take Ben and his friends to a burger bar," she said. I could see the idea didn't appeal.

"Well, my own grandchildren love it," I said.

I'd overheard Ben talking to his friend the other day, saying how he's not looking forward to going to a stuffy restaurant. That he doesn't like Gordon Blue.

"Why not ask Ben what he'd like, Lady Tara?"

But I could tell she was having none of it. "There'll be no burger bar," she said, firmly. "Over my dead body."

Well, it very nearly was. Over her dead body, I mean. Ben had left his skateboard on the first floor landing that same afternoon and Tara found it. When I say found it, I mean she stood on it accidentally, performed a rather amateurish back-flip and hurtled down the staircase like a whirling dervish.

A trip to A & E ended with her sporting a plaster cast on her right leg, a bandaged wrist and severe bruising.

As soon as she arrived home, she had me ring Figaro's to cancel.

"Ben will be so disappointed," she said. "But I can't go out in public looking like this."

"The party can still go ahead," I said. "OK, maybe not at the restaurant, but how about we do something here?" I was remembering a time when the house would be filled with people every weekend. Tara doesn't even have her book club friends over anymore.

"No, I couldn't," she said.

She's so infuriating sometimes, I want to shake her. "Now look here, Tara Pumfrey, it's about time you stopped all this self-pity, stopped waiting for that useless excuse of a husband to come back and started living again."

You know what I was saying about life coming with an 'undo' button. Boy did I need one then. Lady T pursed her lips so hard they almost disappeared into her pretty face and I was waiting for the fallout when she unexpectedly said,

"You forget something, Patricia. The cook's on holiday. Where would I get a party planner at this late stage?"

"You don't need one," I said, relieved she hadn't sacked me on the spot. "I could do it. How difficult can it be to manage a simple tea-party for a bunch of five to seven-year-olds?"

She had no choice.

I smiled and dashed to my computer for a spot of online collaboration with Delia Smith.

So, come the day of the party, I waved Lady T and Ben off in a taxi. She was taking him to visit Santa while I trimmed the Christmas tree and tried to coax the contents of the fridge into a tempting finger buffet. Having qualified in secretarial management, my cooking abilities are limited to microwaving and defrosting. When faced with anything that requires a recipe, I'm hopeless.

I seemed to have been baking for ages, yet I'd only produced one sorry-looking quiche and a runny blancmange. Two attempts at a jelly are lurking in the sink and my banana custard was a disaster. It was so thin you could've emulsioned the ceilings of Pumfrey Manor with it.

I was cursing a reluctant trifle when the front doorbell chimed.

"Hi," said a voice behind a bunch of helium balloons as I opened the door.

It was the entertainer I'd booked. Almost two hours early. I grabbed him by the lapels and dragged him inside.

"I hope no-one saw you. Weren't you told to use the tradesman's entrance round the back?"

"No. And anyway, it's difficult to walk in these. Especially as the ground's icy. I reckon there'll be snow by teatime."

He pointed to his oversized boots with the soles hanging off. He was sporting baggy tartan trousers held up by enormous braces, and a bright yellow jacket. A plastic daisy poked out of a battered top hat perched precariously over bright blue acrylic hair. And he'd been over-enthusiastic with the face paint.

"There must be a mistake," I said, taking in his appearance.

Lady T would have a fit if she saw him. She'd left specific instructions. 'Make sure you order top class entertainment, Patricia'.

"I ordered a magician, not Coco the clown. I was promised the best one they had. Top hat and tails. The lot. Not this." I fanned a hand at him.

"Yeah, sorry," he said. "We double booked. Didn't realise till the last minute, so they sent me to explain in person to Lady Pumfrey. And it's Zippo, not Coco. And yes, it's my real name before you ask." He takes off his red plastic nose and sniffs. "Look, I don't mean to cut short my apology, but can I smell burning?"

"Oh no, the cake!"

I ran back to the kitchen with him flip-flopping behind me. I opened the oven door and grabbed the tin. In my eagerness, I failed to shove my hands into the oven gloves first. The cremated sponge hit the kitchen floor and sat there accusingly.

"Not a very good cook are you?" he said, laughing.

"I'm not the cook," I said, assuming Lady T's best haughty voice, whilst plunging my blistered fingers under the cold tap. "I'm Patricia, Lady Pumfrey's assistant. At least I was. She's going to be livid."

"No she isn't," said Zippo, scooping the cake off the floor and into the bin. "Not if we get a move on. How many people are you expecting?"

"Why?"

"As you pointed out, I'm no magician, but I think I can conjure up something tasty."

I gasped as he slipped out of the jacket, pinged his braces and started unzipping his trousers.

"What?" he shrugged. "You don't think I'm going to cook with this lot on do you?"

He was wearing a pair of shorts under the baggy pants and a T-shirt beneath the bright yellow jacket. He grabbed a tea-towel, fashioned it into an apron and started 'peaking' egg whites. Heaven knows what Lady T would've said if she'd known there was a half-naked man with blue hair whipping up meringues in her bespoke kitchen.

Still, it seemed he knew what he was doing so I left him to it and got on with the Christmas trimmings.

Thankfully, Zippo had finished the party spread and was back in the clown outfit as Lady T and Ben returned.

"Wow! Cool! A clown!" shouted Ben. And he flung his arms around his mother's neck. "Thanks Mama. This is the best party ever."

"Ben's impressed," I said, as he hugged me too, but Lady T looked less than pleased.

"Is this your doing, Patricia?"

"There's been a slight mix up, yes, but if it weren't for Zippo here…what I mean is…he did all the party food. Wasn't that clever of him?"

Zippo took off his hat and gave her a low bow, sweeping the daisy in front of her face. "Zippo the Clown at your service, Ma'm," he said, producing a bunch of silk roses from nowhere. Then he took her hand and kissed the back of it. "And between us grown-ups, the name's Steve." And then he winked at her.

Lady T's face went from purple to a rose-blush. And knock me down with a snowball if she didn't flutter her eyelashes and giggle.

Before long, the house was filled with excited children. Tara seemed to be enjoying herself too. And what's more, I noticed her slipping her husband's photo in the dresser drawer.

Zippo aka Steve, did what he obviously enjoyed: keeping the kids amused. Ben didn't leave his side. He doesn't see his father much, what with him living abroad now. I suppose he missed not having a man about the house more than we'd realised.

"I don't know when I last had such fun," said Lady T, hobbling to join me by the Christmas tree. I noticed she taken the hint about the orange-striped concoction and is looking delightful in an aquamarine dress that matched her eyes. Definitely more butterfly than bee. Even with her leg in plaster she looked stunning.

"It's so good to see you laughing again," I told her. "And I know it's more than the tree lights that have put the twinkle back in your eyes."

She looked across to Steve and blushed. "Thank you, Patricia. For everything."

"Why not tell Steve how much you appreciate his hard work?" I suggested.

But Steve was already making his way over to us. "What did I tell you? It's beginning to snow quite heavily," he said. "Can the children go outside to build a snowman?"

"I'm not sure," Lady T said looking at me. "What do you think Patricia?"

"Why, Tara Pumfrey, are you asking my opinion?" I laughed.

She thought for a moment then turned to Steve. "No," she said unsmiling. "I think not."

Steve smiled politely and turned to walk away.

"Not unless you ask me to come too," she whispered after him.

As I watched the tree lights twinkle and the first snowfall of winter settle on Pumfrey Manor's bell tower, I just knew it was going to be a very merry Christmas.

Perfect Meringues

Ingredients

3 large fresh organic egg whites
6oz caster sugar
organic cream, whipped
pinch of salt
a little icing sugar

Method

Whisk the egg whites until very stiff, so that they will stand in peaks. Gradually fold the sugar into the stiff whites using a metal spoon. Disturb the whites as little as possible. Put two flat baking sheets, covered in greaseproof paper, brushed with olive oil, ready. Shape the meringues with two dessertspoons. Take one spoonful of egg white and sugar mix and then use the second spoon to ease it out onto the prepared baking sheet. When all the mixture has been used, sprinkle a little icing sugar over the meringues. Bake in a very low oven (around 75ºC) for 3-4 hours or longer. The meringues should not brown but should be dry and crisp right through. Cool and remove meringues from paper with a dampened, flat knife. Stick two meringues together with a generous amount of whipped cream and serve immediately.

Diamonds Aren't A Girls Best Friend
By Phil Trenfield.

"To remove cat hair from your upholstery. Dampen your hand and rub it gently along the surface of the furniture. The fur sticks to your hand and then just rinse it off under the tap." Amy folded the letter and put it in her 'accept' pile.

"Have these people never heard of Dysons?" Katie said, eyes watering after a giggling fit.

"Well, according to Mrs George from County Durham, that is the best way to remove unwanted pet hair." Amy replied, mockingly.

"Let's just hope no one walks in on you while you're doing it to find you have hairy palms." Katie started giggling again.

"That joke only works if it's a man doing the cleaning." Amy said, trying to stop giggling.

"Oh, you do cheer me up reading those letters every day." Katie said sipping her water.

"I'm glad I keep you amused." Amy replied. "I just wish I had a more exciting job, I hate being on the mail bags. It is so boring."

"It's not that bad. You got that great recipe last week for sausage casserole from Mrs Smith of Glasgow," Katie said, sparking a new giggling fit.

"It was Mrs Matthews actually and it was very tasty, I tried it out myself before it hit the magazine." Amy retorted. "Look stop taking the mick, I need sympathy. What are you working on at the moment?"

"Nothing that exciting, just a seven page spread on the Baftas." Katie replied without looking away from her computer screen.

"What do you mean? That's mega exciting. I'm so jealous." Amy pouted.

"Look if you are really that miserable then go to the editor and see if you can get put on to something else."

"I've already tried that." Amy replied. "She said I was *essential to the efficient running of the incoming mail department*."

"Well maybe you should try moving to another magazine?"

"I could never leave, I've got too many friends here." Amy replied looking shocked.

"Well, I'm afraid I can't help you then." Katie said.

"Mmm, well, I'm off to lunch now. I'm going to cheer myself up by eating three chocolate brownies."

Katie chirped, "Bring me back a brownie or two." Amy picked up her Prada bag (which still hadn't been paid for as her credit card statement reminded her every month) and walked towards the lift.

The lift door opened and out stepped a man carrying a large black case.

"Please tell me this is the floor that has the photo studio on it," he said with a sexy Irish accent.

"I'm afraid not." Amy replied.

"The studio is situated on the fourth floor. I'm going down so will drop you off on the way."

"Great, I'm Brendan, the new photographer working on the Bvlgari Diamond account."

"Wow, that's impressive. I'm Amy working on the mail bags." She replied as they entered the lift. Amy couldn't help but notice Brendan staring at her hands.

"So how long have you worked for Sanctuary magazine?" Brendan asked, realizing he was staring.

"About two years now, I started when it launched," she replied. "Here we are the fourth floor. Now if you go left and walk straight ahead, the studio is at the end of the corridor."

"Thanks ever so much. Hope to see you around," Brendan said and walked off quoting her directions out aloud.

Amy stood outside the bakery and opened the brown paper bag, pulled out a chocolate and raspberry brownie, lifted it to her lips and slowly savoured the taste. An image appeared in her head – an image of Brendan. She imagined him feeding her brownies, as they lay in bed together. Suddenly, aware of her public surroundings, Amy shook her head and dismissed the thought as quickly as it came.

"Your brownies, that's seven quid you owe me now." Amy quipped as she threw the brown bag on to Katie's desk..

"You'll have forgotten all about that in a few minutes. I have a message for you. Someone called Brendan?" Katie taunted playfully.

"Oh my God, he's the new photographer on the Bvlgari account. What did he want?"

"He just asked if you could call him urgently and left his mobile number." Katie ripped the message off her notepad and handed it to Amy.

Looking at the piece of paper as if it contained winning lottery numbers, Amy picked up her phone and dialled the number.

Katie leaned over her desk, trying to eavesdrop.

"Well, what did he say?" she asked the moment Amy hung up.

"He said that the model they have got for the shoot is awful and he wants me to go and do the shoot with him. That's why he was staring at my hands in the lift." Amy replied excitedly.

"Pull the other one." Katie said, rolling her eyes.

"I'm serious, he's cleared it with the editor and I'll be in next month's issue as the model for Bvlgari."

"That is so amazing. I'm speechless, and that is a very rare thing for me," grinned Kate.

The photo shoot was everything Amy had dreamt of and more. Music playing. A stunning outfit. Make-up that made her skin flawless and dewy and jewels that would make Catherine Zeta-Jones jealous.

A beautiful diamond ring and necklace were placed on her by one of the jewellers. "These items come with a mandatory four security guards who are positioned by the only exit watching your every move." He said matter-of-factly.

"If you can just hold your hand up to the necklace for me, so we can see the ring as well." Brendan called from behind the camera.

The camera clicked and whirred as he cajoled her into various stances. Time went on and she soon felt an urgent need to pee. Her expression became very intense as her bladder reminded her of the urgency with every passing minute.

"Fantastic, Amy. Keep your face just like that. That's the one." He announced. "That's a wrap everyone."

"Wow, that was so fantastic. I've wanted to do something like that ever since I was a little girl." Amy gushed, while crossing her legs.

"Well, you were very good at it. Would you like to join me for a drink after the magazine is released, you know, to celebrate? Maybe a spot of dinner afterwards?"

"I'd like that very much," Amy replied. "Give me a ring and we can set a date." With that she made her excuses and ran off towards the ladies' room.

"Oi, love! Where do you think you're running off to with those?" One of the security guard blocked her exit and retrieved the diamonds from her before letting her go.

The next few weeks were torture for Amy. Her whole family had been briefed on the publication date and the local newsagent's would be overrun with relatives snapping up copies of Sanctuary magazine.

The day finally arrived and Amy, like an excited girl on Christmas morning, flipped through the magazine.

"Oh my God," she said out loud.

"What is it?" Katie asked without looking up from her copy of a rival magazine.

"They've cut my head off. It's just my neck, shoulders and hand in the picture."

"You're still in the magazine." Katie replied.

"But who's going to know its me." Amy growled as she picked up the phone and stabbed out Brendan's number.

"It's Brendan, leave a message after the beep."

"Brendan, Amy here. I can't join you for drinks tonight as I seem to have lost my head!"

She slammed down the phone, sighed, closed the magazine and picked up a new pile of mail.

Chocolate And Raspberry Brownies

Makes 16

Ingredients

350g Dark Chocolate (good quality chocolate is best)
250g Unsalted butter
3 free range eggs
250g dark muscovado sugar
110g sifted, plain flour
1 tsp baking powder
pinch of salt
175g fresh raspberries

Method

First preheat the oven to 170ºC/325ºF/Gas Mark 3. Grease a 9" square cake tin.
Melt the chocolate and butter together making sure it doesn't burn. Then leave to cool slightly.
Whisk the eggs until thick, then gradually add the sugar and beat until glossy. Then mix in the melted chocolate mixture. Gently fold in the flour, baking powder and salt.
Pour half of the mixture into the cake tin. Scatter the raspberries over the mixture. Then cover with the remaining batter.
Bake in the oven for about 40 minutes or until the surface is set. Remove to a wire rack and allow to rest for 20 minutes. Cut into squares and remove from the tin when cold.

Desperate Housewife
by Lorraine Winter

"Sounds fantastic. Dead romantic too," I said wistfully as Maggie enthralled me with the details of hers and Rob's Caribbean cruise.

"Hey, it's a great bargain, if you book last minute. Isn't your wedding anniversary coming up? Why don't you and Mike book one?"

I sighed deeply and looked out the window.

"No change on the romantic front, I see?"

I shook my head. For what seemed like months, Mike had been uninterested, distant even.

"Definitely a cruise then. Lazy days at sea, starry moonlit nights on deck, intimate dinners – it's a recipe for romance if ever there was one."

"Ah, but how do I get him to agree to it in the first place? Mike doesn't seem very interested in anything lately, except perhaps football." I launched into the litany of how deadly dull our love life had become. I'd already bent her ear a while back.

"Alice, you have to work at these things," Maggie scolded.

"I did nibble his ear like you said," I protested.

"And first you created the mood – dinner by candlelight, music in the background…"

I was guiltily quiet.

"Well?" She'd put down her cup and was looking intently at me.

"Uh, maybe I should have waited till after the Cup Final," I said sheepishly.

"Alice, really!" she tutted. "Now, let me think. This calls for something special, something that even Mike will find irresistible."

"Oh yes! You said if I nibbled his ear, he would find me irresistible. You didn't mention I would have to shop and cook and even be a DJ!" I was great at shopping and could fathom the workings of the CD player but cooking…*me*?

Maggie silenced me with one of her looks.

"Listen. Here's the plan. Buy some of those sensuous candles and make sure you get some massage oil in the same scent for later. Very effective. When I get home, I'll e-mail you some fabulous aphrodisiac recipes and…"

"Aphrodisiac recipes?" Was she joking? I struggled with roast chicken.

She threw me another 'look'. "While you're shopping, buy yourself some sexy new underwear, red will suit you. And get your highlights done. You'll knock him dead! Don't forget the accessories, red napkins, soft red lighting. Then zap him with it. More ear nibbling, when he's in the right mood this time. We'll meet for lunch the next day and you can tell me all about it!"

I didn't dare argue. And, I had to admit, Maggie knew about these things.

It had been hard work but now the scene was well and truly set for romance. I lit the candles I'd bought earlier. "I want some candles and massage oil in the same scent, something sort of – sensuous," I'd whispered in the candle shop, sure I was blushing from ear to ear. "I need to create an atmosphere that's romantic and uh…"

"…sexy," the assistant said in a bored tone of voice that was anything but sexy, automatically reaching under the counter. Under the counter stuff. Blimey! "Guaranteed to arouse passions, even those that have been dormant for years," she recited, parrot-fashion. I could feel my cheeks were on fire. Did I have an air of desperation about me? 'Pleasure Garden', the label read. I'd stuffed them in my bag, paid and hurried out.

But I was pleased with my efforts. The table was set with our best cutlery and crockery, heart embossed red napkins in exotic Moroccan holders (fingers crossed they'd evoke memories of our honeymoon in Marrakesh – steamy nights after smoochy evenings), sensuously scented candles, aphrodisiacs simmering on the stove, *20 All Time Greatest Love Songs* playing softly in the background. And that was only for starters!

If that failed to ignite a spark, well… I supposed I could always perform the dance of the seven veils. How did it go? I raised my arms, pushed out my chest, swaying my hips as I waved the tea towel around, giggling. Maybe it had been a bit early to start on the red wine.

It was nearly seven. Mike worked late every Thursday and would be home any minute. I felt a little quiver of excitement shoot through me.

It wasn't fair to blame Mike completely. I hadn't exactly been Miss Dynamite. And I don't suppose Mike was all that different to ninety-five per cent of British males, ninety-five per cent of the time, after a few years of marriage. Probably just a case of having got out of the habit of being attentive, or even noticing I was there sometimes. But I was eager to rediscover the romantic side of him I'd known in the early days of our relationship.

In fact, if you'd asked me then, I'd have sworn he had romance coursing through his veins. He'd surprise me with tickets for a concert he knew I was keen on, or book a romantic meal for two out of the blue. Even occasionally turn up with a book of poetry and a box of Belgian chocolates. We'd sit on a park bench in summer or curled up on the sofa in winter and take turns reading them, sensuously sharing a chocolate between each poem. Romantic or what? And then there was that passionate, serious side to him. Like when he'd hold me tight, look deep into my eyes and whisper "Oh, I do love you, Alice Johnson." I know it sounds drippy now but I swear at the time it was dead sexy. Ooh, I come over all weak just thinking about it.

I even had tears pricking my eyes. But that could have been the onions. Four onions did sound a lot for two people but I'd followed Maggie's recipe to the letter. Onions are a potent aphrodisiac according to the Greeks and Romans and if they were good enough for Antony and Cleopatra, they were good enough for me and Mike.

Maggie said she had some frog saliva and powdered rhinoceros' horns tucked up her sleeve if the aphrodisiacs didn't do the trick. A picture came into my mind of Maggie wagging her finger at me and withdrawing a mysterious package from her sleeve. This prompted a further fit of the giggles. I poured myself another glass of wine. This mood creation thing was definitely working on me, anyway.

The soup was almost ready. The asparagus and the mussels in garlic and white wine were all ready to steam. Mike didn't stand a chance! And for an encore, Cleopatra's own recipe of stuffed caramel walnuts, deciphered from her very own hieroglyphic, no less. Mike was bound to be impressed by my creativity and culinary skills, if nothing else.

I'd been so wrapped up in the 'mood creation' I hadn't noticed the time. He was late! Only fifteen minutes but it wasn't like Mike not to ring to warn me. For the next two and a half hours, I paced the floor, my heart thumping wildly all the time. He must have had an accident on that stupid bike of his. He could be lying under the wheels of a lorry, seriously injured or even crushed to death. I'd never see him again. And all I'd been thinking of was getting him in the mood for love! My fun, carefree mood had disappeared.

Visions of hospital visits flashed through my mind. I saw him swathed in bandages, hooked up to drips and monitors, the doctors and nurses looking on with anxious expressions. If he was still alive, that was. What had Maggie said about knocking him dead! Oh my God!

Something serious must have happened, but the police and the hospital had no record of any accidents. He wouldn't stop by the pub or go off anywhere else without telling me, would he? He always came straight home. I needed something stronger than wine. Where was the brandy?

I'd lost count of the number of times I'd rung Accident and Emergency and the police. But I'd have to ring again. Then Mike came into view, pushing his bicycle up the garden path. Dropping the phone, I ran out to meet him.

"Mike. Oh, Mike. You're not dead." I breathed, flinging my arms round his neck and smothering him in kisses.

"Of course I'm not dead!" He gave me a funny look.

"But you're never late. I thought you'd had an accident, come off your bike and…"

"Got a puncture, didn't I. I stopped off at Joe's to fix it."

"Until this time? But why didn't you ring?"

"I did! The battery was flat on my mobile, I tried to ring several times from Joe's but the line's been permanently engaged."

"Yes, because I was on the phone to Accident and Emergency and the police, worried sick about you!"

"You were that worried?" He looked shame-faced but also managed a smile.

"A bit worried. Why didn't you just come home earlier?"

Mike shrugged his shoulders and shifted uncomfortably. "Spent ages trying to fix the puncture but couldn't. Joe was watching the European Cup qualifier on the telly, he offered me a beer and I just…"

"…forgot about me!" I could feel my face aflame with anger as we went indoors. All the effort I'd gone to and this was my reward.

His nose twitched. "What's that smell?" A pungent odour of wax filled the air.

"Oh, my candles! They've burned out."

Mike's gaze rested on the table set for dinner, the half empty wine bottle and the food on the stove. He looked back at me, his eyebrows raised quizzically. "What's this?"

"This is onion soup, followed by mussels in garlic and white wine with – oh never mind. It's probably ruined now." I snapped, tears pricking my eyes. "I'd planned a nice romantic evening together. Like we used to…"

"Come here." Mike pulled me towards him and dabbed at my tears. I stiffened. He wasn't going to win me over that easily after this evening's fiasco.

"I'm sorry. I haven't been paying you much attention lately, have I?" He could say that again. "It's well… you see, I've had things on my mind. I should have told you…"

An affair! Had he been having an affair? That would explain the way he'd been acting.. I was aware of my heart pounding.

"…but I didn't want to worry you." He paused and looked down. "I found a lump a few weeks ago and…"

"A lump!" I could feel the anger subside and the colour drain from my face. I gasped. I'd been so selfish...

"It's O.K. It's nothing to worry about. I got the test results on Monday. All clear." He stroked my hair tenderly.

"Oh, Mike! You should have told me. You went through all that on your own…"

"Never mind. It's all done with now." He said cheerfully, as he wandered over to the stove, lifting the lids off the saucepans. "Hey, this is amazing. Bit adventurous for you though," he teased as he poked at the onion soup. "Blimey! How many onions did you use?"

"Only four." I mumbled. "They were rather large though."

"Only four?" He laughed. "They'll play havoc with my digestive system! Don't tell me you've forgotten Maggie and Rob's barbecue when I over-indulged on the hot dogs and produced enough methane gas to fuel the whole neighbourhood's barbecues for a month."

I had. Completely. I giggled.

He reached for me and pulled me close. "I don't think the after-effects would be very romantic, do you?" he grinned.

"No, perhaps not, but maybe we could reheat the mussels and asparagus." I suggested.

"I've got a better idea." He gave me a long, lingering look. "Why don't we just go to bed and take the wine with us. I'm a bit tired after pushing that bike home. And I'm not really hungry now anyway," he smiled. "For food, that is. Would you mind? After all that effort you've made."

"Mind?" Was he kidding? "No. All that cooking's sort of spoiled my appetite." I paused. "But I'll bring Cleopatra's walnuts to nibble on, shall I? I made them earlier."

"Cleopatra's what?" Mike laughed.

"Walnuts with almonds dipped in caramel. The recipe was deciphered from one of Cleopatra's hieroglyphics and…"

His eyes twinkled at me just like they used to. "Oh, I do love you, Alice Robbins."

All this and not one aphrodisiac had passed his lips. The plan had gone out the window, but I wasn't complaining.

He poured us both a glass of wine, then rummaged in a drawer and pulled out two wrapped parcels.

"I went shopping on Monday on my way back from the hospital. I found these for our wedding anniversary but I think now's a good time."

I stared at the beautifully wrapped gifts. How many more surprises tonight?

"Go on. Open them."

I carefully undid the ribbon and the paper of the first package.

"Belgian chocolates…"

Then I untied the second package to reveal an exquisitely bound book with entwined hearts embossed on its cover.

I stared, open-mouthed. "Love Poems," I read. "Love Poems and Belgian chocolates." I could feel my eyes misting over.

"I was planning to give them to you when we celebrate our anniversary with a meal on board the Empress of the Seas. Mussels, oysters, lobster galore. And maybe even Cleopatra's walnuts for afters."

I just stared at Mike, open-mouthed. "What?"

"I'm talking about a Caribbean cruise, silly! I had a long talk with Rob and Maggie. They were saying how much they enjoyed their cruise. Maggie said we should be able to get a last minute booking…"

I was still staring.

"Well, say something then."

"Oh, I do love you, Mike Robbins," I giggled. "Now, lend me your ear. I want to nibble it. I'm suddenly feeling very, very hungry." Antony and Cleopatra, eat your heart out!

Stuffed Caramel Walnuts From Cleopatra

Ingredients

50g almond flour
50g sugar
1-2 tbsp orange essence
30 walnut halves
50g sugar

Method

Mix the almond flour (milled almonds) with the sugar and enough orange essence to form a paste.
Place a little of this paste between two walnut halves and press.
Melt the sugar in a pan with a few drops of water and when it starts to turn to caramel, remove it from the heat source and dip the nuts inside to coat them with caramel.
Set them out on greaseproof paper to dry.

Strawberry Surprise
by Gill Lammas

Alison gave herself a contented smile as she looked at her new shape in the mirror. She turned this way and that as she admired her body form. She closed her eyes and let her fingers gently caress her breasts, just as Mark had done all those months ago. Whatever would he think of her now? It had taken her months to achieve this new figure. He'd certainly see a change in her since she kissed him goodbye at the airport a while back, but hopefully he would be as pleased as she was with her new look.

Her hand moved slowly down to her belly, her fingers deliberately pausing on her shapely hips. Alison continued rubbing in the essential oils, paying particular attention to her stomach. She chose vanilla scented oils, as it was Mark's favourite. The one he used to massage her after they'd showered together…just after the feast they'd had with the strawberries and cream or the chocolate spread. They certainly needed a shower after that lot!

Mark could do some amazing things with strawberries and cream, she recalled. And his expertise with chocolate spread made her go weak at the knees. She allowed a smile to cross her lips at the thought of Mark coming to see her in a few hours time. He'd be surprised to see her looking this good; there was no doubt about it. But whichever way he'd react, the fridge was well stocked with the fruits of her desire. Just in case she needed them.

Alison smoothed the remainder of the oil into her thighs then laid out her new clothes on top of the bed. She'd bought the dress especially for the occasion. Not too figure hugging, but one that would leave Mark in no doubt about her new found womanly charms. The choice of colour…bright red was also one of his favourite colours. When she'd tried it on in the shop, she couldn't resist buying it.

The shopkeeper had raised her eyebrows as Alison sashayed around in front of the mirror, in the red number with the plunging neckline. But she didn't care. This creation was for Mark's eyes only. After all, tonight was a very special occasion and she wanted to show him exactly what he'd been missing these past few months.

She'd been shopping a lot lately, in establishments that she'd have normally walked past before. Now it was absolute heaven to buy some decent clothes in her new size.

Alison opened the drawer of her bedside cabinet and took out a shimmering pair of hold up stockings. She rolled them up onto her shapely legs, and decided that they were definitely more comfortable than the support tights she'd had on earlier in the day. The red stilettos, although not practical, complemented her outfit perfectly.

The clock struck six. Mark would be here in an hour's time. There was just enough time to touch up her makeup and have an ice cool drink, before he arrived. Nothing alcoholic…she'd given that up since he'd been away, but in any case she wanted to keep a clear head. The last time they saw each other he was piling his clothes into a suitcase, while she was piling on the pounds. Too many pizzas and plates of spaghetti bolognaise at the Italian restaurant, she thought at the time.

But that had all changed now. The thought of all that stodgy food make her feel positively queasy. Romantic meals for two were a thing of the past. From now on it was healthy eating all the way… with the exception of the strawberries and cream with a dollop of chocolate spread on top!

Alison thought back to those romantic meals for two when they first got together. Their eyes meeting across the table at expensive restaurants with low music playing in the background, followed by moonlit strolls along the riverbank hand in hand. Then it was back to her place for afters.

Before long his feet were well and truly under the table, then it was all day breakfast in bed! But she wasn't complaining. Neither was he. They both had healthy appetites, and with what she had on the menu they never went hungry. Anyway, enough reminiscences, he would be here any minute, and they had a lot of catching up to do after his six months overseas work assignment.

Alison took one last look in the mirror and checked her makeup. She rolled her tongue over her lips, her taste buds savouring the strawberry flavoured lip balm she'd applied with the tip of her little finger. She couldn't wait for Mark to taste it too.

Mark gazed at the woman before him and didn't utter a word. He was spellbound by her appearance. Although she'd already given him her good news over the telephone, he wasn't expecting her to look this good. He always thought she was a stunner, but now she looked even more beautiful and surprisingly sexy. He pulled her towards him and gently stroked and kissed her face before working his way down her neck, then further down her body. Finally his hands came to rest gently on her stomach. He traced the outline with his fingers. Yes, he definitely approved of her new shape.

Alison took his hand and led him to the bedroom, but first of all they stopped off at the kitchen where she gathered up a few ingredients.

"You don't mind, do you?" Alison gestured towards the bowl of fruit.

Mark gave a knowing smile as he watched her dive into the strawberries, topped with lashings of whipped cream and gooey chocolate spread. She'd been craving for it all day.

"Mmm… tastes heavenly," was all she could manage between mouthfuls.

"Satisfied?" He asked, drawing her closer to him, after she'd finished.

Alison nodded and gave a sigh of contentment, "Yes, I think we're both satisfied now."

Mark pushed the empty dish to one side and patted her swollen belly proudly.

"What a recipe for happiness," he said lovingly, "You, me and our first baby on the way!"

Strawberry Shortcake

Ingredients

275g / 10oz self raising flour
pinch of salt
75g / 3oz butter
50g / 2oz caster sugar
1 egg
few drops of vanilla essence
5 tbsp milk (plus extra for brushing)
For the filling
450g / 1lb fresh strawberries
2 tbsp orange liqueur or orange juice
254ml / 1pint whipping or double cream
2 tbsp icing sugar
small sprig of mint for decoration

Method

Remove the green hulls from the strawberries, slice and place in a bowl. Sprinkle over the orange liqueur / juice, cover with cling film and chill for 1 hour.

Preheat the oven to 230ºC / 450ºF /Gas 8. Grease a baking sheet and dust with flour. Sift salt and flour into a bowl and rub in the butter to make fine breadcrumbs. Stir in the sugar.

Beat the egg. Make a well in the centre of the dry ingredients and add egg, vanilla essence and milk. Mix into a soft dough with a knife and then knead on a floured surface until smooth. Roll out to 1cm / ½ inch thickness and cut out six 9cm / 3 ½ inch rounds with a fluted scone cutter.

Brush the tops lightly with milk and bake for 10 – 11 minutes until golden brown. Cool then cut cakes in half. Whip the cream until it just holds its shape, then fold in 1 tablespoon of icing sugar. Cover the cake bases with half the sliced strawberries. Spoon or pipe the cream onto the fruit, then add the remaining strawberries. Gently press on the tops, sift over remaining icing sugar. Decorate with mint springs and serve.

Perfect Timing
by Daisy Jordan

It's all in the timing with soufflés. That's what the cookery book said. But I've never been terribly good with instructions, which is probably why my soufflé looked more like a cow pat, and definitely why I was sitting here.

I switched off the ignition and considered the sky bleakly. It was raining nine-inch nails and blowing a gale and I was in posh-frock-and-full-hairdo regalia. Typical. If I hadn't massacred the soufflé, I wouldn't have had to rush to the supermarket. If I hadn't rushed to the supermarket, I wouldn't have been in the supermarket car park, And I wouldn't have – ohmyGod – pranged Justin's car.

But even in a gale, some sounds are unmistakeable. I groaned. Then I swore. Then I opened the car door. There was a tall man outside wearing big muddy boots. I reached for my umbrella.

"Didn't you see me?" he asked me. Terribly politely.

"See *you*?" I said, wide-eyed. Surely he had hit *me*?

It soon became obvious what had actually happened. We'd both reversed out of opposite parking spaces, and our cars had sort of kissed in the middle. Justin would blow a gasket. And possibly a piston. If only I'd made him get the wretched shopping. If only. They were his friends that were coming to dinner, after all.

I bent down to assess the damage. It didn't *look* that bad, but I knew it would be. It was that kind of car.

The other car was worse. The bumper was hanging off. And if it was my fault…could it have been my fault?

But as my hair would soon be doing an impersonation of my soufflé I felt very cross indeed.

"You hit *me*!" I told him crisply. "Weren't you looking?"

He blinked rain from his eyes. I didn't proffer the umbrella. I couldn't afford to. And besides, he didn't need it. He didn't have a hairdo. Just a raggle-tag of curls, each one tipped with a raindrop.

"Of course I was looking!" he said.

My eyes lighted upon his car now, which was elderly, dirty, and full to the brim with all sorts of strange stuff.

I pointed. "But you have no rear vision at all!"

He looked defiant. "I checked in my wing mirrors," he said.

"That's hardly sufficient," I said, feeling sniffy and sounding it. "I was probably in your blind spot."

"Both wing mirrors," he said, wrestling with his bumper while the rain fell in stair-rods on his back. "Anyway, how do you think lorries manage?"

Which was, I had to concede, a reasonable enough point. And I had, I knew, reversed in rather a hurry. I had been in a hurry. I was in a hurry now.

The rain was coming at us sideways now. "Just bad timing, I suppose, then," he said equably. "'Look. There's no point us both getting soaked while we debate it. I have to be somewhere, and it looks like you do too. Let's exchange details," he added, almost cheerfully. "We can sort the whole thing out on Monday."

Justin, who had come round early to help, was watching TV when I returned

"You OK?" he said, inspecting me. "You're looking very dishevelled."

"I'm feeling dishevelled," I told him. 'I have pudding to prepare in ten minutes flat, and someone has just reversed into your car."

"My car?" he said, galvanised. "How bad is the damage?"

"Minimal," I told him. "Though I've broken my leg."

"Har har har," he said, following me into the kitchen. "Anyway, how did it happen?"

I told him while I unpacked the shopping. With special reference to my faultless driving and the plethora of junk in the other man's ancient and much bashed-up car. As you do.

And then, when I thought about it, I felt a bit bad. Because the more I thought about it, the more I realised the man had been right. It really had just been a case of bad timing. But Justin, being Justin, disagreed.

"It's his fault," he said, while he watched me clear away the dishes once everyone had gone. "From what you tell me, it's definitely his fault. I presume you got his insurance details? And I hope you didn't admit liability."

I shook my head. I hadn't. Because it wasn't my fault. But then, it wasn't really his either.

I'm not very good at heeding any advice, despite having been given it all my life. Particularly from my mother. I never took hers, which is probably why I ended up marrying a rat and failing to finish university. But though that was way behind me, and my daughter was grown up now, even she'd started being rather bossy.

"It's your time now, Mum," she'd told me, before skipping off to university herself. "To do what you want to do. Finish your degree, perhaps."

I didn't take her advice either. Because there was the small matter of supporting her through university. I did go to college, but on a short computer course. Which got me the job with Justin's firm. Justin was a financial advisor, so he was good with advice too.

The man in the muddy boots phoned me on the Monday. His name was Matt and he sounded very nice. We chatted for quite a while.

"How'd it go?" he asked.

"How did what go?"

"Whatever it was you were looking so glamorous for. I hope I didn't ruin your evening."

"You didn't," I said. "It was the soufflé that did that." And then I told him all about it.

He telephoned again on Tuesday. We talked for half an hour. He told me he was a geography teacher and had been returning from a field trip. Hence all the stuff, which was mainly soggy tents. He liked the outdoors, he said. Walking up hills.

"And I've been to the garage," he said.

"Oh, dear. What's the damage?"

"Ouch," he said grimly. "Double-ouch. But I don't want to claim on my insurance because if I do I'll lose my no-claims bonus, of course. If we agree – and we do, don't we? – that it was nobody's fault, shall we just decide to call it quits?"

Justin, naturally, had booked his car in too. I'd thought they'd need a microscope to see it, but I was wrong.

"Two hundred pounds!" I heard myself splutter. I was ironing his shirts at the time. "All that money? Just for one tiny scratch?"

Justin frowned. "There's a small dent as well."

I told him, rather reluctantly, what Matt had suggested. "Quits?" He scowled. "Quits? Well, of course, he would say that. No. It was obviously his fault so he'll have to pay up. You shouldn't let people take advantage."

No, I thought, folding the ironing board. I shouldn't.

On the Thursday, I telephoned Matt. For a change. We talked for a whole hour this time. He told me he'd made a soufflé once, and it had turned out rather well. That he could cook rather well. Being single. I told him he'd have to give me lessons.

"I'm sorry," I said, then, though I really didn't want to, "but my boyfriend wants to go though the insurance."

"'Oh," he said. "Boyfriend?"

"It's his car," I explained. "I had to use his because it was blocking mine in."

"Oh," he repeated, and I could hear his brain whirring. "I suppose you'd better send me the bill, then."

I tried hard to remember, then, exactly what had happened, because my conscience just wouldn't let me sleep. At least I think it was my conscience.

A week later a cheque arrived for two hundred pounds.

"It doesn't seen fair," I said to Justin. "It was just fate. It doesn't feel right to accept this. Not when he's already had to pay for his own car."

Not when he probably earned a fraction of what Justin did. Not when Justin's car, with its microscopic dent, would be traded in for a new one in months.

Justin grimaced. "Are you trying to tell me it was your fault after all?"

No, I thought. No! But that felt wrong too. "Yes,' I said instead. "It was my fault."

As I had Matt's address, I took the cheque back myself. And he smiled such a smile when he opened the door that I instantly remembered what had kept me awake. Not my conscience. It had been his eyes.

And everything else about him. His hair. His big boots. His culinary prowess. “Here’s your cheque,” I said. “I managed to make him see sense.’

“Ah,” he said. “The boyfriend.”

“Er… actually, *ex*-boyfriend,” I told him.

It’s not only Justin who’s seen sense. It’s raining when Matt arrives to collect me, but this time I don’t bother with my umbrella. You don’t need posh hairdos for walking up hills. Or fancy cars, come to that.

I kiss him. Or soufflés. I don’t care what the book says. I think my timing was absolutely perfect.

Chocolate Soufflé With Caramel Sauce

Serves 6

You'll need 6 x 6cm ramekins
To prepare ramekins
1 tsp unsalted butter
1 tsp caster sugar
1 tbsp cocoa powder

Ingredients

Soufflé
100g (4oz) dark chocolate, minimum 60% cocoa solids, broken into pieces
60g (2½ oz cocoa powder
8 egg whites
60g (2½ oz) caster sugar
Caramel sauce
100g (3½ oz) caramel-filled chocolate, broken into pieces
1 tbsp thick cream

Method

Preheat oven to 190ºC/375ºF/Gas Mark 5.

Prepare the ramekins by melting the butter and brushing it over the inside of the ramekins. Mix the sugar with the cocoa powder and sprinkle into each ramekin until coated. Shake out any excess. Set aside.

Melt the chocolate in a heatproof bowl suspended over a saucepan of simmering water. Meanwhile, mix the cocoa with 150ml (quarter pint) of cold water in a saucepan then bring to the boil, whisking continuously. Boil for 10 seconds. Take the melted chocolate off the heat and mix with the cocoa mixture.

Whisk the egg whites until soft peaks form. Add the sugar and continue to whisk until the egg whites stiffen. Add a quarter of the egg white to the chocolate and cocoa mixture and whisk until thoroughly blended. Gently fold in the remaining egg white using a metal spoon. Pour into the prepared ramekins, fill to the rim, and with a palette knife, level off the surface. Run your thumb around the rim of each ramekin, pushing away the soufflé mixture so it does not stick to the edge and will rise evenly.

Bake the soufflés for 10-15 minutes. Remember not to open the oven door while the soufflés are cooking. While they are cooking prepare the caramel sauce. Place the chocolate and cream in a heatproof bowl suspended over a saucepan of simmering water. Stir before serving. (You don't have to use caramel-filled choc, if you don’t want to – ordinary chocolate is fine too.)

Remove the soufflés from the oven, pour a little sauce over each one and serve immediately.

Recipes For Life
by Sophie King

When I look at my mother's writing, so distinctive with its eccentric loops in royal blue ink, I can almost feel her next to me in the kitchen. The exclamation mark after the 'clean' (she knew my hygiene standards weren't as exacting as hers) and the underlining of 'very slowly ' (she was always gently reprimanding me for rushing round life), makes her voice sing in my head. My mother was a marvellous cook. Everyone said so. But not me. I would have liked to have learned but she was the kind of person who didn't want anyone else in the kitchen. So I stuck to books and passing exams.

Now I'm trying again. I've set the oven to 150 degrees as my mother has instructed me on paper, and my own daughter is hovering over my shoulder. "Can I taste?"

I stop her just in time from dipping her finger in. "Not raw eggs. They might give you a tummy upset."

"But you used to." Grace has an answer for everything like my sister at her age. It both irritates me and, conversely, fills me with a sense of pride that my daughter can stand up for herself. "You've told me. Loads of times. How you used to lick the bowl out after granny had made a cake."

"Eggs were different in those days."

So were children. And parents. As soon as Grace was old enough to express interest in cooking, I had set her up with a pinny and clean(ish) hands and a hand mixer. Now Grace wants to take some home-baked cakes to the school craft fair and she's got it into her head that she wants to make almond macaroons and nothing else will do. So she's doing it herself and no thank you, she doesn't want any help from me.

She examines her grandmother's recipe carefully and my heart tightens. Grace can't remember my mum (she was barely two when she died) but she grasps every remaining memento to make her real. And that includes the hand-written cookery book that I found amongst my mother's possessions when I had to clear out her house. Luckily, there were two books; each with different recipes. One for my older sister and one for me.

"When do you first remember granny making almond macaroons?"

What a question! But Grace has always been full of them. "My mother used to make them every Sunday afternoon. Your auntie Florrie and I used to love the rice paper best. It seemed naughty, somehow, eating paper but it dissolved magically in our mouths like sherbert flying saucers."

"And did she make them EVERY Sunday? What if she was doing something else?"

Grace's social life is such, even at twelve, that she finds it hard to believe someone can do the same thing every week. I struggle to maintain her beloved grandmother's reputation. "Most Sundays."

"Did she stop when she got ill?"

Heavens, this was getting hard. My daughter and my mother's recipe were bringing back memories that I thought I had locked up, years ago. "Yes," I lie.

And then I begin to wash up vigorously, so my daughter can't see my face. The truth is that my mother stopped making almond macaroons on the Sunday that my father left. I knew exactly why he had gone because I had heard the noise upstairs when I'd been studying in my bedroom. The walls were thin and I could hear my mother crying so I flew down to try and keep the peace again. By the time I'd got there, he had gone and she was sitting at the kitchen table, her head in her hands and a blob of almond paste on her hair. I put my arms around her and after that, I never had another macaroon again.

"I don't want to make almond macaroons any more."

I look up from the sink sharply. "Why not?"

"I don't know. I think granny wants me to make Three-layered Frosted Walnut Cake. Look. Here. On the third page."

That's something else. It doesn't take a psychologist to tell me that Grace has been harbouring romantic visions of her grandmother since her new best friend Sophie joined her class. Sophie has two grandmothers, both of whom spoil her rotten. Grace, who has only one grandfather, whom she sees at Christmas, feels cheated. That's another reason for her interest in the cookery book. It's something tangible that her granny once held in her own hands.

"Three-layered Frosted Walnut Cake is very difficult to make. Even your grandmother used to say it was time-consuming." As I say this, I can clearly see my mother's intense expression as she whisked the egg whites (no electric mixers then) and the way she would whistle with concentration as she coaxed the icing into the right consistency. My sister and I loved the way it melted right into our tongues and the soft pouches of our cheeks. It was a birthday cake and also one for special occasions. I distinctly remember her making it for my sixteenth birthday after my father had left and we'd moved into a two bedroom flat that was so much smaller than any of my school friends' homes.

"There's a stain on the recipe," says Grace reverently as she stroked it. "Did granny make it?"

The things that remain after you've gone…

"Probably. When you're cooking, it's easy to smudge ingredients onto a cookery book, just like you do when you're eating and reading at the same time."

Grace nods. She can see that. Like me, she's an avid reader but she somehow manages to have that practical gene from my mother at the same time.

My daughter is urgently leafing through my mother's recipes. They are glued into a hard-backed book but since Grace discovered it, one or two are getting torn. Perhaps I should carefully tear them out and put them into plastic pockets. Yet I am loathe to change something that my mother did. It would, I am sure, take the flavour away.

"What about Victoria Sponge?" I suggest.

Grace shakes her head. "Everyone else will be doing that."

Very true. My mother used to make that when she disapproved of whoever came to tea. That included Mr Green, my geography master who sometimes came round until I overheard my mother (in the kitchen again), saying that she was very sorry but it was just too soon. She also made it for Brian when he came to pick me up. By then, I was nearly eighteen and had filled out my university form. My mother was terrified that Brian – who worked in the local garage – would somehow make sure that I didn't go. Her Victoria Sponges were somehow never up to the usual standard of her other cakes and both Brian and Mr Green would often need another cup of tea to make them go down.

"Wedding Cake!" Grace gasps. "I haven't seen this one before."

That's because it's right at the back. The ink has blurred as though someone was crying on it while trying to cook at the same time. Or maybe it just got splashed with water. 'Did granny make the cake when you and Dad got married?'

"Yes, she did." I force my face to look normal. One thing I learned after my parents' break up was that I would never, ever put my own child through the same thing. So when I found that my husband was being fed by another cook, I made the second-best decision. I determined that ours would be as civilised a break as possible. Which is why Grace has tea at her step-mother's house every other weekend, even though it's shop-cake fare.

Grace is tempted, I can see. But we both know that a Wedding Cake would look a bit out of place at the school craft fair. Flapjacks? Mummy used to make those for Philip Green whom she started to see soon after I got married. All right, I suppose, but both were a bit too gooey for my liking. Butterfly cakes? She made those for Grace's christening. By then, she was clearly unwell although she kept telling me not to fuss. Of course she was going to do her granddaughter's christening tea.

Shortbread? Florrie and I tried to make that for her funeral but it was a complete disaster. Neither of us could concentrate and in the end, we made do with cucumber sandwiches, which would have had our poor mother turning in her grave.

"I don't know what to make." Grace's eyes are panicking and I can see both myself and Florrie and our mother in her face. "Sophie's grandmother is helping her make Brownies this afternoon. I wanted to find something really special."

"I could ring Florrie," I venture. "She's got granny's other book. Maybe there's something in there."

We live near each other, my sister and I. We didn't have a lot in common as children but after mummy died, we became inseparable, like two halves of a sponge. Florrie was round within the half hour, one twin on each hip and the book in her hands. Grace was engrossed.

"Don't tell me it doesn't get easier," says Florrie as she tries to calm one twin while I jiggle the other.

"Afraid not."

"Remember what mummy used to say? Bringing up a balanced child was like making a cake. You need to add the right ingredients and then give it time to rise in the right conditions."

Really? I don't recall that one. But it sort of makes sense.

"There's a recipe here for me!" Grace jumps up to show me. "Look."

I had to look twice to make sure but there it was. In our mother's very distinctive handwriting. 'Grace's Gorgeous Guzzle-Cake.' And then, underneath. "For when she's old enough to cook on her own."

"I haven't seen that before," says my sister. "Mind you, I haven't really looked through it properly. It's so much easier to buy ready-made when you're working."

"We got the wrong books," I say. "She left two, didn't she? And we just took one each without looking at them."

"She must have written it towards the end," says my sister shakily. "Look at the writing. It's sloping in a funny way. And her 't's' are different."

I squeeze her hand and put the kettle on. Meanwhile, my daughter is busy weighing out the ingredients and Florrie's twins are exploring my kitchen floor which hadn't been washed properly for a week because I've been writing. How like my mother, I thought, to leave something special for Grace. She had loved her first grandchild – the only one she was to know – with a passion. And during those last days, when I had sat by her bed, Grace had clambered over her counterpane and played with her glasses. I can still see the raw pain in my mother's eyes and the unspeakable knowledge that this was one child whom she wouldn't watch as she grew up.

"That smells delicious!"

I hadn't heard the door opening. Smiling, I put up my face to be kissed.

"Grace has been cooking again."

My husband pats his stepdaughter's shoulder. "That's my girl. What are you making?"

So we told him the story and his eyes twinkle. "Just so long as it's not Victoria Sponge. Do you know, Grace, when I first knew your grandmother, she disapproved of me so much that she used to leave out the sugar in her cakes. It was all I could do to eat them."

"Really!" My mother twinkles in Grace's eyes. "But she'd like you now, wouldn't she?"

"Yes," say Florrie and I firmly.

"Do you know," says Brian thoughtfully as he watchs Grace carefully take the golden-brown mixture out of the oven. "I know someone else who might enjoy this."

And that's how we came to have the mother of all tea parties. Florrie and I weren't sure at first but Brian assured us it was the right thing to do. And it was. After all, he only lived an hour away. And life doesn't go on for ever.

Grace's Gorgeous Guzzle Cake had almonds that made you salivate and cherries that juiced in your mouth and icing that crunched like snow. It made me remember the days when my parents had laughed happily together and when we'd gone on picnics with a red tartan rug and a thermos. It took away the taste of the bitter years that followed and replaced them with a taste for the future – and, to my surprise, the present.

"This is delicious," says my father who looked greyer and somehow smaller, since I'd seen him last year. 'Did you really make it, Grace?'

She nods, pleased. "I baked two, actually. You lot are my guinea pigs. But because you like it, I'm taking the second one into the school craft fair tomorrow."

Dad looks around for a napkin and I hastily handed him a creased square of kitchen roll. "I'll have to come. The boys would like it."

My father had had a second (and a third) family over the years. Talk about having your cake and eating it.

"Know what, Grace?" He wipes his mouth. "Your grandmother was a wonderful cook."

It was the first time he had ever mentioned my mother in front of me since the divorce. And for a second, I saw something that was more than a hint of regret flash through his eyes. So I hug him. And he hugs me back. And I feel wonderfully warm and somehow 'risen', inside.

"I wonder," says my dad in a strange sort of voice. "Do you think I could have a second piece?"

Almond Macaroons

Ingredients

3 egg whites
6oz sugar
4oz ground almonds

Method

Whisk three egg whites in a large, bowl. Add sugar, very slowly. Carefully, pour in ground almonds and mix into a smooth paste. Drop by teaspoonfuls onto slightly oiled baking sheet. Bake in moderate oven 190ºC/375ºFGas Mark 5 about 15 minutes. Remove from oven. Set baking sheet on wet towel for a few minutes. Remove macaroons with a wide spatula.

How To Improve Your Love Life

by Zoë Griffin

I have never been very good at following instructions. If the weather man predicts a rain storm, then I'll forget my umbrella. I don't understand the wotsits on video recorders, and I have wobbly thighs because I cannot stick to a calorie-controlled diet.

Luckily, I have friends that understand. My best friend Sally, sitting opposite me in my kitchen, sees me staring at the majestic looking carrot cake on the table between us. She takes the knife, and plunges it through the moist pile of heaven.

She scoops it on to a plate and passes it to me. Delicious.

Sally picks up a fork and dips it into her portion, spiking a bite-sized blob and running the fork over the top to get a big dollop of icing. The lot disappears in a second and she grins wickedly.

Sally's got a lot to answer for. If it wasn't for her then I'd never have tried carrot cake in the first place. My dieting books all tell me that carrots are good and that cake is bad, and I've always thought it rather confusing.

I was thirty years old when I tried my first slice – and it was the day after Sally told me she that she was engaged. I didn't have a steady boyfriend and lived with a few goldfish in a poky flat. My fridge was constantly empty because I was always on a diet. (I've tried low fat, low carbohydrate, grapefruit and cabbage soup).

But as soon as Sally hit me with her 'happy' news, I had a craving for a big slice of chocolate fudge cake or a nutty brownie or a large, gooey muffin.

I took a trip to the café at the end of my road. It was a cold wet day, and it was uncomfortably warm in that small café. As I looked at the goodies in the display cabinet, I couldn't help but think that the chocolate assortment looked like mud. Mud that I'd stepped in as I fought my way to the café, mud that splattered up my jeans and made my ankles wet.

That's when I spotted the fluffiest slice of carrot cake you could imagine, covered in creamy vanilla icing. There was magical-looking glitter dusting its top and it was calling my name.

I brushed a strand of sopping wet hair from my cold, red face and ordered it. I asked for a cappuccino for good measure, and walked carefully through the crowded café carrying my fluffy, glittery wedge of cake and my frothy drink.

I placed my precious load on a coffee table in the corner of the cafe and threw my bags on the armchair next to me. A bright pink book fell out of my handbag and I cringed as it crashed loudly on to the floor displaying its bold title; How to Improve Your Love Life: Without Even Trying.

My mother had bought it last Christmas. I've never really been into all that psychology mumbo-jumbo and it had sat on my shelf untouched until the day that Sally announced she was engaged. She broke the news during one of the Saturday brunches that we used to have to soak up the alcohol after a heavy Friday night on the town. When she told me she was getting married, I knew that Saturday brunch would never be the same again.

The book was in my handbag because I was going to take it back to the bookshop and exchange it for something more worthy like a Lonely Planet travel guide. The problem was it was so pink, and pink has always been my favourite colour, and I felt compelled to open it.

I gobbled down a few forkfuls of carrot cake and began to read.

Chapter One – Pamper Yourself

You will never meet Prince Charming unless you are ready to go to the ball.

Never go out in old jeans and trainers. Have regular manicures and book a hair appointment every six weeks.

I put down my fork. I was wearing mud-splattered trousers, my hair was starting to go frizzy from the rain and my nails were bitten stumps. I knew I would never be able to follow all those rules and toyed with the idea of hurling the book across the room.

I decided against it. I didn't want to get thrown out of the café before I'd finished the cake. I scooped a large dollop of glittering icing and shovelled it into my mouth. The sugar gave me a sudden rush and I decided to tackle the next chapter.

Chapter Two – Grab Every Opportunity

Cinderella would never have found her prince if she was too tired to go to the ball

Get out on to the social scene. Look at the potential around you, on public transport or in cafes.

At last I was doing something right. I was in a café. I did what I was told and searched the room.

At the table next to me was a ginger man engrossed in a crossword. One of my ex-boyfriends was ginger, but dyed it black and spent the whole time inspecting his roots. Another boyfriend did a crossword every day. It took him more than an hour and he wouldn't let me help.

Never mind, I thought to myself as I scraped the last of the glittery icing from the cake, I was going to exchange the book for a Lonely Planet guide. I sipped my cappuccino to wash down the sweet frosting and that's when I saw him. He was tall, dark and handsome and standing behind the counter, looking straight back at me.

I licked my lips, wondering where he'd sprung from and what he was doing behind the counter, and cursing the fact that my Mr Potential had to appear when I had a milk moustache. I blushed as I went back to my book and continued reading.

Chapter Three – Appear Confident and Secure

Prince Charming searched the town for Cinderella when she left the ball early.

Get a life! Men get a thrill from chasing busy, successful women.

I scooped up another morsel of cake and thought about what I could do to appear exciting and interesting. For inspiration, I took another bite and looked through my handbag. Apart from a mirror and some red lipstick, all I could find was the reporter's notebook that had been in there since I took minutes for my boss's meeting on Friday afternoon. That would have to do.

I could feel Mr Potential's eyes on me, and made a big show of pulling out the notebook. I threw him a brief glance and turned away flicking my hair. That bit wasn't in the book, I thought to myself smugly.

I placed the notebook on the table and delved through my bag for a pen. My coffee cup was being pushed further and further towards the edge of the table, but I was oblivious until it crashed to the floor with a bang. My frothy cappuccino became a neat puddle, and the china smashed into tiny pieces.

I raised the book to my eye level to hide my blushes, while a sulky-looking youth was sent over to mop up the mess. I read another few pages of dating dos and don'ts with the book held high up in the air, until I realised that its bright pink cover with its screaming bold title was broadcasting my unexciting love life to the entire café.

Feeling self-conscious, I placed the book back on the coffee table. As I did so, I couldn't help but notice that Mr Potential was still watching me from his spot behind the counter. My stomach lurched and I felt weak. I craved another mouthful of cake, but I had eaten it all. Perhaps it was time to go.

I stood up and brushed the crumbs from my trousers. He was still staring at me. I don't know what came over me, but I winked at him. It was rather a quick wink, really more of a blink than a wink, but it did not have the desired effect. My contact lens started shifting about in my eye and the room became blurry.

It was definitely time to leave. I scrabbled in my bag for my purse, threw a couple of pounds on the table and ran out of the door.

I was halfway down the road when I realised that someone was running after me. As they got closer, I was struck by a strong waft of cinnamon. A large, manly hand tapped me on the shoulder.

"Is this your book?" asked Mr Potential.

I couldn't talk. I nodded and grabbed it back.

"And you have some frosting in your hair." His hand swept through my tangled mane. He brushed my hair and slowly brought his hand towards my right cheek, tentatively stroking it with his index finger.

"I wanted to do that for the past half hour. The name's Jack."

He offered his hand and I took it. "I'm Karen."

"Karen and the carrot cake." He raised my hand to his mouth.

Sally pokes me with the other end of her fork. "Sugar rush? You're awfully quiet."

"I was just thinking about us having our Saturday brunches after all these years."

Sally smiles. "Only now they're much better. We have unlimited carrot cake now that you're married to Jack."

Carrot Cake

Ingredients

Cake

225g butter
225g soft brown sugar
225g self-raising flour
4 eggs (lightly beaten)
1 tsp nutmeg
3 tsp cinammon
300g grated carrot
100g juicy sultanas

Icing:

225g icing sugar
50g plain greek yoghurt
Water to mix
1 tsp cinnamon
Edible glitter sparkles – available from specialist cake decorating suppliers on the internet and at Jane Asher

Method

Pre-set the oven to 190ºC/375ºFGas Mark 5.
Cream the butter and sugar in a large mixing bowl.
Form a well in the centre of the mix and pour in half the egg. Stir gently.
Fold in half the flour.
Add the remaining egg and stir.
Fold in the remaining flour, cinnamon and nutmeg.
Add the carrots and sultanas and stir well.
Place the mixture in two greased Victoria sponge dishes.
Bake for 45 minutes – until top is firm.
Place on a wire rack to cool.
Mix the icing sugar, cinnamon and yoghurt, with water if desired.
Spread over the cool cake. Add glitter to decorate.

If Flapjacks Be The Food Of Love

by Alison Baverstock

We were in the very beginnings of our relationship, but even then I was so attuned to you, so aware you were near. I could recognise your tread as you strode up the gravel on the garden path that Sunday morning. Strong steps – not to be distracted. I stood in the kitchen counting the seconds between you ringing the doorbell and me opening it. Trying to restrain myself. Trying not to look too eager when what I wanted to do was feel your arms around me. It was so hard to appear cool when that was the last thing I felt inside.

I opened the door and there you stood, that familiar half-smile on your lips. Do you know you don't move your upper lip when you smile? Your lips sort of crinkle at the corners, but your top lip remains stiff. You smile with your eyes. I went towards you and we kissed briefly. You smelled of the shower, your hair still wet, and that salty taste on your lips, half you, half toothpaste. Cold lips, slightly apart, warm depth beneath.

We looked at each other and smiled. "Hello" you said. It seemed profound.

You followed me into my house. The one I shared with my three flatmates, none of whom were yet up. It was still only ten a.m., exactly when you had said you would arrive.

We were students, far away from home. Whereas at home you would take a boyfriend into the sitting room, hoping that your younger brother was not there or that your parents would not come in and make polite conversation, here there was no one to tell us how to behave. Student lives are conducted in bedrooms, even in the very early stages of a relationship. There is nowhere else to go.

You had just come from your hall breakfast, I was full up with butterflies and needed no sustenance, yet we went through the formalities of hospitality, you following me into the kitchen, the cold of the red floor tiles eating into my socks.

I put on the kettle for some coffee, the great student displacement activity. No one wanted all that instant coffee, and only a small proportion of it got drunk, but it was the social glue that bound us all together. "Do you want some coffee?" The standard greeting – a cheaper version of offering people a beer.

In the centre of the kitchen table sat a plate of flapjacks, neatly arranged; a petal-like structure stretching out from the two rectangular stamens in the middle. One of my flatmates had recently been through a difficult end to a passionate affair, and she had channelled her resentment into cooking. The recipes she chose reflected her mood. Whereas she had cooked crème caramel and sauces for her lover, now she combined unyielding ingredients into solid fare, items that would nourish and withstand – and which could be thrown. These flapjacks were no exception, hard and unyielding, their shiny surface tension dusted with caster sugar. Not for now the softer, malleable sort that leave fingers and mouth sticky and for which saliva is needed to moisten, chew and swallow.

You spotted them, asking if I had been cooking. "Hardly", I replied, "I have been out with you most of the time". You smiled. I asked you if you wanted one. This is a complicated area in flat-sharing. The ingredients belonged to us all, the effort to her alone. You took one and I moved the others round to hide the gap.

You bit the edge, offering my mouth the other end; taking the opportunity to come and stand beside me, next to the sink, our backs together touching the cold surface. We bit again, one after another, our teeth marks moving closer along the surface of the biscuit. We giggled, you brushing sugar from my top lip. Our hips rotated us towards each other. The kettle began to hiss.

I heard a noise on the stairs. We looked at each other and realised the significance, I took the biscuit from your hand and slipped it into the top of your pocket. Your jeans were not tight and it went in easily. We tried to look casual as my flatmate Jen burst into the room, wearing jeans and a tee shirt with her dressing gown on top.

She avoided eye contact. She was all resentment and bustle.

"Michael, are you here already? I did not hear the bell go." The implication that this was too early for visitors was very strong.

She caught sight of her plate, looked at it suspiciously and then looked at me, "These seem to be going down rather quickly." I seized the initiative.

"Would you like a cup of coffee? Michael and I are just about to have one."

"We seem to be running low on coffee," she replied "Who is drinking it all?"

She bustled around the kitchen and around us, taking her provisions out of the cupboard, putting the remaining flapjacks in a tin and slamming the lid down firmly. It teetered on the edge of the table, precariously. We all said nothing.

You and I sheltered closer, united by her hostility and complicit in our secret. Her suspicion was clear, but our mouths were shut. Our backs pressed closer into the steel rim and our hips into each other. Both warmed slightly.

The kettle boiled and I moved away from the sink, making two mugs of coffee. Jen moved into another room with her tin. We headed upstairs to my room, bed already made, warmed by the sunshine, a lazy view out over the valley, the early summer breeze making the branches move.

You followed me in, holding the door for me to pass through with the mugs. Where to sit? Neither of us wanted coffee, but we went through the motions, drinking a few small sips. You asked about the books on my desk, did you really want to know? We were killing time. You sat down beside me and put your arm around me. I could feel my stomach turning somersaults. I leaned into you and let my head fall on your shoulder. Even now I love it when you kiss the top of my head. We sat there primly, my head on your shoulder, rocking slightly to and fro. Outside we could hear the rest of the Sunday morning going on, lawnmowers starting to run, children shouting, Jen banging around downstairs – Sunday morning was the time for cleaning out her room. I wished there was a lock on my door.

"Are you hungry?" What a stupid question. You were not. I moved closer to you and something dug sharply into my ribs – I looked up at you. We both laughed – 'The flapjack'. Very gingerly I slid my hand towards your pocket, this time allowing my fingers to probe down. I passed the rough denim facia without difficulty, and slid on into the cotton lining, you moving to accommodate me. I pushed down, finding the edge of what I was looking for. You lay back to give my probing fingers more room; easing my search. I reached the bottom of your pocket and let my fingers roam, the morsels were floating in the moleskin space inside, loosely held but firm.

I looked up at you, and all the while maintaining eye contact, grasped the individual fragments. One at a time I pulled them out and fed them to you. One at a time, you bit each piece in half and slipped my share into my mouth. All the while we looked at each other; serious – deliberate.

Such a simple task, so utterly absorbing. Lying side by side we explored each others' mouths, let the crumbs drop in, chewed each fragment and gazed intently. Then we lay together, fed and content, fell asleep to the sound of the mowers and the chatter, the hoovering and the washing machine, the bed beneath us growing warm and deep, like a large mouth, well moistened. Our own private space.

Even now, looking back many years on, I can feel the fullness that came not from food but from our total obsession with each other. Throughout that summer, each time I met you it was the same, each time I felt it was impossible to be any more involved. It was like falling off a cliff in slow motion.

They say avocados and oysters are the perfect aphrodisiac, but nothing ever filled me up quite so completely as those few fragments of stolen flapjack.

Chewy Flapjacks

Three top tips for these to ensure success every time:

1. Grease the tin before you start
2. Take them out of the oven just before you think they are ready - once they look ready they are overdone
3. Cut them into pieces whilst they are still warm and in the tin, once they harden they are much harder to cut

Ingredients

8oz demerara sugar
8oz margarine
4 tbsp of golden syrup
8oz porridge oats
½ tspof salt

Method

Put the sugar, margarine and golden syrup in a pan and heat gently until melted. Remove from the heat and stir in the dry ingredients. What kind of tin you choose depends on your taste – whether you like them shallow and finger-like or square and fat. Whatever kind of tin you choose, cook at 180ºC/250ºF/Gas Mark 4 for 20-25 minutes. The mixture should be just set, with a crust formed, but not solid (see top tip above).

On the Menu
by Josephine Hammond

"Bastard", I shouted as with a resounding thwack I slapped his face.

"Bitch"

"I've really done it now," I thought. "He will never speak to me again", I knew I had brought it all on myself because of what I had been involved in. To this day I can't explain, even to myself, why I went along with it. I was young and naïve that is for sure. I was also a mere student, an apprentice both in life and in the kitchen. I was expected to do as I was told.

It all happened while I was doing my catering course. I was determined that I was going to become the Elizabeth David of my generation. Food is my passion – real food, not the pap that passes for food in all the fast outlets or even most restaurants.

I was sent to one of the smartest hotels in the world to gain experience, working in a top-flight kitchen. The Hôtel George V in Paris was a revelation. In the run-down British seaside resort that I come from, the most expensive room in the most expensive hotel was £70 per person per night B&B. At the George V the rooms started at £200. Perfection and attention to detail were the watchword of the hotel.

My first tour of the kitchen was terrifying. It was an assault on all five senses. Every surface was shiny, stainless steel, reflecting the bright lights that lit the work areas. There were so many things and so many people it was hard to take it all in. The chefs all shouted at one another and at the waiters, "Ça marche, deux saumons à l'estragon, deux coquilles St. Jacques." I realised I was going to regret not having paid more attention to my French lessons.

I began work in the part of the kitchen where the entrée dishes were made. I was to help create the small delicately flavoured preludes to the meals. A peppery-tempered individual named Michel was responsible for the tantalising titbits that awoke the palate and aroused the appetite. On our first meeting he looked me up and down, "Ah, une Anglaise" he said dismissively. Then he ran his forefinger gently down the side of my face and neck, moving on to my chest where he stopped just short of my breasts with a little sigh, "Not bad."

All that week I washed, peeled and chopped hundreds of vegetables and salads but also watched with what deft hands the dishes were prepared. Mushrooms quickly sautéed in a garlicky butter. Red peppers roasted and skinned, dowsed with oil and balsamic vinegar. Soups strained and seasoned with care. All were finally presented with such artistry that each plate should have been exhibited at the Tate. Every one was examined by Michel and, if not perfect, would be returned to the luckless cook with shouts of "Idiot, espèce d'andouille" At the end of the first week Michel said to me "You have worked very hard – for une anglaise. You must come and have a drink with me." I couldn't refuse. It was more a royal command than an invitation.

That evening, washed and changed, I met Michel at a little bar along the road. We had a simple meal of tomato salad and plain grilled steak washed down with a bottle or two of good wine. Then he introduced me to the delights of a Marie Brizard sur glace. This is a liqueur based on aniseed. Served with ice it is fantastic, after several of them you are very mellow indeed so when Michel suggested we go back to his place taking a bottle with us I was happy to continue the evening.

I sat on the sofa in his tiny room. He poured two more glasses of Marie Brizard and sat beside me. We were talking happily when he suddenly put down his glass and placed one hand on my knee "You are a very beautiful woo-man, Helen." There was something about the way he pronounced the word that made it seem the softest, sexiest thing I had heard. He began to nuzzle my neck and I felt his hand stroking my thigh, pushing my skirt away and moving further and further up my leg. It was already too late to protest and, by the time his probing fingers were stroking at my knickers, I was enjoying myself far too much.

After my first fortnight in Michel's department, I moved on from preparation to some actual cooking. He and I continued to meet outside work. We often shared a meal, bottles of wine and his bed. But soon I had to move on to the fish department. Looking back now, I know that I had expected to continue to enjoy Michel's company and I didn't understand when our outings and nights together stopped. So here I was in the fish area of the kitchen, under the guidance of Pierre, missing my evenings out.

Pierre was a gangly individual who seemed to have more than his fair share of arms and legs, not unlike the squid and octopus that he worked with. His mood was tranquil, in contrast to the fieriness of Michel. After checking the beautifully arranged dishes of seafood or fish he would pronounce them good. Then with a shrug of his shoulders, "but the customer will complain anyway." As before, I started with the most menial of tasks but I quickly moved on to filleting and cutting up fish and knew that by the end of my stay with Pierre and his team I would be putting together whole dishes on my own.

Monday was always the quietest day of the week. So it was then that several of us had our day off. An outing was proposed – a trip to the forests and some fishing in the river. As if we needed to see more fish! We took only bread and salad with plenty of wine. The plan was to catch our fish and barbecue it there and then. It was perfect weather. Sunshine dappled down through the trees and we had a wonderful meal on the riverbank washed down with lashings of wine. A great sleepiness seemed to come over the group and people started to drift off to have a quiet moment alone.

Pierre called me over to him.

"Look, I have something special for us to share," he said as he took a bottle of Marie Brizard out of his rucksack. I did vaguely wonder how he knew about my penchant for it, but I was already too woozy with wine to give it much thought. He led me further into the forest away from the heat of the sun and the sparkle of the river.

It was hushed and still all around us as we sipped our drink from the tiny glasses he had brought. Pierre moved closer and kissed me, just gently at first but soon I could feel his tongue pressing urgently against my lips as he held me to him. He pulled back for a moment and looked at me as I sat there, already helpless with the heat of my feelings.

"You know, I like breasts. All day long in the kitchen I see legs, soft floppy ones of octopus and the hard shell-covered ones of crab and lobster. Fish do not have breasts. But you, Helen, you have the most beautiful poitrine. Tu permets?"

And with that he gently slid the straps of my T-shirt down off my shoulders and cupped my breasts in his hands. Then groaning with pleasure, he bent his head to kiss them. It was some time later that we rejoined the rest of the group.

Pierre was very different from Michel but just as exciting in his way. His sea-green eyes were gentle. I spent a month in the realm of my Fisher King. In that time we became great friends as well as lovers, but it was also during that time I first met Richard. We were introduced because we were both English. He had already qualified and was now part of the pâtisserie team. For me it was love at first sight. My Cœur de Lion was tall but well muscled with the tightest bum you ever saw. He seemed completely uninterested in me and made it clear that he was here to be with French people, not English, and to that end was busy with one or other of the waitresses most nights. So with a Gallic shrug of the shoulders (I was getting into the vernacular by now), I turned away disappointed but not defeated.

Meanwhile, I carried on with my soulful Fisher King. While I was working in the fish department I didn't see Richard at all. However, the time came for me to move on to the area where the meat dishes were prepared and cooked. Here, I used to catch the occasional glimpse of him going about his work with the patisserie, or giggling with one of the waitresses in a hidden corner of the kitchen, but I was biding my time and thinking up a strategy.

The meat department was ruled over by a tyrant named Henri. He was famous for his culinary achievements and was one of the reasons why the hotel had three Michelin stars. Within the hotel he was renowned for his extreme perfectionism. I saw with my own eyes how he rejected a delicious plate of magret de canard because the watercress garnish had not been placed at quite the right angle to the meat. His signature dish was Châteaubriand steak. The steak was cooked to such perfect tenderness that it shivered apart with a mere stroke of the knife. It was served with a Béarnaise sauce, light crisp pillows of potatoes and fresh green salad.

Once again I started with all the menial tasks and I think Henri took to me because I was enthusiastic and worked so hard. He had been known to give a good grilling to any apprentice who fell short of total dedication or who didn't cut the mustard. Pierre and I had stopped seeing each other the minute I moved on to Henri's team. This time I was not surprised and when Henri came to me after work late one night, bearing a bottle of Marie Brizard and suggesting that we relax together, I knew exactly what to expect.

Henri led me to a tiny private room he had at the back of the kitchens, little more than a cupboard with a bed in it.

"Sometimes when there is a big important party that continues late into the night, I am too tired to go home so I sleep here. Are you too tired to go home, little one?"

No one had ever called me that before, as I am tall and willowy. I rather liked it. But then Henri was even taller, quite a hunk in fact.

"Mmmm," I replied vaguely, holding my hand out for the drink he was offering. It was delicious, iced to perfection and I began to relax as the glow of it gently slid down my chest and into my stomach. Henri took one of my hands in his and, turning it palm up, began to kiss it. The velvety touch of his lips on my hand was a revelation of softness and when he realised the way he was making me feel, he ran his fingers up and down my naked arms.

"You have such beautiful skin, little one," he murmured, "et que tu es bien parfumée," as he sniffed and snuffled against my neck. We undressed and fell onto the bed where his hands were soon caressing my thighs. My thighs fell apart under the lightness of his touch like one of his Châteaubriand steaks being stroked by the knife. And so it was that Henri became my lover, a most passionate and exciting one.

Much as I enjoyed being with Henri for the month I spent on his team, I never once forgot Richard. I would often catch a glimpse of him kneading dough or rolling out pastry. I tried to be as friendly as possible at all times, always smiling, always bright-eyed and bushy-tailed. The waitresses he frequented all had a tendency to the gothic. They had dark eyes, sultry mouths and rarely smiled. I believed that being different from them was my only hope.

Occasionally during the weeks that our paths crossed in the kitchen he even spoke to me. It was never more than a gruff "hello" or a slightly more cheery "hi" but those things mean a lot to a Yorkshire man. They have to be the most undemonstrative people on the planet, but then the strong silent type is irresistible because you never can be sure what they are thinking and that is so tantalising. Each time he even nodded in my direction I spent the next two days shredding daisies as I agonised over the meaning of the small gesture. Eventually my turn came to work in the pâtisserie team where we were working together, rubbing shoulders with one another. He was even giving me orders. Our hands often touched in the course of our work as I handed him eggs or a rolling pin or helped to sieve the flour. It sent shivers down my spine every time.

I was longing to run my hands up his arms and over his broad shoulders or to nestle my head against his well-muscled chest. Frequently I caught him looking at me and I had the feeling that he liked what he saw. He even seemed to be paying less attention to his waitresses. Whereas before, he used to pick them up and whirl them around the kitchen for a laugh, he suddenly seemed much more serious. He spent more time than he needed to, showing me how to make the Tarte Tatin, Vacherin or Gâteau St. Honoré that were the specialities of the house.

Then one day I decided it was time to be bloody, bold and resolute. After work when we had finished cleaning up the kitchens for the day I rushed to the loo to arrange my hair more prettily and dab on a touch of lipstick. From my bag I took out a bottle of Marie Brizard and walked up to him smiling. Holding out the bottle I said, "My place or yours?"

"Oh, my God, you don't think I would do that!"

"What's wrong with relaxing together?"

"Nothing, but I've heard all about you and your liking for Marie Brizard, you've worked your way through every chef in the kitchen, from what I've heard."

"So? What about you and your waitresses? It's no different."

"You're just a tart!"

And that was when I slapped him. I was just thinking "I've really done it now, He will never speak to me again" I had really screwed up. Then to my shock and horror <u>he</u> slapped <u>me</u>. I reeled back, cheek stinging, mouth open in astonishment. It really hurt. Anger took over, with a rush of adrenalin I shouted at him, "That is taking equality too far and you don't even believe in it." I looked around for a weapon and found a gorgeous raspberry tart we had been making earlier. With a cry of, "I'll give you tart!" I hurled it at him. It hit his face with a very satisfying splodgy squelch and seemed to hang on the end of his nose for aeons before finally slithering to the floor. It left behind a mixture of squashed raspberries and gooey custard all over his annoying fizog.

He had evidently got the equality bug big time now because I then got a large tarte au citron in my face. It's hard to look dignified or angry with slices of lemon stuck on one's face. He seemed to be laughing which made me even angrier. As I lunged to grab another missile I slipped on the custard-coated floor. I think he intended to stop me falling. He put out his hand to grab me but as I fell into the mess he lost his balance and fell on top of me. We lay there panting with our exertions. For several seconds we glowered into each others eyes. Then suddenly he bent his head towards me and holding my arms back either side of my head kissed me hard. I struggled a bit at first, just for show really, – what moi, a tart, never! – but then quickly succumbed to his passion. After all it was what I had wanted all along.

Sweet Surprise
by Jill Stitson

"So, you make a roux for the main dish and you've got to blanche the vegetables as well." Tricia's voice droned on and Jackie stared at her cappuccino, watching the chocolate disappear as she stirred it. That was as far as her culinary expertise went, she thought.

"Don't forget the pate sucre and of course you've got to glaze the ham." Kate's voice joined in enthusiastically.

They might as well be speaking a foreign language, mused Jackie.

"The only thing that's glazing over is my eyes." She suddenly realized that she had spoken aloud as her two friends stared at her and then smiled, patronisingly, Jackie thought.

"Well, you know I can't cook. Just the basic meat and two veg," she added defensively.

"Yes, but you're good at other things," they chorused as they always did.

Jackie grinned, her good humour restored. These two were her best friends. Her rocks in times of trouble. But they were expert cooks and she was not.

"Read any good books lately?" she said, trying to distract them.

Books were her passion and she regarded them as her friends. Many were so old and thumbed that they were falling apart. She had joined a book club two years before and enjoyed the monthly meetings and discussions, but none of her friends there meant as much to her as Trish and Kate. Probably because the three of them went back a long way, having met in the playground taking their kids to school for the first time. They had all been near to tears, though it was the children who should have been upset, not the mothers, she had managed to joke at the time.

And here they were ten years on, Trish and Kate still exchanging recipes, Jackie still reading and all still worried about the kids.

Kate was anxious because Liam showed no interest in football, but dancing of all things! Then the film 'Billy Elliott' had come out which had almost, but not quite, allayed her fears - not that his sexuality mattered at all, she kept saying.

Then Jackie's own daughter was caught smoking pot and had been banned from school for two weeks. She had tried every possible approach ranging from 'well of course I tried it myself, but you know it can be dangerous in the long run', to shouting and finally 'grounding' her. Tamsin had just looked bored and continued painting her finger and toenails black and having another piercing when she was finally allowed out.

Tricia's two boys were remarkably 'untroublesome', but she worried anyway.

"So, when are we coming again?" Jackie gathered her thoughts and looked at her friends. They met up at their local health club three times a week, usually in the evenings, as they all worked, but occasionally during the day if they could get time off.

"Well, it's 'Body Blitz' tomorrow," said Kate, "which you've both got to do because I'm going to feed you a million calories when you come to dinner on Saturday. I've got this fantastic new recipe…" Jackie ordered another cappuccino and let her mind drift.

An amazing idea came to her as she drove home. I'll show them, she thought, I'll cook a wonderful meal for Rob.

He always said the same thing when she moaned that she couldn't cook.

"I married you for two reasons and one was that you're good at ironing." He gave her his 'Brad Pitt' grin when he said that, trying to look sexy and sardonic. As he wasn't in the least like the actor, being of average height with ginger hair and glasses, this always gave Jackie the giggles, but she loved him to bits and gave up a thankful prayer to whoever was in charge for their solid, eighteen year marriage.

That afternoon, Jackie sat in her kitchen surrounded by all the cookery books she had ever bought. As there were only three, it didn't take long for her to leaf through the remarkably unthumbed, glossy pages and then shut them again, as she had so many times before. Rob didn't seem to need cookery books, he just liked experimenting and his meals were always delicious. A new paperback bought that morning beckoned, but she knew that if she opened it and started reading, she would be lost.

Oh, damn it, she thought, I'll just do a roast. I know he likes that. She turned quickly, knocking one of the cookery books onto the floor. Tricia's neat handwriting, on a piece of crumpled paper, caught her eye. She remembered having hastily stuffed it into the front of the book months ago.

"You can do this, anyone can make a Raspberry Pavlova," Trish had said when, in a weak moment, Jackie had actually asked for a recipe.

Yeah, I can do this, she thought, glancing at the piece of paper. Egg whites, sugar...it didn't seem difficult at all.

Jackie's spirits rose. Roast chicken, roast potatoes and veggies followed by her very own pavlova, not one bought from Marks or Waitrose.

Humming to herself, she turned on both ovens - one for the chicken and potatoes and the other for the pavlova. She peeled the potatoes and put them on to boil for five minutes. It was then she realized how hot she was. Outside, a perfect July day shimmered, the temperature almost hitting 80 degrees and the heat from the ovens made things even worse. Oh God, not the day for a roast, but she was committed now and determined to produce a perfect pudding for once.

Sweat trickled between her breasts and down her back. So, whipping off all her clothes, she put on one of Rob's big aprons. The Naked Chef, she giggled, although Jamie Oliver always kept his clothes on, more's the pity. She pulled herself together. Time to concentrate on the task in hand.

'Whisk the egg whites until very stiff,' she read. Frowning, Jackie tried to remember how to separate the yolks from the whites. She thought there must be some sort of gadget that did it for you nowadays, but of course she didn't have one. Thinking for a moment, she managed to dredge up distant memories of disastrous school cookery lessons and vaguely remembered tapping an egg with a knife and tipping the yolk from one half of the shell to the other whilst the white dripped into a basin. Fifteen minutes later she looked triumphantly at the pale liquid in the mixing bowl and wondered what to do with the yolk.

"Mum, what on earth are you doing and what the hell are you wearing or rather not wearing?"

Tamsin stood, leaning against the kitchen door, her school shirt hanging out over a miniskirt revealing long legs ending in huge, clumpy shoes. Jackie had long since learned not to question her daughter's idea of fashion or her language, unless it was the 'F' word.

"I'm making a pavlova and I'm very hot." She was not going to bandy words with her daughter at this crucial stage.

"You have no idea what you look like from the back!" Tamsin rolled her eyes in disgust.

"Exactly what you'll look like in a few years, I should imagine," retorted Jackie.

Tamsin smothered a grin. She was secretly glad her mum was 'a bit different'. Like all her friends she was an over-the-top feminist and it was good for her 'street cred' that her dad did most of the cooking.

"I'm going to Sophie's." Tamsin turned and made for the door.

"OK. Be back by seven." Jackie had not raised her eyes from the egg yolk still, still in its shell and dripping slightly onto her hand and up her arm. Making a decision, she decided to ditch the yolk into the sink and concentrate on the egg whites.

She whisked them and folded in the sugar as the recipe said. Suddenly she could hear Tricia's voice saying something about the mixture being so stiff you should be able to hold the basin upside down and it wouldn't come out. Hmmmmm…she wasn't about to do that little trick without being very careful!

The front door slammed. As usual, Tamsin must have forgotten something. Gingerly, she held the basin up and tilted it slightly.

"You gorgeous, sexy creature." Two strong hands came up behind her and enveloped her breasts, jiggling them up and down. The basin flew into the air and the contents spilled over Jackie's neck and trickled down her boobs.

"Rob, how could you! This was going to be your surprise pudding," she wailed.

"What do you expect? I come home and find my delectable wife in the kitchen wearing nothing but an apron. Every man's dream."

He started licking the mixture from her breasts. "Got any raspberries to go with this? Oh yes, I've found two – delicious!"

"Oh, Rob, stop it. I'm all sticky and look at this mess." Jackie didn't sound very convinced about the 'stopping'.

"Right, the kitchen we'll clear up later, but you, my love, need a shower and so do I."

In true Gone With The Wind style, he picked her up and headed for the stairs and the 'big-enough-for-two' shower.

"When are you going to remember that I didn't marry you for your cooking? It was for your ironing and one other thing," he whispered jokingly, soaping her all over very slowly.

Jackie smiled and started to do the same for him. Trish and Kate can keep their recipes, she thought. I'll stick to ironing and…the other thing.

Raspberry Pavlova

Ingredients

3 egg whites
175g (6oz) caster sugar
2½ ml (½tsp) vanilla essence
2½ ml (½tsp) vinegar
5 ml (1 level tsp) cornflour
½ pint double cream, whipped
fresh raspberries (or strawberries)

Method

Preheat oven to approx 135ºC/300ºF/Gas Mark 1. Draw an eight inch circle on oiled parchment paper or non-stick paper and place the paper on a baking tray. Beat egg whites until very stiff then beat in sugar, half at a time then beat in sifted cornflour, vinegar and vanilla. Spread some of the mixture on the circle, put the remainder in a piping bag and pipe onto the edge of the circle . Bake in a cool oven for 2 hours. When cool, carefully remove from baking tray, whip cream and pile into middle of meringue. Top with raspberries. Serves 4

Gingerbread Man
by Tina Brown

Ella looked at the clock, on seeing the time she threw down her spatula and dashed toward the window, hurtling over furniture to hide behind the curtain of her parents' cottage front window.

"What are you doing?" Jackie looked totally baffled at her friend's impromptu behaviour.

"Get over here quick." Ella turned to the window and waited. Jackie grumbled as she made her way around the furniture.

"Don't stand there. He'll see you. Get over behind the other curtain."

"Who are we spying on?" Jackie asked.

"It's Maggie's teacher. He jogs past every evening at this time."

"What are we going to do? Throw eggs at the old coot?" Jackie mocked. "I thought you grew out of that years ago."

"Very funny. Just wait and see." Her heart skipped as she saw a figure coming down the street. Anyone taking her pulse right now would think Ella was the one doing the jogging. She watched every bare muscle visible as he came closer into view. He had a sleeveless T-shirt exposing smooth, toned perfection.

His concentration seemed intense. Every time he ran past he was looked straight ahead. He never stopped to acknowledge a neighbour, nor did he look at the gardens – his concentration was set.

"Stop drooling. He's mine." Ella jeered at Jackie as she stood there with mouth open and eyes popping. Ella looked back to the man and gasped – he was looking straight at the house! Straight into the window as if he knew they were there spying on him.

He was still jogging, but his concentration was now aimed at the house. Ella felt her heart jolt painfully. Felt her cheeks flame with embarrassment and the disappointment of discovery.

As he jogged out of view, Ella stumbled back and landed in her dad's favourite arm chair.

"That's Maggie's teacher?" Jackie had a delighted look on her face, as if she'd just won the lottery.

Ella was too stunned to answer. He had never looked before. Had never even acknowledged that she was there watching him. Why today? How did he know?

Jackie cursed as her mobile phone started to play a cheery tone in her handbag. "I've forgotten to pick Joe up." She grabbed the bag. "I'll have to go. He'll kill me!" Jackie looked at Ella playfully. "I want to know everything tomorrow."

In a dazed state, Ella got up and went back into the kitchen to finish the baking.

Twenty minutes later, Ella was sliding some freshly baked gingerbread cookies out of the oven. She was just pulling the oven mitt off when there was a knock on the door.

On opening the door her eyes widened. "Oh." Her thoughts went into a panic. Was he here to confront her about her spying? Her cheeks flamed.He looked just as shocked as she did. "Er... Mrs. Peck, I'm Anderson Blake. One of Maggie's teachers. I just wanted to speak with you about your daughter..." Ella was about to melt at the sound of his sexy voice when she heard the words 'Mrs.' and 'daughter'.

She laughed. "Maggie's my sister." It was his turn to laugh, but self-consciously. Then he cleared his throat and held out his hand.

"Call me Andy."

"What was it you needed to discuss? My parents are overseas on family business and I'm Maggie's guardian until they come home." Ella replied, reeling from his touch.

"Oh well then..." He took in a deep breath as if to start a long story, then his eyes widened. "Gingerbread?" He had the oddest smile on his face. Then as if realising what he had just said and what he was doing, he straightened and cleared his throat again. "I know it's inappropriate to be here, but I'm very concerned about Maggie and I would like to discuss it with you. I didn't want to alarm you over the phone or for Maggie to know that I'm here. What I have to say is private. I know she'll be held up with netball practice for the next hour or two."

"Please come in." Ella stepped back in invitation. "Keep going through to the kitchen. I just have to pop another batch of gingerbread in the oven."

"So what's the problem with Maggie?" Ella asked, concerned, as she motioned for Andy to take a seat.

Andy perched on a stool near the bench close to Ella and the decorated gingerbread men. "Don't let me interrupt what you were doing." He eyed the cookies with a lick of his lips.

Ella went to the other side of the counter. "Would you like one?"

Andy paused for a fraction of a second before shaking his head and patting his very taut stomach. Well, it looked taut and muscle-tight under a T-shirt that was clinging to his body like a second skin.

"So what trouble has Maggie got herself into now?" Ella pulled her stool over and sat opposite as she pushed a tray of cookies aside.

"Oh she's not exactly in trouble, well, not yet." He leaned his elbows and forearms on the bench and Ella's eyes did a detour over firm rounded biceps. She licked her lips and trailed her eyes back to his but he wasn't looking at her, he was eyeing the gingerbread men. "I'm not sure if you know of the Mallory's."

At the mention of that name, Ella almost snarled. "I know of them. Who doesn't? They're nothing but a bunch of…"

Andy sat up abruptly and crossed his arms in front of his chest in a very defensive way. "My mother is a Mallory."

Ella sat back on her stool and felt the red heat of shame rising to her cheeks. "Oh!"

"Yes. I'm starting to realise that admitting to being related to the Mallory's isn't such a smart idea, but I'm loyal to my family and I hate lying. Pete told me you'd react like that."

"Pete!" Ella sat forward this time. "So you're here on his behalf then. I should have known it." She jumped off her stool. Her earlier thoughts of devouring this hunky man vanished now that she knew he was connected with the Mallorys.

"Can I at least have a gingerbread man before you throw me out without hearing what I have to say?"

She was so stunned by his audacity that she paused and turned to him with a frown. He picked up a cookie and bit the head off one of her gingerbread men.

"Give that back." He ignored her and took another bite.

"Mmm. These are nice cookies," he said through a mouthful "Actually one of the best damn gingerbread men I've ever had. You need some more practice to beat my mother's though."

How dare he! Ella folded her arms over her chest this time and leaned back against the bench. "Say what you have to and leave, Mr. Blake, and believe me the school will be hearing about this little visit of yours."

He didn't look fazed or intimidated at all. "What! No coffee?" His hand snaked out and snared another gingerbread man.

Ella was quick, but not quick enough as she tried to slap his hand away from the cookies. It was already in his mouth and the poor gingerbread man's feet were disappearing between even white teeth and a firm ruthless mouth.

"If I tell you these are nicer than my mum's will you relax and listen to me?"

"What happened to family loyalty?"

"I hate lying, remember." He raised an eyebrow waiting for her response.

Cheeky, Ella thought and she almost smiled. "Speak and keep your filthy hands off my gingerbread men."

"Are you as protective of all the men in your life or just your gingerbread ones?" "OK." He sighed when he didn't get a response from her. "Judging by your reaction you don't like Pete."

"I don't know Pete and I don't want to and I don't want Maggie to hang around him."

"Don't you remember what it was like to be fifteen years old or is that too long ago for you?"

Now his true Mallory colours were showing, she thought. "Not as long as it was for you," Ella quipped back.

He shook his head. "I'm not here to exchange insults with you. I'm here out of concern for Maggie. Her grades are dropping. Her attention span is minimal and her attitude is worse."

"It's since she's been sneaking around with your cousin…"

"So it's his fault?"

"Pete's not to blame. It's actually the other way round."

"What!" Ella spluttered. "You have got to be joking. Maggie has never been in trouble in her life before…"

"Neither has Pete. Not all the Mallory's are bad you know."

"Well of course you'd say something like that. You're one of them."

"Who was it?" Andy glared at her hard.

"What do you mean?"

"Which of my Mallory cousins broke your heart?"

For one fraction of a second Ella didn't respond. "A Mallory break my heart! Get real." She scoffed and turned away. She turned back to see another of her gingerbread men disappear into his mouth.

"Hey! They're for the fête tomorrow."

"Then I'll pay for them and see you again tomorrow for some more, so make plenty."

"Have you got more to say on what a bad girl Maggie is?" Ella asked in mock innocence. "I don't need you to lecture me on how to bring my teenage sister up." She watched him nibble on the other end of the poor gingerbread man.

"I'm not lecturing..." He stopped at the sound of the front door and Maggie calling out.

"Netball was cancelled."

The look on Andy's face was comical. He swore and glanced around. "I don't want Maggie to know that I'm here discussing her," he whispered. He was already on his way to the back door. He turned suddenly, almost knocking into Ella who was moving behind him in bewilderment. His arm went around her waist to steady her as he leaned past and thieved another cookie from the tray. Noticing that he had taken the largest one, Ella started to cry out, "Not that one," but before the words could come out, his lips landed on hers in a quick, warm, silencing kiss.

"This is our secret for now – please. I'll explain more later." And then he was dashing through the door.

"Who was that?" Maggie entered the room behind Ella.

Ella swung around and for once in her life felt speechless.

"Where's all the cookies? Ella! Where's my special one?"

"Ummm..."

"You didn't eat it?" Maggie gave her a death look.

"No, I didn't."

"Then where is it?" She saw the two coffee cups. "Who's been here?"

Ella opened her mouth to tell Maggie all about her teacher, but the words 'No one' came out.

"No one?" Maggie gave her that 'you must think I'm an idiot' look. "You had two cups of coffee and you ate half a tray of gingerbread on your own?"

"Well Jackie was here but then Joe called. She apparently forgot to pick him up again, so she dashed off." Ella started cleaning the cooking mess up, not looking at Maggie as she spoke.

"Jackie ate all the gingerbread, including my special one? But she's on a diet."

"What was in that so called special gingerbread man anyway?" quizzed Ella.

Maggie shrugged. "Just some extra spices."

"What kind of extra spices?"

"Nothing illegal," Maggie huffed, "if that's what you're worried about."

"I'm worried that it might make the person who eats it sick."

"It's got grandma's love potion in it. The person who eats it will fall madly in love with the first person they kiss but since Jackie had it, it doesn't matter since she is already married, unless, that is, she kisses someone else before she kisses Joe." Maggie stood with hands on hips.

"It wasn't me. I take it that special gingerbread man was for Pete Mallory."

Maggie's jaw fell open.

"Listen, I've got to go." Ella grabbed her car keys and made for the door. "I won't be long and then we'll talk about how you got that recipe and about Pete Mallory." Ella said over her shoulder as she left.

Ella drove along the main road into town and sure enough she saw figures jogging in front of her, but neither was Andy. It was a neighbouring farmer and his wife. How strange, Ella thought, and then she saw the reason why. Running along the edge of the road was a pig. Ella laughed as she slowed down to pass. Further along was a cow. This time Ella slowed right down until she passed the cow. Ahead Ella could see a horse galloping through the paddock. The horse was heading straight for Andy.

Andy looked through the passenger window as Ella pulled up and then lookedover his shoulder. He swore as he opened the door and squeezed into Ella's small car. Through her rear view mirror she saw the horse jump the fence of the paddock., on to the road.

They both looked at each other. Ella put her foot down and sped off just as the horse's breath washed the window of her car.

"What the…?" Andy looked out of the back window at the horse that was still following them.

Finally they out-drove the horse. Ella's suspicions were awakened now. She looked at his hands. No special gingerbread man.

"Did you eat that cookie?" Ella's heart rate was pacing back to normal after leaving that crazed horse behind.

"I'm not sure I liked it."

"But you ate it?"

"Uh huh."

"Where do you live?" Ella asked. "Will your wife be wondering where you are?"

"Not married," he said, as he turned to look at her. She concentrated on her driving but felt the heat of his gaze.

"Your girlfriend?"

"Haven't got one, but I'm free tonight if you're after a hot date."

"No." Ella flashed him a look. "Why would you think something like that just because I was being polite."

"Sorry. I misunderstood. It sounded like you were sussing me out to see if I was single or not."

Ella blushed. Well she had been, but not for the reasons he was thinking. She pulled up in front of his house. What if he kissed the wrong person after eating that cookie? She had every reason to believe that the love potion would work, it was after all the same one that had been passed down for generations and all her ancestors had had happy marriages. She knew this from family gossip.

"Um...have you...kissed anyone since leaving my place?" Ella's cheeks flamed red.

He groaned in reply. Concerned, Ella asked, "Are you feeling alright?"

He was holding a hand to his stomach. "I think I ate too much of your gingerbread. I wonder if the fox got a tummy ache too?"

"I think you are the Gingerbread Man. You have the same cheeky quality, and what about the farmer and those animals?"

Ella helped Andy into his flat. Just inside the door, Andy whispered something that Ella didn't catch.

She leaned closer to hear more clearly.

"Come a little closer." His words whispered.

"What's wrong?"

"All the better for me to eat you." He nipped Ella on the ear.

"Ouch! You're quoting the wrong tale. It's suppose to be 'Run Run as….' No!" Ella tried to pull away as he ran his lips along her jaw towards her mouth.

"If I'm the gingerbread man then I want to be caught by you," he whispered as he arched her over his arm.

Ella opened her mouth to try and explain about the special gingerbread man, but it was too late. He was giving her an extra spicy gingerbread flavoured kiss.

Gingerbread Men

Ingredients

125g butter/margarine
½ cup brown sugar
⅓ cup golden syrup
1 egg
2 cups plain flour
⅓ cup self-raising. flour
2 tbsp ginger
1 tsp Bicarbonate of soda
Icing:
1 egg white
½ tsp orange juice
1 cup icing sugar
food colouring and dried fruit or choc chips for decoration

Method

Preheat oven to 180ºC/350ºF/Gas Mark 4. Spray baking tray with cooking oil.
Beat butter, syrup and sugar until light and creamy. Beat in the egg.
Sift the dry ingredients and combine with a knife or metal spoon.
Knead the dough onto a floured board until smooth.
Roll the dough out and cut out into shapes. Place shapes onto prepared trays and bake for 10 minutes or until lightly brown. Cool biscuits on the tray for a few minutes. With a spatula gentle slide under the gingerbread so as cookies won't stick to tray. Leave to cool.
Using the icing mixture and a small piping nozzle, pipe clothes and hair onto the gingerbread men. With a little icing mixture stick dried fruit/lollies or choc chips as eyes, nose, mouth and buttons.

Midsummer Rose
by Liza Granville

"But why didn't it work?" wailed Rose, "I done everything exactly like Gran said."

"Because all that Midsummer's Eve love charm business is a load of nonsense, that's why!" snorted Mrs Palmer, slapping the lid on an enormous gooseberry pie. "And she's a silly old woman who ought to know better, filling your head with such rubbish."

"But…"

"Conjuring up visions of your own true love indeed! Love. See how long that'd last on a labourer's wage with half a dozen grizzling babies to feed."

The old cook flicked up the edges of the pastry with a practised hand. "Take it from me, you silly young wenches, marriage is a good bargain for a poor working man, but a life sentence for his missus."

Rose and Dot hid pitying smiles. What did she know? The Big House kitchen was Lily Palmer's whole life. She'd never married. The 'Mrs' was only a courtesy title.

Dot lowered her voice. "It ain't too late, Rose. Our Mam says if you hang a pod with nine peas in it over the door on Midsummer's Day, the first single man that comes in will be the one you'll marry."

"Let's hope it ain't daft Tommy Handcorn bringing the milk then," Mrs Palmer snapped. "Because he couldn't string the words together to ask you. And you can keep your hands off them there peas."

"Or we could try the hempseed charm," Dot persisted. "Trouble is, you've got to say it walking twelve times round the church at midnight."

"Leave this house at night, *madam*," warned Mrs Palmer, brandishing the rolling pin for emphasis, "and you'll be looking for a new situation."

She peered into the bowl. "Pair of you ain't got very far with topping and tailing them gooseberries neither. There's another two baskets waiting to be done. Better make a start on the ironing, Rosie Carter. That'll put a stop to your chin-wagging."

Sticking out her tongue at the cook's broad back, Rose flounced into the stifling atmosphere of the back-kitchen.

Outside it was unbearably hot. A heat haze had set the meadows shimmering. Nothing moved. The cattle lay exhausted in the shade of the great elms.

Indoors it was like a furnace. The scent of roses drifting in from the garden was so strong that it drowned the everyday smells of kitchen and stable yard. It dulled the senses. Stopped you thinking. Grew until it was so intense that it was almost a taste.

On top of that, thunder threatened. The air seemed thick, heavy, short of oxygen. Far away in the west, the sky had turned a peculiar leaden-yellow colour.

Rose defiantly made as much clatter as she could setting the flat-irons to heat on the back of the blazing range. Who cared what old fat bum Palmer said? She would go on trying to see a vision of her own true love. As Dot said, it wasn't too late. It was still Midsummer's Day.

A fierce longing rose in her. Clenching her fists, screwing up her face, her longing exploded to something nearer prayer. If only, if only…she'd do anything, sacrifice anything, just for a glimpse of him.

Her skin prickled. She had a brief sensation of something lurking, listening, pouncing on the thought. Rose opened her eyes hurriedly.

Nothing was amiss. Through the open door, she could see Dot concentrating on nipping the ends from the hard green fruit. Mrs Palmer was measuring sugar into the vast preserving pan.

Rose spread and damped the linen. She lifted the first flat-iron, spitting on it to test the heat. The metal sizzled. She turned back to the table.

But in that instant the room disappeared. The air tingled. Vibrated. An icy wind flickered at the damp tendrils of hair escaping from her cap.

She caught her breath. Her eyes widened. There was nothing. Nothing. She was surrounded by a softly lapping white mist.

For a brief moment she could still hear Mrs Palmer giving Dot another earful, pots and pans rattling, water splashing… Then these sounds were muted, smothered, gone.

The iron was too hot to hold. Rose looked wildly around. There was nowhere to put it down!

Hissing with pain, she tried to change hands. The cloth slipped. There was a moment's searing pain. She glanced down. A small livid heart-shaped mark glowed at the base of her thumb.

The mist cleared abruptly. Rose was still in the kitchen, but it had been transformed. With its pastel walls, curtains and furniture it felt as if she was standing inside a flower.

The wall into the scullery had been knocked down. The old pump was gone. In its place were shelves holding more books than she thought existed in the world. Plants and pictures everywhere. Steam rose gently from a bright blue cup. A man sat reading a newspaper.

Her heart leapt. He was not exactly young, not exactly handsome. She didn't know him, and yet it was as if she'd always known him. Clear grey eyes, a determined chin, the rumpled brown hair was as achingly familiar as the crooked little finger on his left hand.

He looked up, half rose and for a fleeting moment they stared into each others' eyes, both as startled as the other.

Then his gaze dropped to the throbbing burn. He frowned, moved towards her, his lips moved and it was over.

Outside, a dove began to croon a mournful love song on the stable roof. Mrs Palmer went on with her scolding. The irons were still sizzling and popping on the hob.

Rose bit her lip as the pain intensified. Her first impulse was to run and tell Dot what had happened. It had worked. The old stories had been right. Her Gran had been telling the truth. But the thought of Mrs Palmer's sharp tongue stopped her. Besides, they might not believe her.

She remained standing by the range, the iron now cool and useless in her throbbing hand. It would be her secret. Their secret. She wouldn't tell anyone. Rose smiled to herself. They would know soon enough when he came. And he would come, she was sure of that. It was just a question of time and patience.

She would wait forever if necessary, she thought recklessly.

Ben Armstrong never felt quite the same about his new sitting room after seeing the girl.

What a looker! There she'd stood, bang in front of the fireplace, utterly charming in her quaint clothes. He wryly wondered what money-spinning look fashion designers would latch onto next.

Heaven only knew how she'd got there. So much for all the cash he'd spent on security locks. Then she'd just as inexplicably disappeared.

He strode over to the window – not a sign of her. All that was left was the extraordinarily intense smell of roses from the beds outside the window.

Shy, he supposed. He wished she'd waited. At the very least he would have liked to have done something for that burn. These things should never be neglected. Left, it would almost certainly scar.

Still, on with the work. He wanted to keep up what had been a good start in his new practice. Little-Miss Mystery would turn up sooner or later. Netherwood was a small place. Being the only doctor meant he'd get to know everybody in time.

He hoped it would be soon. As he unlocked the car door he could still see her in his mind's eye. The enormous violet eyes, that hardly concealed mass of tumbling hair.

It was unbelievably hot today. Thunderstorms were forecast. The fierce midsummer sun scorched his shoulders as he mounted the steps to his first call.

The scent of roses seemed to have followed him. It was stronger here than it had been at home. Over-powering. Made you light-headed.

Ben glanced over the neat lawns and saw that one or two of the old folk were sitting out under the trees. Doing nothing, as usual.

That was the trouble, he thought. People who'd often been incredibly active all their lives were expected to sit passively, waiting for what?

The inevitable.

One of the care assistants at the Home opened the door. "Oh, good morning doctor. I'm glad you've come. I'm afraid she's sinking fast."

He followed her through a labyrinth of passages.

Take this old dear, for instance. She proved his point. According to his records, she'd gone into service at Netherwood

Manor when she was only fourteen. An enormous old place. Must have taken an immense amount of work to look after it. Thank God those days were over. It was all he could do to keep up the bit he'd bought, and that was only the kitchen wing.

She'd slaved away all her life. Working and waiting. Gradually progressing through the old-fashioned below-stairs hierarchy to become Cook. Now she had come to the end, gently drifting away, hardly knowing who or what she was, but still pretty with her clouds of soft white hair.

How was it that some women retained their femininity all their lives? Just another of life's mysteries, Ben supposed, something else that science couldn't provide an easy answer for.

He lifted the frail soft claw to take the pulse. As he did so he felt a tingling shock run up his spine. His heart began to pound. The tiny hand clutched at his. Tightened and turned slightly.

Below the thumb was a bright heart-shaped scar.

The old lady opened her faded violet-blue eyes. Pure joy shone from them as she stared full into his face. She smiled.

"I waited," Rose whispered, "I kept our secret. Never gave up. I knew you'd come to me in the end."

Travelling Man
by Carolyn Lewis

It had been her idea. I told her it wouldn't work, I told her it wouldn't be the same, but she wouldn't listen to me. She said the same thing over and over again. "Let's just take off, let's sell everything and travel the world."

Daft. That's what it was, a daft idea. But she wouldn't stop, on and on she went and in the end I had to ask her, "What about our jobs, what will we do for money?" She laughed and put her arms around me, "We'll sell everything: the house, the car, the whole lot."

She's got amazing eyes, my wife, hazel they are and when she's excited they get a sort of glint in them, a copper glint. It was one of the things I first noticed about her. We met at work; I'm a chef at a French restaurant and Cheryl, she was a waitress. She started work three years ago and I fancied her straight away. Always laughing, always got a smile for the customers and for me.

Before we got married, we bought a house, not a big one, just a small starter home the estate agent called it. I thought it was perfect. The kitchen was the biggest room in the house and we bought a large, double oven with a halogen hob. "We can invite people around for dinner," I told Cheryl.

"Oh, no, I don't think so, we spend all day feeding the hungry masses, last thing we want to do is to do it when we get home."

Seemed a shame to me, I like cooking, preparing dishes, seeing the way people enjoy what I've cooked for them, but if Cheryl didn't want that, then that was fine by me.

About six months after we got married, she began grumbling about our lives, "God, don't you get sick to death of doing the same thing, day in, day out?"

I didn't know what she was on about. My hours are long, but we've managed to get days off on the same day, I thought she liked that. We go to the supermarket, I cook something nice, we watch the box then we go to bed. I thought that was fine.

I'd made Sole Veronique, it was one of her favourites but she pushed and prodded at the fish, she sighed a lot and stared out at the garden. "Aren't you bored, Col? Don't you want to do something exciting?"

"Like what? Do you want something different to eat? What about Coq au Vin? I can make that for you if you like."

"No! Not the food, not the bloody food. I mean, us. Don't you want us to do something different?"

I still didn't know what she was talking about.

We had a few more sessions of sighing, mooching about the house, getting up in the middle of the night and staring into space. I tried different recipes, I went to the open air market, I bought strawberries, plump raspberries and the best Cornish cream. I tried a new recipe with mussels, another one using fresh crab. It was costing me a fortune and nothing worked. She still sighed and flounced around a lot.

Then she said it. "Let's sell everything, the house, the furniture, everything!"

"Why?"

"We can travel, see the world, see different places before…"

"Before what?"

She said she didn't know, she just looked at me with those amazing eyes and smiled.

She wanted to buy a camper van. "They're brilliant, Col. They're luxurious, they've got showers, fridges, central heating, everything!"

"But what will we do with a camper van?"

Just for a moment, her eyes flashed, almost like a warning, then it was gone and she smiled at me. "We'll travel in it, we can go anywhere in one of those. We could drive over to France, Italy, we can tour Switzerland, think about it, Col, we could go anywhere in the world."

I did think about it and I didn't like the thought. I wasn't sure if I wanted to go anywhere in the world. Some places I simply didn't fancy. But she kept on, each night when we got home, she'd start on it again.

"Col, what do you think?"

She wore me down. Each day the same question, the same thing said over and over again. "Let's do it, before we get too old, before it's too late." I didn't know what she meant by 'too late.'

She was fixated on the idea of a camper van. She dragged me to caravan shows, where smiling salesmen talked about cubic weights and demonstrated the various ovens. "Just like home from home," they all said that. What could I do? I gave in.

Seemed to me that it took a long time for us to buy all our furniture and no time at all to sell it. The lot went, the leather three piece suite, the glass coffee table, the bedside lamps, even the cooker. It grieved me seeing the cooker being carted off in the back of someone's van. I tried to tell the man who bought it about its temperature control, about the special grill it had. Cheryl frowned at me, "Give it a rest, Col." So I did. I didn't offer to help, just watched the cooker being hauled into the van.

Cheryl's plan was to sell everything we had and use the money to spend a year travelling. "Think about it, Col. Think about the places we could go, places we've never seen before."

She knew I'd never been abroad. When I was a kid my mum and dad took us to Barry Island every year. We had a caravan and I played on the sands. Never thought of going anywhere else.

Cheryl organised everything: the passports, the ferry crossing, she got maps from the AA, she sorted out the lot. "France first, Col. You'll love it there, I know you will." She sounded so positive, I thought it was because she'd been there before on a school trip.

The last week at the restaurant went quickly, too quickly. It felt as if I'd been hanging on to my job by my fingertips and slowly, one by one, my fingers were unhinged until finally it was the last Saturday and Cheryl and I were standing there, in front of the rest of the staff, whilst Bernard, the owner made a little speech about "travelling, seeing new pastures." He said there'd always be a job for me, "and Cheryl," he added quickly. When we got home Cheryl said we'd never go back there, "Not once we've seen the world, he can keep his poxy restaurant."

I quite liked France. The markets were bigger than the ones at home, I bought cheese, delicately smoked ham, olive oil and duck pate.

At the first campsite, I saw other people eating plates of sandwiches, beef burgers, nothing French at all.

"Look at them," I said to Cheryl. "You'd think they'd try something different."

I have to admit, the cooker in the camper van wasn't at all bad and, with the fresh ingredients, I soon made Poulet a l'Estragon, 'Chicken with Tarragon,' I explained to the middle-aged man who wandered over to where Cheryl and I were sitting. "Here, I've made enough for four, would you and your wife like to try it?"

The next night I made Porc Farci aux Pruneaux, and this time a woman stopped to ask what we were eating. "Pork stuffed with prunes." She brought the casserole dish back the next morning and said it was the best meal she'd ever had.

Cheryl said, "I hope you're not going to be cooking your way around the world. We came away to get away from all that."

We drove to Italy next, making our way towards Tuscany. I knew a little about that, the restaurant bought Italian olive oil and I wanted to see the fields of olives. Cheryl said the sunflowers were nicer.

Our first night, other campers were sending out for pizza, the sound of bells on delivery bikes could be heard all over the campsite.

"Let's do that," said Cheryl. "Don't do anything fancy, just order a pizza."

"Why eat pizza when I can make a fresh risotto?" She frowned at me, the Italian sun shining on her hair. "Why do you always have to be different, can't you forget you're a chef?"

I didn't answer her, the rice was at that tricky stage, when I had to stir it slowly until almost all of the liquid is absorbed. I didn't see Cheryl flounce off, just heard her muttering, `What's the point?'

The markets in Italy were just as good as the French ones. Cheryl wanted to see Pisa and Florence as did I, but I always looked for the markets. Cheryl liked wandering around with a guide book in her hand, I held a shopping bag so I could buy fresh herbs, cheese and once, when I found a recipe for artichokes, I carried them back to the camper van. "Look at these," I said, holding them up for Cheryl to see. She ignored me and showed me the miniature tower of Pisa she'd bought.

I only asked where she was going to keep it, "It's not as if the camper van is designed for ornaments, is it?" That was all I said and she stormed out.

She hadn't come back by the time I'd cooked the artichokes. I'd sautéed them with olive oil and garlic. I'd also bought fresh lamb and the recipe I found used fresh rosemary and more garlic. The smell wafted through the open door of the camper van and it must have reached other campers because as soon as I'd put the dishes on the table, two women appeared. "Would you like some? I've made quite a lot and I seem to have lost my wife…" Before long their husbands appeared and by the time Cheryl came back, there was nothing left for her. She ignored me for the rest of the evening.

I told her I'd like to stay a bit longer in Italy, "A few days won't be enough, I'd like to see some of the smaller villages." She brightened up when I said that, grabbing my arm and smiling at me. "I knew you'd like it, travelling, I knew it."'

I didn't tell her that I wanted to look at the restaurants, to look at the food they prepared. I knew she wouldn't understand.

Each day we toured, driving the camper van through tiny cobbled roads, stopping near vineyards, looking at the tall cypress trees and the smiling faces of the sunflowers. When Cheryl explored the walled towns, I explored the restaurants, gazing at the menus; I wandered into shops, handing over money for the local cheese, fresh pasta and bottles of wine.

We stayed in Italy for another week. Each night I tried a different recipe, Gnocchi alla Marinara, that went down well at the campsite. I soon had a queue of people standing outside the camper van door.

Another night I made pizza. I thought Cheryl would like that, after all it was the first thing she wanted to eat. She didn't seem at all pleased when I told her that I was making enough for ten people. "Whatever for?" She stood with her hands on her hips, her eyes glaring at me.

"Because that's what everyone asked me to do," I was busy trying out the food processor I'd bought. The recipe for pizza dough calls for a processor and before we left home, we'd sold ours so, without telling Cheryl, I bought another one.

"What people?" her voice had risen.

I kept my back to her, `The people on the campsite, they said they fancied fresh pizza, like the Italians make.'

"Well, let them go to a pizza parlour," she almost screamed the words at me. I turned the processor on full speed so I couldn't hear anything else she might have said.

That night some of the campers brought their tables and chairs over, a red-faced man in baggy shorts brought a case of wine and before long the area around the camper van was full of tables and chairs and wine glasses. I didn't see Cheryl at all until I was clearing up. Even then, at first I didn't see her, I sort of felt her presence as I scrubbed at the dishes. One of the first rules of being a chef is always to keep your kitchen clean and tidy. I did too, I never went to bed without clearing up. I could see her out of the corner of my eye as I wiped the units.

"Have you finished?" her voice was cold.

"What, clearing up? Yes, I think so…"

"I didn't mean the clearing up." Her voice didn't sound like Cheryl's voice, it was hard, flat as if it had been left out in the sun to bake.

"I don't know what you mean." To be honest I was a bit tired, too tired to have a row. I'd been cooking for hours. Nearly everyone had wanted second helpings.

"I thought when we left the UK, you'd be spending more time with me, just the two of us exploring various countries."

"We are, we've done a lot of sightseeing." I didn't have a clue what she was on about.

"The only sights you see are what's on the market stalls."

I put my hand on her shoulder; she flinched and moved away, the movement abrupt as if I'd burnt her.

"Look, Cheryl, love, I'm a chef. That's what I am and I'll be a chef whatever country I'm in. I thought you'd understand that."

"But can't you forget that you're a chef? Can't you just be a tourist, looking at the sights without working out ingredients?" Her voice was loud and I thought she'd wake the rest of the camp.

"No, I don't think I can." For the first time I understood what Cheryl had done; this wasn't just about packing up and moving away, it wasn't about a new start, a new life. She didn't like what she'd had in her old life – me.

We stood there in the camper van, the overhead light illuminating the shiny hob, the stainless steel sink, the bottles of spices in the rack. We stood there and stared at each other. I don't know what Cheryl saw in my eyes but in her eyes I could see disappointment. A large well of disappointment. Pity too because suddenly I realised the colour of her eyes wasn't just hazel, it was the colour of the biscuits I'd made that day. Biscotti alla Nocciola, Hazelnut biscuits.

Biscotti Alla Nocciola
(Hazelnut Biscuits)

(makes 12)

Ingredients

9 tbs butter, softened
1 egg
1 tsp vanilla
2 cups flour
1 cup ground hazelnuts
½ cup sugar
½ tsp baking powder
egg glaze made by beating 1 egg with 1 tsp water.

Method

In a bowl, using an electric mixer, cream the butter. Add the egg and vanilla and beat until combined well. In another bowl, combine flour, hazelnuts, sugar and baking powder. Add the hazelnut mixture to the butter, a little at a time, until the mixture is incorporated. Divide the dough in half and form each half in a 3 x 8" rectangle. The dough should be rounded at the sides, slightly higher in the centre and tapering off towards the ends. Wrap the dough in plastic and chill for one hour.

Preheat oven to 180ºC/350ºF/Gas Mark 4.

Arrange the rectangles of dough on a buttered baking sheet, brush them with the egg glaze and score the top of each at ¼" intervals. Bake for one hour or until the rectangles are golden brown and dry. (Should they brown too quickly, cover with foil) Let the rectangles cool on wire racks for 5 minutes. Cut into ½" slices and allow to cool completely. Store in airtight containers.

All The Time In The World
by Catrin Collier

"Uncle Henry was a good age." Daphne preceded Irene into her own house.

"What is a 'good age' to die?" Irene handed her hat and coat to her 'daily', Annie. Henry had been her husband for sixty years. Daphne was his niece, but she still felt aggrieved by her remarks.

"Uncle Henry was ninety-five…"

"And active until he had a heart attack last week," Irene interrupted. "He played bridge, visited his club and enjoyed a social life."

"You stopped giving dinner parties years ago."

Irene was tempted to say, 'because Henry couldn't stand you or your money grubbing bankrupt husband.' But Daphne was a Marsh. She had the sensitivity of a cactus and was equally prickly. "Henry preferred supper parties. He liked to choose the food himself."

"I heard he was friendly with a woman in the delicatessen." Daphne eyed the etchings hanging in the hall.

Irene knew about Henry's mistress – had known for over thirty years but she wasn't going to give Daphne the satisfaction of pitying her.

"She allowed Henry to sample before he bought." Daphne's husband, Anthony, roared at his own crude joke.

Daphne glared at him. "I always think supper buffets rather scrappy, Aunt Irene."

"The buffet at the hotel was a bit of all right. You gave old Henry a good send off, but I wouldn't like to get saddled with the catering bill. There must have been two hundred there." Anthony looked out of the window as a car pulled into the drive.

"Sheer extravagance, Annie could have laid on food here." Daphne saw two women step out of the car. 'I didn't know Peggy and Susie were coming back here?'

"I invited them." Irene opened the door to her best friend, Peggy, and her own niece Susie. She knew why Daphne and

Anthony had insisted on driving her home from the hotel. It would be only a matter of time before Daphne asked. But she was damned if she was going to offer. Let Daphne demean herself. She didn't have to wait long. Daphne pointed to the canvas hanging over the fireplace as soon as they entered the sitting room.

"That is the painting that used to hang in grandfather's study? The Sickert, Uncle Henry had re-valued."

"If you want it, take it." Irene couldn't bring herself to be gracious.

"It belongs to the family and you have no children to leave it to."

Irene winced. Daphne never missed an opportunity to remind her of her childless state. 'Why don't you and Anthony look around, Daphne? If there's anything else you want, take it.' Irene saw Peggy's shocked reaction and realised she had been too blunt. But not for Daphne.

"We will." Daphne called to Irene's daily. "Annie, coffee for everyone."'

Irene shook her head at Annie when she walked in. "I don't want anything after the buffet."

"I do," Daphne persisted, "Arabica coffee with milk, not cream, and a plain digestive." She sat on the sofa. Anthony took Irene's easy chair. Feeling unaccountably guilty, Irene perched on the one that had been Henry's.

"It was good to see so many people paying their respects to Henry," Peggy observed.

"It was." Irene couldn't suppress the uncharitable thought that if Henry had been well regarded it was because so few people really knew him.

"Remember, I am only a phone call away." Peggy pulled a chair close to Irene's.

"I know." Irene smiled, the sensation felt odd. But it was the first time she had smiled since the police had called to inform her that Henry had collapsed in the delicatessen.

Annie brought in a tray and set it on the coffee table. "Can I get you something, Mrs Marsh?"

"No, thank you, Annie." The day Irene had dreaded was passing, just as Peggy said it would. But Peggy knew what to expect. She had lost her own much loved husband six months ago.

"The Sickert, Rackham etchings and the mahogany desk and bureau bookcase belonged to my grandfather…"

"Poor Uncle Henry has just been cremated, Daphne." Susie remonstrated.

"Irene told us to take what we wanted," Daphne smirked.

"Put your pickings in the hall, Daphne. I want to check them before you cart them away." Still feeling guilty, Irene sat back in the chair.

"I've been meaning to ask for years, Auntie Irene, where did you and Uncle Henry meet?" Susie knelt on the rug at her aunt's feet, just as she had done when she'd been sent by her working mother to Irene and Henry's for school holidays.

Irene suspected what Susie meant was 'how come you married a stuffed shirt like Henry.' "In 1942, in an air raid shelter below the War Office."

"Uncle Henry was involved with vital war work." Daphne abandoned her coffee and lifted a watercolour of Venice from the wall.

"Vital?" Irene repeated. "Hardly, he balanced the army's accounts while wooing me with lamb chops."

"Lamb chops!" Anthony snorted, as he left the room.

"It's difficult to explain to a generation brought up on plenty what luxury a lamb chop represented in wartime. Food was rationed. The only meat available on coupons was a few ounces of offal, tripe, lung or pancreas."

"I had no idea you worked in the War Office." A crash resounded from Henry's study.

"I'll just see what that is." Daphne left the room and closed the door behind her.

Susie gripped Irene's hand. "Tell us about it."

"It was odd," Irene looked inward to a world that existed only in memory. "We believed ourselves immortal, yet expected to die at any moment. And thousands of us did. Young men and women, who said 'see you later,' and disappeared. The worst was the sirens. They went off night after night. At the first wail, there was a mad rush down to the shelter in the basement. And there was Henry. Long before he said a word, I sensed he was looking out for me."

"You knew he was the right one for you from the outset." Ever a romantic, Susie had been married twice and was planning a third foray up the aisle.

"We were issued with an army blanket and pillow. The loneliest nights of my life were spent lying on bare concrete surrounded by people. Every one of us quaking in terror, as bombs exploded overhead. It was all so grubby, only two lavatories for hundreds of people and one washbasin, no privacy. When the bombing stopped there was always a terrible silence before the all clear. That was when we wondered if anything had survived above us."

"And Uncle Henry?" Susie prompted.

"Always set his blanket down close to mine. One morning I opened my eyes and he was smiling at me. I felt under my pillow and found a newspaper wrapped lamb chop. The next air raid, it was mince. Then, the ultimate luxury – two whole steaks. That night there was no siren. I went home with Henry. We cooked the steaks over a gas burner in his room and ate them in guilty secret."

"And then you married," Susie sighed.

"Not until after the armistice in 1945."

Irene hadn't mentioned love. Henry had been thirty five to her twenty-eight. But he had been old before his years, stooped, round-shouldered, and myopic. But he'd loved her and she thought him kind, not realising his kindness was prompted by obsession.

Daphne breezed in. "We have everything we can take in the car, Aunt Irene. We'll hire a van for the rest."

Irene went into the hall, Peggy and Susie followed. Annie was at the door watching Anthony reverse his car up the drive.

The pictures had been wrapped in towels, the brand new ones Irene had stored in Henry's wardrobe. Daphne flicked through the frames. "The Sickert, the Rackhams, my grandmother's watercolours…"

"Your grandparents' will divided their assets between your mother and Henry," Irene broke in.

"But you have no one to leave them to, Aunt Irene."'

There was a set of leather bound Dickens that Irene had bought for Henry. His antique globe, leather blotter pad, pen case, and briefcase were in a separate pile, as were the first editions he had assiduously collected over the years.

"You've cleared Henry's study?" Irene picked up a book.

"We couldn't find all of Uncle Henry's first editions." Daphne said shortly.

"Possibly they are in his bedroom."

"They aren't, we looked." Anthony picked up the Sickert.

Irene's huge leather trunk and suitcases had been hauled downstairs. "What are in these?" she asked.

"Uncle Henry's clothes. We have a charity shop near us."

"The one you work in, Daphne, so you can have the pick of the donations?"

"I thought I'd save you the trouble of getting rid of them. But if you don't need my help…"

"'Take, them, but leave the suitcases."

"They're battered and all those old labcls…"

Irene looked Daphne in the eye, they both knew 1930 luggage of that quality with those labels would fetch a decent sum at auction. "I need them, Daphne."

"Don't be ridiculous, you'rc cighty-eight…"

"Here." Annie stepped in and handed Anthony a roll of black plastic sacks. He opened a case and started transferring the contents.

Irene retrieved a wooden box from the suitcase. Daphne held out her hand. Irene ignored it. "These are Henry's gold tiepins, and cufflinks."

"They should go to our son. It's high time you considered the children's future, Aunt Irene."

Irene emptied the box on the hallstand and halved the contents. Scooping one up, she dropped it into the open sack Anthony was holding. The other she handed to Susie. "For Frank when he's eighteen."

"Frank isn't a blood relative," Daphne protested.

"He is Henry's great great nephew."

"There's the house and the furniture. If you give your assets away seven years before you die your heirs won't have to pay death duty."

"I know, Daphne. Please, take your spoils and go."

"The dining room suite…"

"I'm still living here, Daphne."

"There is a marvellous place near us. We would visit you every Sunday. I'll bring the brochure…"

“Goodbye, Daphne, Anthony.” Irene held the door. Anthony loaded everything into the car. When they drove away Irene didn’t return Daphne’s wave.

“Why did you let Daphne take those things?” Peggy followed Irene and Susie back to the sitting room.

“Because things aren’t important, and because now she has them she’ll leave me alone for a while.”

“Shall I return the cases to the box room, Mrs Marsh?” Annie asked.

“Please, Annie.” Irene glanced at the clock. There was plenty of time, two hours yet.

“Would you like wine and a few smoked salmon nibbles, for three?”

“You know me so well, Annie, thank you.”

Annie brought wine and canapés. After she left, Peggy lifted her glass and toasted. “To Henry.”

“Wherever he may be.’ Irene added.

“You didn’t tell us how you came to be working at the War Office.” Susie curled up on the rug again.

“I was posted there in 1942. My father had an influential friend; it took him three years to arrange my release from the internment camp I had been sent to when I came back from Germany.”

“You were in Germany before the war!” Peggy exclaimed.

“Not all Germans were bad, Peggy.” Irene hadn’t mentioned the war in over thirty years. Peggy’s brother had been killed at Dunkirk. She thought it something best left.

“I studied languages in university, after graduating I worked for a shipping firm in Hamburg. There, one magical, moonlit night, I met Graf Horst von Plewe, and yes, Susie, we fell in love and became engaged. Every Friday night he would pick me up from my office in his car and drive me to his family’s castle. His mother and grandmother lived there and for all their titles, and aristocratic accomplishments, they adored cooking.’”

Irene handed her glass to Susie, closed her eyes and slipped back. Once again she sat in the castle’s enormous kitchen, sipping schnapps with his mother and grandmother who had shooed the servants out for the afternoon.

“Horst loves Prussian Marzipan. Make notes.” His grandmother thrust a small notebook at her. She still had it.

"This family recipe is over two hundred years old," his mother said proudly.

"Five hundred," his grandmother corrected.

"One pound of finely milled sugar… icing sugar will do," his mother reassured. "Twenty grams of bitter almonds…"

"Not so much," his grandmother amended.

"Perhaps fifteen grams, it is the final quantity that is important. One pound of sweet ground almonds, four tablespoons of rose water, make your own, dear. Put everything in a bowl and knead it well. Leave for an hour…"

His grandmother's blue eyes twinkled, "then work the marzipan the way you work a man. Pummel until pliable, lift it from the bowl, roll it out, not too thin…"

Horst's mother rolled it half an inch thick and punched out hearts, diamonds and spades with metal cutters.

"Roll the off cuts, so." His grandmother twisted them into ribbons and edged the shapes, turning them into shallow cups. "Grill them."

"Lightly." Horst's mother pushed a loaded pan under a gas grill for minute. Half an hour later the room was filled with the aroma of roasting nuts and light brown marzipans covered the huge table.

"Make royal icing, coat the inside of the cups," his grandmother iced the cups and decorated the tops with glace cherries and angelica.

"Food of the gods." Horst was behind her, his hand lightly caressing her neck.

Later – much later – they had stood on the balcony outside his bedroom in the moonlight, eating Prussian marzipan. But it had been the summer of 1939.

"Auntie Irene?" Susie's voice, sharp with concern, shattered Irene's reverie.

"Sorry," she opened her eyes. "I was revisiting my youth."

"Your German fiancé, did you seen him again?" Logic dictated otherwise, but Susie still hoped.

"A major in the Wehrmacht and a British secretary who would be interned when war broke out?" Irene retrieved her glass. "Our love was doomed from the outset. My employer paid a fortune for a ticket on the last train out of Germany for foreign nationals. It was my only hope of reaching neutral Switzerland before hostilities. He asked me to take out two children. A boy and a girl, two and three years old, Jews of course. It was too late to save their parents but they had a grandfather in London.

Horst came to the station to say goodbye. He insisted we'd meet again but I knew he didn't really believe it. We kissed, I cried, the children were bewildered. The carriages were crowded. I found a place in one where a man was shaking like a wet dog. He had no papers. A fat lady from Luxembourg started shouting that we'd all be shot. I slapped her face and from that moment was elected leader of our group. I collected all our papers, the children's were forged, but good. I handed the bundle to the guards who checked us at every stop, "to save them trouble."

Not one official thought to count the passports or match them to the passengers, one even called me 'a kind lady' but I was half-dead from fear when we reached the border. Four hours of waiting and the train was shunted over it. I used the ten marks allowance – all anyone was allowed to take out of Nazi Germany – to hire a taxi to the British Embassy. I fought my way through the crowds. A hatch opened in a door, a face appeared,

"We're inundated with refugees, we can't help." The door slammed. The children were hungry. I used one of their ten marks to catch a bus to a Red Cross centre. The Swiss laughed. What if the children were hungry? People were starving everywhere. The country was full of beggars, why didn't we go back where we'd come from?

I bought bread with the last ten marks. The children ate. I made beds for them in the waiting room of the station. We moved in with hundreds of others who'd been stranded. I sent telegrams to the children's grandfather and my parents. I paid for them by selling my clothes and when I had nothing left to sell, I begged.

I washed the children and their clothes in the station washroom. The Americans who were passing through Switzerland were the kindest. I never received a crust of bread or penny piece from the Swiss. I sold my jewellery. The charm bracelet I had inherited from my grandmother, my great aunt's sapphire earrings but not Horst's engagement ring – that I hid.

It took two months for the children's grandfather to wire tickets and money. We travelled first class to London and ate in the buffet car. We landed at Tilbury. The children's grandfather and my parents were waiting. But someone on the ship had reported that the children and I spoke German. The children were considered too young to be a danger, so the grandfather was allowed to take them, but I was arrested and interned.

I had expected to be put to work as an interpreter. Horst and I had discussed it. We hated the thought of hurting one another and our families but as Horst said, we owed a duty to our countries, and some things were bigger than love.

My father went to the authorities, but he couldn't argue against the facts. I had lived in Germany for a year. I was engaged to a major in the Wehrmacht, therefore I was a spy. Never mind that I had brought out two Jewish children, or that I was British, or my sisters and brothers were in the army. I was a spy. But the camp could have been worse. After three years I was posted to the War Office."

"Where Henry wooed you with lamb chops." Susie said sadly.

"I told him I loved Horst and could only offer him friendship. In 1944 the children's grandfather visited me. He had a letter from Horst's mother. I never knew how she managed to send it. She wrote that Horst had been killed in Russia, even in her grief she had thought of me."

A dense silence closed in on the room

"I wanted to die, but Henry loved me and insisted he couldn't be happy without me. I married him a week after VE day. A year later Horst knocked our door. He had spent months searching for me. He had a girl with him, someone he had met after he'd been released from a POW camp. She loved him but he wouldn't marry her until he knew whether or not I had survived."

"What happened?" It was a ridiculous question but Susie still asked it.

"What could happen? Horst saw Henry. He returned to Germany and married the girl."

"Henry knew you loved another man. All those years he knew?" Peggy murmured.

"Henry was happy as long as the house was run like clockwork and his meals were on time."

"And, after his retirement, he was drunk every morning by eleven."

"It was his choice and his life to waste, Peggy."

Peggy recalled the short stories Irene had published when Henry had been working and she'd time to write. The novel that was half completed when he retired. His insistence that Irene set aside her own life to chauffeur him to his club so he could drink himself into a stupor every day. Perhaps he'd lived to ninety because the alcohol had acted as a preservative. And, had Irene's life been so terrible? Wasn't marriage synonymous with subservience for most women of their generation?

"Sorry, I didn't mean to depress you." Irene left her seat. 'If you don't mind, I'd like to be alone now."

"I'll call in tomorrow, Auntie?" Susie kissed Irene.

"Please don't. Annie will take care of the housework. If there's anything else, I'll telephone you." Irene unlocked a desk and drew out two envelopes. She handed one to Susie. "Henry and I put our assets into a trust fund ten years ago. He didn't want anything to go to Daphne. The trust is yours after my death. These are all the papers you'll need."

Tears filled Susie's eyes. "Auntie…"

"Don't thank me. You told me years ago you didn't want anything. Give it to your children, but don't tell them about it until they need it or they may not make the effort to find their own way in life. Peggy, you've always admired my gold brooch. Here." Irene unclipped it and placed it in Peggy's hand.

"Irene…"

"No sentimental nonsense, off with both you." Irene ushered them out. When Susie was helping Peggy into her car, she called out. "Talk to my solicitor, Susie. He knows where the Sickert and Rackhams are."

"But Daphne…"

"Took copies. Bye." Irene closed the door and leaned against it.

"I've cleared the sitting room, Mrs Marsh."

"Thank you, Annie." Irene handed her the second envelope. "I know you come here by bus, but you can drive, can't you?"

"Yes."

"Take Henry's car."

"The Mercedes… I couldn't possibly."

"You'd be doing me a favour. The log book, keys and everything else you need is in there. You have made up the guest room?"

"Yes, Mrs Marsh and tidied up after your niece's rummaging."

"She's no niece of mine, Annie. You've laid coffee in the dining room?"'

"Yes, Mrs Marsh."

Irene went into the kitchen. She picked up the bowl that held the lump of marzipan she'd mixed that morning. She sprinkled icing sugar on the table and rolled it out. Cutting the shapes was therapeutic. Soon she had trays of hearts, clubs, diamonds and spades, just like Horst's mother and grandmother all those years before. They wouldn't have approved of the ready mixed royal icing, neither had she grown and sugared the angelica and glace cherries, but when she finished decorating the marzipan she was satisfied with the results. She set a hand crocheted doily on her largest plate and filled it.

"They look nice, Mrs Marsh."

"Try one, Annie."

"Mmm…"

"Food of the gods." Irene set the marzipan next to the smoked salmon sandwiches on the table. The silver gleamed. The linen was pristine, glossy with starch.

"I could stay, Mrs Marsh."

"I won't need you until tomorrow, Annie. Don't forget to take your car. I'll be glad to see it gone." Irene did something she'd never done before. She kissed Annie goodbye.

She didn't have to check the house. If Annie said it was perfect, it was. She went into the sitting room and waited. Half an hour later the doorbell rang.

Her heart beat erratically when she rose from her chair. "Please, not a heart attack. Not now."

Fifty nine years, and she would have known him anywhere. His back was bowed, his shoulders hunched, and when he lifted his hat she saw his blond hair had turned grey, but even though his skin was wrinkled his eyes were as blue and so very, very loving.

"Please come in. Let me take your hat and coat." She hung them in the cupboard.

"How are you, Irene?"

It wasn't an idle enquiry. He had lost his own wife ten years ago. "'Good now you are here, Horst."

He saw the table set for coffee. "Prussian marzipan?"

"What else for our reunion."

"You've not changed your mind about leaving with me tomorrow?"

"No."

"My chauffeur will be here first thing. I thought a ferry crossing best. It is longer but…"

"At our age, Horst, we have all the time in the world."

Prussian Marzipan

Ingredients

1lb finely milled sugar (icing sugar will do)
15g bitter almonds
1 lb sweet ground almonds,
4 tbsp of rose water

Method

Put everything in a bowl and knead it well.
Leave for an hour.
Work the marzipan the way you work a man. Pummel until pliable, lift it from the bowl, roll it out, not too thin
Roll it ½" thick and punch out hearts, diamonds and spades with metal cutters.
Roll the off cuts. Twist them into ribbons and edge the shapes, turning them into shallow cups.
Grill them lightly for 1 minute.
Make royal icing, coat the inside of the cups decorated the tops with glace cherries and angelica.

His Last Wife
by Heather Lister

His last wife is extremely thin.

She's always been thin. I've known her for years and she's never been through what you'd call a 'plump stage'. If I make a comment about her, in a kind sort of way, my husband smiles and says, "She always did have trouble putting on weight."

I wonder if she's really trying. Out shopping one day, I see her at the salad counter in Tesco. I'm just passing, on my way to the bakery section, and there she is, making a song and dance about choosing a handful of cherry tomatoes and a stick of celery. She gives me a tight little smile, and I arrange my face to look pleasant.

Then blow me if I don't run into her again by the condiments. Now she's casting a critical eye over a bottle of low-cal extra-dry vinegar dressing. No doubt she's planning to drizzle it over a shred of lettuce by and by.

And imagine how my heart sinks when I come across her again in the dairy section, selecting a pot of Greek yoghurt with nought per cent fat...She gives me a sidelong glance, sizing me up. It must be at least a minute we're standing there, saying nothing. Sizing me up is not something that can be done in a few seconds.

You've got it, I'm jealous. When I look at her, it's as if she belongs to a different species. A superior one. When she's picking up her bags at the checkout I can't help noticing her narrow waist and trim little derriere, and I feel my mouth twisting in a sneer. I watch her tiny ankles twinkling out of the shop, and I'm wishing for uneven paving stones and concealed rabbit holes.

Out in the car park I bulge and sag and brood behind the wheel of my car. It is only after a considerable interval of boiling and grousing that I manage to drive off smoothly.

She's put me right off my stroke for the day. When I get home I begin punishing myself, though I couldn't say whether it's for being too large or for having dark thoughts about *his last wife.*

Now I've seen her, I know I should have started off the day with half a grapefruit rather than croissants, so I compensate by going down the garden and chopping wood.

The logs split easily under the axe, and it feels good. I can get four big pieces from each log. As I throw them in the wheelbarrow I'm still thinking of her. I reckon I'm large enough to make at least three of *his last wife*. Perhaps four. She doesn't have to chop wood because, while we're stuck out here in the sticks with solid fuel, her little town house has gas central heating. I know this because sometimes he has to go round and relight her pilot light. It's easier for a thin woman to be helpless. Dear God, please don't let me become jealous and bitter.

At lunch-time I eat a banana, and drink a cup of tea without milk. I am ravenous. I hoover the house from top to bottom, trotting briskly up and down the stairs. Later I take the dog for a walk. I set her free in the fields, and she tears around in circles, leaping the long grass. She's a mixture of breeds, all born to be skinny. Every now and then I break into a run myself, but it's not in my nature. When I do, the dog orbits me anxiously. Above me in the cold air, birds skim the budding trees. New lambs frisk in the fields. Everything mocks my ungainliness and weight. How can he love me?

I reach home just as darkness is starting to close in. He'll be home before long. I light the fire and draw the curtains. I've made up my mind we'll have a salad for supper. I think I've got a tin of salmon to go with it. And we'll follow it with fresh fruit. It's not as though we both couldn't do with losing a couple of pounds.

I rummage in the fridge, but all I can find is one flaccid cucumber, which I drop in the bin. As I crouch there, despairing, his headlights sweep across the kitchen window, and my heart lifts. I go to the door, he gets out of the car, and we hug as if we haven't seen each other for weeks. He is huge and warm in my arms.

I think to myself, bugger the salad. "When would you like supper?" I ask, hopefully.

"Soon as you like," he says. "I'm starving."

He follows me out to the garage, where we keep the chest freezer. As I haul out frozen packages, he stands behind me with his arms round my waist. He can just about reach to clasp his hands in front of me. He squeezes me, holding me tight against him.

"Let's have something," he says, "that doesn't take too long."

I turn in his arms in the darkness of the garage, so that I can kiss his mouth. The frozen peas crackle between us. I say nothing about seeing *his last wife.*

Soon we're having supper, sitting close together by the fire, the low table before us laden with food. We have plump herby sausages from the local farm shop, along with peas, roast potatoes, and carrots from the garden. Everything's swimming in hot thick gravy. I have a glass of smooth red Rioja with mine, and he has a pint of beer and a wedge of crusty bread and butter with his. What's more, we have large helpings of apple crumble and custard for pudding.

Not long afterwards we are lying in complete and utter peace, our arms around each other. The moon is at our bedroom window, and outside the house the sleeping meadows stretch away to infinity. He is speaking my name. I run both my hands down his back and all I touch is solid and smooth and warm. He is my beloved husband. His waist is not slender. But he has fine strong arms, and lovely heavy downy thighs. I am smiling as I tease and caress him. I can see his face above me and his breath is in my hair. He holds me and strokes me, gathering me up, insisting, and I yield myself to him.

As I lie loving him I am all soft hollows and wonderful curves – and it is at this moment I know I am beautiful.

Apple Crumble

Serves 4-6

Ingredients

700g apples
100g brown sugar
1 tbsp water
a good pinch of ground ginger
a little grated lemon rind.
2 ttbsp of lemon juice
100g wholewheat flour
100g porridge oats
100g butter

Method

Pre-heat oven to 180ºC/350ºF/Gas Mark 4
Wash, core and slice the apples. Leaving the peel on adds flavour, texture and fibre. Place in a 850ml (one and a half pint) pie dish and sprinkle with the lemon juice to keep the apples white. Add 75g of the brown sugar, the lemon rind, the ground ginger and the water.
Place the flour and porridge oats in a bowl and rub in the butter. Spread this mixture over the fruit, covering it completely. Sprinkle with the remaining brown sugar. Immediately place the dish in the oven and cook for 45 minutes, or until golden-brown.

Serve with fresh whipped cream and /or custard.

Renaissance
by Maggie Knutson

I am in Florence on a warm October day. A gentle sun smiles on me and I lift my face in gratitude. It is so good to be alive. I am wearing jeans and a loose cotton top, with a silk scarf around my neck. It is my favourite one, the colour of soft orange and muted lemon. It falls languorously in front of me, swaying rhythmically as I walk, delicate as a feather. My hair is free, falling beyond my shoulders. I am free like my hair, my auburn hair, which is like the colour of the tiled roofs in this ancient city. I belong here. I am a Renaissance painting come alive, gliding along the cobbled streets of Florence.

But it is too busy. Gangs of tourists block my path like obstacles. I head towards the side streets, searching for serenity, but churches, museums, statues litter the way. And everywhere are tourists. I am not a tourist. The past does not interest me, or the future. It is the present I wish to inhabit.

Walking is tiring. I find a tiny restaurant tucked away behind a row of planted bushes, their dark green tentacles offering privacy. It looks full but there is a lone man sitting by the open door and opposite is an empty seat. I ask in broken Italian, "Excuse me, may I have this seat?"

"Please," he says in perfect English, "be my guest." I smile. It is good to hear such politeness. We fall into conversation, he and I, as naturally as with a friend. First we talk about Florence, the weather, the nuisance of tourists. We discuss the menu, agree on a shared bottle of wine and as he talks, I absorb every detail of his features, as a tourist would view a Botticelli in the Uffizi Gallery. Black hair, thick as glossy paint, it layers towards his neck, heavier than my scarf. His skin is olive brown, flawless. I like the shape of his face. It is long, angular. I watch his lips as he talks. Strong lips outlining perfect teeth. But it is his eyes, as warmly brown as autumn leaves, which I am drawn to the most. His direct look seems to sear through my layers of defence. I want to melt into his eyes, his beautiful, piercing eyes.

I know what Kay will say when I describe this man to her. "You see, your luck *has* changed." The thought pleases me.

"What is your name?" he asks. I pause, unwilling to break the mood. I do not like my name. "Margaret," I reply reluctantly, "but I prefer Maggie."

His reply surprises me. "I shall call you Mar-gar-et. It is such a beautiful name. Mar-gar-et." He gently savours each syllable. I am used to people saying my name quickly, tripping over the middle section carelessly, making it clipped, abrupt, ugly. But he makes music out of my name. I am a Spanish princess, a Russian ballerina, a beautiful countess. I am Mar-gar-et.

He tells me his name is Misha. I want to say that his name reminds me of the sea at sunset, but all I can say, in such a banal way that I feel immediately ridiculous, "That's not a very Italian name."

"So, you think I'm Italian! I'm flattered."

I look at him in surprise. " But of course."

He laughs. It is a deep, joyful laugh. "I suppose since we are in Italy and my hair is dark, it's an easy assumption to make, but no, I am Croatian. I come from Sarajevo."

So simply said. Sarajevo.

I have seen too many news items about the war there not to react, and instinctively I search his face for signs of a story. It is as if he can read my mind.

"Yes," he says softly, "I was a soldier for a time when my country needed me."

What can I see in his eyes? Pain? Loss? Anger? He looks away from me and I understand that he does not want to remember, that it is still too painful, and I respect that. " Do not look so sad," he commands. "We who have lived through war and destruction have learnt to enjoy life while we can."

"It is a good philosophy for us all," I reply, and for a moment our eyes lock together. Green and brown merge in shared understanding. I am the first to look away. Yes, it is a good philosophy. I have learnt that the hard way.

I want to hold him in my arms, tell him that everything will be fine, kiss away the unshed tears, but I am too fragile. I have no right to offer the comfort that I myself need.

We eat spaghetti and drink Chianti and he talks about his career as an architect. I tell him about my work. He is interested and I feel the stirrings of the old enthusiasm although I have not worked for months. The time passes like gently falling snow. We are leaning closer towards each other, listening intently to what the other says. He smells like soft bracken and tender moss. We have coffee and I pray that this meal will never end.

"I leave tomorrow," he says quietly. "Back to Sarajavo. Please spend today with me."

I look away, confused, examine a painting on a nearby wall. It is an amateurish attempt to reproduce the San Lorenzo Church opposite. But temptation to be reckless surges through me. I know that I should graciously decline. He is, after all, a stranger.

"Please," he says again. "The day will be lost otherwise." His eyes are intense. It is not passion, although the physical electricity between us is tangible. Is it pleading? Desperation?

My instincts have always served me well, I tell myself. "That would be lovely," I reply, and his face softens into a smile which makes me want to sing for joy.

We walk together past the San Lorenzo Church and then onto the impressive Duomo Cathedral and into the Piazza Della Repubblica. I do not mind the tourists now. They part as we approach. They think we are lovers. He tells me about the architecture of the medieval buildings. I am having my own intimate, personal history lesson. We head down towards the Piazza Della Signora, arms gently touching from time to time. We admire the replica statue of Michelangelo's David. There is strength and beauty in the pose but it hurts me to see such perfection in a naked body. Always, I am aware of Misha's presence, the way he moves, the scent of his denim shirt and corduroy trousers. His shoes are the same colour as his eyes. I reach to just below his shoulders, my hair occasionally floating against his arm. Sometimes the bare flesh of hands meet.

We cross the Ponte Vecchio bridge, ignoring the jewellery shops and dodging the Japanese tourists taking photographs, and stroll towards the Boboli Gardens of the Pitti Palace. Misha tells me that Florence is known as the 'city of stone' and that these gardens are the only tranquil space to escape the crowds and noise and heat of the buildings. My soul cries out for the green of nature, the shade of trees, but there is safety amongst the throngs of people. I am about to enter this hidden place with a man who does not know the secret in my heart and I feel frightened. His strong body is beside me, his hand guiding me up the narrow stone steps.

The gardens are too formal for my liking. I prefer a random abundance of wild flowers, but the view of the city is irresistibly impressive and the shade provides relief from an October sun that does not acknowledge that summer is over. We ignore the notice that tells us to keep off the grass – this is Italy after all – and we settle down under a sycamore tree. My fate, whatever that will be, is sealed.

At length, Misha speaks. "This is not my kind of city. I prefer open spaces, the sea, a quieter pace, but now I'm glad I came to Florence." I do not ask about why he came, or his past, or his family. I think we each have a secret. Perhaps, like me, he cannot utter the words that still give so much pain.

We lie down on the dry grass and look up at the sky in-between the kaleidoscopic shapes of leaves. It brings back magical memories of a childhood of laughter and innocence.

"When I was a young girl on holiday at the seaside," I say, "my brother and I would lie spread-eagled on the beach and daydream about our futures. He wanted to be an astronaut. I wanted, of course, to be a glamorous film star or a famous singer. It was freeing just to feel sand on bare legs and arms, to feel the warmth of sun on faces. You know, it always seemed to be sunny during the summer in England when I was a young girl."

Misha laughs. "So it is true what they say about you English. You are always talking about the weather! That's one of the first things you said to me. 'Wow! Isn't the weather great for October!'

I shake him gently on his shoulder as a mild reproof for his teasing and he takes hold of my hand. My heart skips a beat. Can he tell, just by holding my wrist, the effect that his touch has on me? But I tense up. I want so much for him to touch me tenderly, passionately, longingly and yet it is impossible. Tears sting my eyes. The dream is about to be broken. "Misha, "I say in a whisper, "there is something I must tell you."

Softly, so softly, he lifts a finger to his lips. "Shush," he murmurs. "I know." He strokes my cheek. It is such a gentle touch. Then he runs his fingers through my hair as if he's touching velvet, and he leans towards me and we kiss, long and slow and with such tenderness that we are trembling. His lips and tongue taste of spaghetti and Chianti and kindness. I close my eyes and enjoy the flavours. Mind and body relax and shyly I lean into denim shirt, corduroy trousers, firm body. We lie in each other's arms and I almost feel complete.

Later, a cooling breeze floats off the river and we make our way out. He wraps his arm protectively around my shoulder. I do not mind. I am not embarrassed. I am enjoying the moment. Yesterday is not important, tomorrow is too far away. Today is everything.

I return to my hotel, shower, change clothes. This time I do not try to hide my body. I have chosen a short, lacy black dress, no sleeves, a dress that tells the world that I am a woman. No scarf this evening. I scoop my hair up, spray a delicate perfume over my exposed neck. I pick up my black pashmeena and drape it over my back and arms.

Misha is waiting for me in the foyer. Again, I am overwhelmed by his beauty, his smile, his body. He is wearing denim jeans and a crisp white shirt. I take a mental photograph of how he looks this evening so I can keep it in my own private gallery hidden away in my mind.

"You look beautiful," Misha says and he bends down and lightly kisses me on the cheek. A shiver of ecstasy runs down my spine and I feel light-headed. I reach up to his cheek and softly caress it with my fingertips. His skin is pleasing to the touch. I feel free with this man whom I do not know. I am freer than I have ever been. He is teaching me how to show love with a touch, a smile, a sense of closeness. I wonder how I was ever satisfied, before, with anything less.

We dine at a little trattoria in one of the back streets. All around us, in this atmosphere of romance, are lovers. Misha and I cannot be lovers tonight. Perhaps sometime in the future we will be so. But for now we are guiding each other through the darkness of troubled souls.

And afterwards, he returns me to my hotel and we stand outside the entrance and gaze up at the glorious stars in the clear sky, more precious than diamonds. The intoxicating smell of a foreign city envelops us. Finally, I ask, "How did you know what I tried so hard to hide from you?"

Misha takes his time before replying. "I knew someone who had the same problem. But she wasn't as lucky as you. She did not survive."

He looks at me with those gentle brown eyes. I see a touch of tears. "People are damaged in many ways," he murmurs. "You learn to find the person within. That is what's important."

A car passes but we continue to consider one another carefully. I have never felt such communication, such intensity, such depth of feeling from another human being. The world has stopped and we are the only ones left. Have I never understood nor experienced the power of silence before?

I would like to stay like this forever. Tears trickle down my cheeks like shaken dew. He leans down and kisses me on the lips, a long, hard kiss with passion and longing, then he gives me his handkerchief. It is made of fine linen and I dab carefully not to spoil it but I can see, as I attempt to give it back to him, that there is writing on it. A phone number

"My lovely, sensitive Mar-gar-et," he breathes, this man who has captivated my pounding heart. "When you are ready, come and visit me in Sarajevo. I will show you my country, which is undergoing its own Renaissance. You will love it, I'm sure." And with that, he turns round and walks back down the street, his footsteps echoing between the tall buildings. I watch him until he turns the corner and disappears from sight. I am trembling with cold and longing and sadness and joy.

Back in my room, I undress slowly in front of the mirror. I have not had the courage to do this since the operation. Naked, I drink in every part of my body greedily, like a man deprived of water finding a well in the desert. I slowly touch this body which I had learnt to hate. Face, hair, neck, arms and hands, feet and legs, my stomach, my left breast and then the place where once I had a right breast. There is flatness where there should be soft, luxurious skin. I am like Boadicea, I think and laugh at the idea. I am a modern-day warrior, triumphant after the battle. I am not afraid any more. I have been given a second chance. I am alive! It is so good to be alive. I dance round the room naked and collapse onto the bed, laughing and crying at the same time. What did Misha call it? Renaissance?

Yes, I am Renaissance Woman!

Ice Cream With Macaroons
(Created by John Knutson)

Ingredients
Ice-cream
3-4 level tbsp Splenda (15g)
2 egg yolks
250ml So-Good soya milk
half a vanilla bean
large Elmlea Light (284ml)
Macaroons
2 egg whites
100g ground almonds
2 tbsp Splenda

Method
Cream together egg yolks and Splenda in mixer (10 minutes or until it turns a light yellow creamy colour).
Simmer milk on low heat with vanilla bean (10 minutes).
Slowly add hot milk to egg and sugar cream. Beat until consistency is even.
Set a heat-resisting bowl containing mixture on pan of simmering water. Whisk occasionally for 10-15 minutes until mixture thickens.
When cool, mix in Elmlea.
Churn in ice-cream machine following machine instructions or leave in freezer compartment of fridge and periodically stir well to avoid ice crystals forming.

Method for Macaroons
Beat left over egg whites in mixer until stiff.
Fold in ground almonds and Splenda.
Shape into balls.
Place on greased baking tray.
Place in heated oven 200°C/400°F/Gas Mark 6 on middle shelf until golden brown (10-15 minutes).

Honeymoon
by Della Galton

"We could stay in bed all day if you like," Ken purred, letting his fingers trail across my shoulder suggestively.

"I think that's a great idea. But shouldn't we go down for breakfast? Won't they be expecting us?"

"I'm not very hungry. Are you?"

I shook my head.

"Then let's stay here. If we get peckish later, we can always order room service. I doubt if anyone will bother us – especially if I put the 'do not disturb' sign on the door." He gave me a sleepy wink. "After all, we are on our honeymoon!"

I smiled at him and sat up in bed. I had a hazy recollection of falling into it at some unearthly hour. But now, in the shafts of morning sunlight slicing between the heavy curtains, I took a proper look at our surroundings. The room had been described as luxurious and it was. Thick, pale carpet stretched towards the door, which was some way away. In one corner a glass coffee table was flanked by two cappuccino coloured leather armchairs. On the table was a bowl of fruit and a vase of pink roses, and beside them an ice bucket, which had contained a "complimentary" bottle of champagne that we'd drunk last night.

A step led up into the en-suite bathroom, which was all marble floors and mirrors and contained a sunken bath and a Jacuzzi. No doubt we'd be in there later. I smiled and snuggled back down in the four poster bed, which had lace drapes that could be drawn across to ensure privacy. Ken was right. Why not make the most of it. It had cost us enough.

It was a beautiful hotel room and all ours for a week. Not that we were going to stay in it all week, obviously, it'd be nice to go out and explore our surroundings. Apparently there was a lake in the hotel grounds, where guests could go boating and there were marked out woodland walks all over the estate. Deer roamed the grounds. But we had plenty of time. And we had more pressing things to do than walk.

I glanced at him. "Fancy a massage, love?"

He nodded and moments later I was sitting astride him, my fingers gently circling his naked skin.

"Mmm, that feels good. I could just lie here all day and let you do that."

"That's not very fair. I might want a turn." I pouted and he smiled. And a few minutes later we reversed positions.

His hands felt wonderful and I took a deep breath of contentment.

Some time later I woke up. Ken was still asleep beside me. When I glanced at the clock I saw that it was almost three. I shook him gently awake.

"Love, I think we've missed lunch, too."

"I'm still not that hungry," he murmured sleepily. "I could do with a drink though. How about you?"

"Yes please."

I watched him make it, loving the movement of muscles in his strong back as he lifted the kettle, and feeling an ache in my throat. I loved him so much. Marrying him was the best thing I'd ever done.

"What are you thinking?" he murmured as he came back with two steaming mugs and clunked them onto the bedside table.

"Only how sexy you look."

"Is that so? Well, shift over and let me back in then. It's cold out here."

A moment later he was beside me, his arms around me. And neither of us noticed the time again until it was almost five.

"We're not going to miss dinner as well as lunch, are we?" I asked him. "All the hotel staff will be gossiping. Anyway, I think I could probably eat something now."

He reached for the room service menu. "They do oysters," he said, with a wicked grin. "Ever tried them?"

"No, and I hardly think we need to eat oysters. Smoked salmon's more my style. A sandwich will do."

I let Ken answer the door when our food came. He didn't get dressed, just pulled on his robe, and I stayed where I was, hidden behind the drapes until I was sure the coast was clear.

"He didn't say anything about us staying in bed all day, did he?" I asked, sitting up in bed and feeling slightly embarrassed.

"Course not," Ken said, grinning. "I think he was probably impressed." He gave me a mock bow. "Is Madam getting dressed for dinner, or shall I serve it in bed?"

"I'm getting up."

"Then I'll lay up the coffee table. Blimey, this place is posh, silver cutlery and linen napkins. And that's just on the take out menu."

"How the other half live, eh."

"Shall we have an after dinner drink?" he asked when we'd eaten. "Or we could make an effort and go for a romantic stroll in the sunset."

"I'm quite happy here," I said and he nodded and went to the mini bar and retrieved a couple of miniatures.

"What have we here? Looks like finest malt."

We sipped our drinks. "So what did that room service chappie say?" I pressed.

Ken laughed. "It wasn't what he said. They're too polite to say anything, aren't they? It was just the look in his eyes. As if he couldn't quite believe that we'd missed breakfast and lunch and couldn't manage to drag ourselves down for dinner either. I think he was quite jealous. And so he should be. Sensual massage, a whole day in bed, with a beautiful woman, only getting up to make the odd drink, and now a nightcap – bliss."

That's what I love about Ken – the way he sees the positive in everything. He could just as easily have said, 'vapour rubs, exhaustion and hot lemon.' Although I do agree with him on one thing. These hot toddies are wonderful – and with a bit of luck, we'll have shaken off this flu by tomorrow, and we'll be able to enjoy our honeymoon properly!

Hot Toddy

Ingredients
1 tbsp honey
¾ glass tea
2 shots brandy
1 slice lemon

Method
Brew tea and fill a tall glass ¾ full.
Mix in honey.
Mix in brandy shots.
Add lemon slice and enjoy.

Contributor's Biographies

Alison Baverstock began her career in publishing before setting up a marketing consultancy. She has published widely, including eleven books, three distance-learning courses and numerous articles for the professional press. She regularly gives seminars at universities teaching Publishing Studies and is Visiting Senior Lecturer within the Business School of Kingston University. She recently contributed to the Richard and Judy strand on how to get published, and has been heavily involved in the Kingston Readers' Festival. Her most recent book is *Whatever, a down to earth guide to parenting teenagers* (Piatkus 2005). She has four children and lives with her husband in Kingston-upon-Thames.

Kelly Rose Bradford is a freelance journalist and writer. Her features regularly appear in parenting, teenage and women's magazines, and her short stories have been published in magazines all over the world. Kelly is 32 and lives in West London with her partner and two year old son. Her interests include shoes, wine, Oscar Wilde and participating in the online writers group she administrates.

Rose Bray was born and grew up in the Isle of Man. Trained as a teacher, she lived and worked in the North of England, Switzerland and Sussex. Married, with a grown-up family, she now has time to write, and studying in a creative writing class has inspired her. She has had several articles and poems published and has won prizes in competitions for her short stories and poems. Living near the sea is one of her pleasures and often features in her writing.

Tina Brown lives two hours south of Sydney, Australia. She penned a winning entry in a Woman's Day/ Mills and Boon Romantic fiction competition. She has contributed to three other titles in the 'Shorts' range and is a professionally trained chef.

Catrin Collier was born and brought up in Pontypridd. Her first novel, *Hearts of Gold* was made into a mini series by the BBC, aired in July 2003. Her latest *Finders and Keepers*, was published in July 2005. *Tiger Bay Blues* will be published in Spring 2006. In addition to fifteen Catrin Collier novels, she has also published four crime books as Katherine John and three modern fiction novels as Caro French. Tŷ Catrin Adult Education Centre named after her was opened in 2002. Catrin is contracted to produce two books a year for Orion publishing.

Elaine Everest is a freelance writer living in Swanley, Kent with her husband Michael and a houseful of Old English Sheepdogs. When not writing magazine fiction or articles for many UK and overseas publications, she teaches creative writing for Kent Adult Education Service. A member of the successful Wild Geese writing group, Elaine is overjoyed to be part of Saucy Shorts for Chefs as she has just celebrated 25 years of surviving breast cancer.

Penny Feeny has worked as a copywriter, editor and broadcaster, but far prefers writing fiction. Her stories have appeared widely in print, on radio and online and have won several prizes. She's lived in Cambridge, London and Rome, but has been settled for many years now in Liverpool with her husband and their five children.

Christine Field was born in Birmingham, now lives in Mid-Wales. Working mainly in legal offices, Christine has travelled extensively throughout Europe and, after a taster of the Japanese language and culture, Japan is now on her wish list. After joining a creative writing class in 2004 she has recently started writing short stories.

Kelly Florentia lives in North London with her husband. Her short stories have been published in women's magazines in the U.K., Sweden and Australia and she belongs to an online writers group. As well as writing, Kelly currently freelances in marketing. She enjoys long walks, various types of music, fine food and wine, and great conversation. Kelly hopes to write a novel in the future.

Della Galton's passion is writing. She lives by the sea with her husband and four dogs and works as a full time writer. She has sold in excess of three hundred short stories to women's magazines and also writes serials and features. She has two novels awaiting publication.

Liza Granville has had a great deal of romantic fiction published in national and international magazines. *Midsummer Rose* won a Writers West award. She also writes dark grey comedy, has two stories in the anthology: *Loffing Matters* (Tindal Press 2006), a novel, *Curing The Pig* (Flame Books). Immanion Press are to publish two novels. *The Crack of Doom* and *Until The Skies Fall*, also in 2006.

Zoë Griffin is a journalist, who trained at *The Daily Telegraph* before becoming deputy editor of the *Mail on Sunday's* showbiz column. Every evening she attends star-studded parties, meeting weird and wonderful people who provide the inspiration for the characters in her short stories. She is currently working on her first novel.

Josephine Hammond grew up in West Africa and took a degree at University College London in French and Italian. After working briefly in France she settled into married life in England and now has four grown-up sons. She taught languages for several years then escaped into her own business selling hampers by mail order. Throughout, she has always enjoyed writing and has had several articles and short stories published. She is currently completing an MA in Creative Writing and is working on a book.

Veronica Henry has written for many television dramas including *Boon, Heartbeat* and *Family Affairs*. Her first novel *Honeycote* 2002 was followed by *Making Hay* in 2003 and *Wild Oats* in July 2004. Her latest novel, *An Eligible Bachelor* received fantastic reviews from the likes of *Elle* and *Hello.* She lives in Devon with her husband and three sons.

Tamar Hodes was born in Israel in 1961 and moved to England with her family when she was five. She was educated at Henrietta Barnett School in London and Homerton College, Cambridge. For the past twenty years, she has taught English to adults and children, and run courses in Creative Writing in schools, prisons and universities. She has had nine stories broadcast on Radio 4 and others published. She now teaches full-time in a school, and is married with two teenage children.

Sue Houghton is a mother of four grown-up children. Since completing a creative writing course she has had over 25 short stories published in the UK and abroad. Sue has won a number of writing competitions and is currently seeking an agent for her first novel *Nearly Dearly.*

Dawn Hudd lives in Hereford with her husband, three sons, a couple of dogs and more than a few cats. By day she is a Teaching Assistant at a local school. By night she studies for a BA in Creative Writing at Birmingham University and writes articles and short stories. She is currently working on a children's novel.

Sue Johnson was born in Kent and now lives in Pershore, Worcestershire. She is a member of the RNA and has had short stories published in a variety of women's magazines. Her poems and stories have been successful in national competitions. She runs creative writing and art workshops and enjoys composing guitar tunes in her spare time.

Daisy Jordan is the alter ego of the novelist Lynne Barrett-Lee, who has contributed short stories for three of the last books in the Shorts range, as well as penning four novels of her own. Daisy's debut novel, *Wild About Harry* was published in September 2005 (Bantam), so though Lynne still enjoys beavering at the keyboard in her Cardiff garret, Daisy's now much too busy being fabulous and gorgeous, and trying to get an interview on Jonathan Ross.

Ruth Joseph worked for IPC magazines as a free-lance journalist. She recently graduated with an M. Phil. in Writing from Glamorgan University. *Red Stilettos* was published in 2004 by Accent Press who also published *Remembering Judith* in September 2005. Ruth is a Rhys Davies, Cadenaz and Lochfield prize-winner and lives in Cardiff with her family.

Kath Kilburn lives in Halifax, West Yorkshire with her husband, Mike and two children. She is a non-fiction writer at heart but has enjoyed the odd foray into short story territory. Kath has had articles in a variety of publications including TES, Adults Learning and Writers' Forum and used to love editing and writing for a local newsletter. She is a member of two writer's groups.

Sophie King aka Jane Bidder trained as a journalist after reading English at Reading University and has since written for most major magazines and newspapers. In the last few years, she has written over one hundred short stories for women's magazines. She also writes a regular parenting page for *Woman* and has had several non-fiction books published as well as a series of children's picture books. Her first novel *The School Run* (Hodder) was released in August under her fiction name Sophie King. Jane has three children ranging from fourteen to twenty-one.

Maggie Knuston lives in Winchester with her husband and dog and has one grown-up daughter. Maggie has spent most of her working life as an English teacher, but now concentrates on writing. She's had a number of articles published in her local newspaper and has a short story soon to be published in *Quality Women's Fiction.* She is currently working on a novel set in Cyprus.

Gill Lammas lives in Swansea with her husband, and has two grown-up sons and a granddaughter. She took up writing short stories several years ago after recuperating from an operation. In the past she has written a weekly grapevine column for a local newspaper and had an article published. Gill is presently working on a book, due to be published next year.

Carolyn Lewis graduated from the University of Glamorgan with an MPhil in Writing and has won several prizes for her short stories. Her work has appeared in two other Shorts anthologies. Earlier this year Carolyn came second in the Mathew Prichard Award. Born in Cardiff, she now lives in Bristol. Working on her second novel, she also tutors part-time in creative writing.

Heather Lister was born in Hereford and grew up in the Midlands. She has worked as an English teacher in England and Africa and, always a keen writer, has had some poems published and plays performed along the way. She now helps run a library for homeless people in Bristol, her adopted city, and encourages creative writing in groups of ex-offenders. She has four sons and a happy second marriage.

Adele Parks lives in London with her husband and son. She has published six best-selling novels to date; *Playing Away, Game Over, Larger Than Life, The Other Woman's Shoes, Still Thinking of You* and *Husbands*. Her books have been translated into seventeen different languages and are published throughout the world. Adele writes articles and short stories for a number of publications in the UK, USA and Australia.

Linda Povey's first writing success was with verse for greetings cards. She now writes short stories for women's magazines. She is involved in running residential courses for writers. Her play, *The Cat-Flap Burglar,* is to be performed in her home town of Bridgnorth early next year. She has given up her teaching job to write full-time and is working on her first novel.

Rosemarie Rose was born in England and now lives in South Wales with her partner and two cats. She has had several short stories published in magazines, and has been placed and shortlisted in various creative writing contests, the most recent being a third place in the King's Lynn Writers' Circle Competition 2005.

Rachel Sargeant has been an assistant teacher, a librarian and a project manager in London and Germany. She has now settled for the best job as a full-time mum, living in Shropshire. A former winner of Writing Magazine's Annual Crime Story Competition, she has just completed her second novel, a whodunnit.

Jill Steeples is a freelance writer, living in Leighton Buzzard with her husband and two children. Her short stories have been published in the popular women's magazines in the UK and Australia. Jill is an enthusiastic member of both her local writers' circle and the international online group, Wild Geese Writers. Her hobbies include white water rafting, abseiling and hang gliding.

Jill Stitson. is originally from London but now lives with her husband in Dorset. She had her first story published at age of twelve and restarted writing five years ago after a long break. I have had articles published in women's magazines and small press publications and last year was a prize winner in the *Writers News* magazine short story competition.

Ginny Swart lives in Cape Town, is married with three children and has been writing fiction for four years. She is a member of the Wild Geese internet writing group. She was the winner of the 2003 Real Writers Fiction Prize. Her stories have appeared in high school text books, anthologies and women's magazines.

Phil Trenfield was born and raised in Cheltenham. He now lives in Cardiff where he works in event management, whilst spending his free time creating the short stories he loves to write. He is currently putting the finishing touches to his first novel.

Wendy Turner is a member of the Verulum Writers' Circle at St. Albans, she is a winner of *Circle's* Lisbeth Phillips Competition. Wendy is also a regular contributor to the *Hertfordshire Countryside* magazine, and recently published an inter-active CD-Rom on sign language and finger-spelling for children.

Jane Wenham-Jones lives in Broadstairs, Kent. Her work has appeared in a wide range of women's magazines and national newspapers. She writes an advice column for *Writing Magazine* and a humorous column for the *Isle of Thanet Gazette*. Jane has appeared on radio and television and is regularly booked as an after-dinner speaker. She is the author of three novels - *Raising the Roof* (2001) *Perfect Alibis (2003)* and *One Glass is Never Enough* (October 2005)

Pam Weaver has had over eighty short stories published in main-stream women's magazines, and her short story *The Fantastic Bubble* has been repeated on Radio 4 and the BBC World Service. Pam recently won a novel opening competition at the West Sussex Writers' Club Day for Writers and is currently working hard to complete the novel.

Lorraine Winter grew up in Northern Ireland but now lives near the beach in Sussex with her husband and dog. When she's not working as a midwife or enjoying the company of her young grand-daughters, she enjoys writing short stories and keeping in touch with her friends in an online writing group.

Betka Zamoyska has written a biography of Elizabeth I, published by Longman's in the UK and Mcgraw-Hill in the USA; *The Burston Rebellion*, published by BBC publications, about the longest strike in history, and *The Ten Pound Fare* about British emigration to Australia in the l950s. Betka is currently working on a collection of short stories.

Message from Breast Cancer Campaign

Thank you!

By buying this copy of Saucy Shorts for Chefs a donation of £1 has been made to Breast Cancer Campaign.

Breast cancer is the most common form of cancer in the UK, with one woman in nine developing the disease. On average 13,000 women will die from the disease every year. Breast Cancer Campaign aims to find the cure for breast cancer by funding research which looks at improving diagnosis and treatment, better understanding how it develops and ultimately either curing the disease or preventing it.

The donations we receive fund independent breast cancer research at any centre of excellence in the UK.

At present, the best way to influence your chance of surviving breast cancer is to detect it early. We encourage all women to be breast aware and know what is normal for them. Look out for:-

- A lump or swelling in your breast that feels different from the rest of your breast tissue
- A lump or swelling in the armpit, arm or around your collar bone
- Any change in the shape or size of the breast or the nipple
- Any change in the position or colouring of the nipple, including inversion
- Any dimpling, denting, scaling or discolouration of the skin
- Discharge from one or both nipples
- A pain in the breast, armpit or arm, that is new for you

Report any changes that you find to your doctor without delay. If you are aged 50 or over attend routine breast screening.

www.breastcancercampaign.org

To find out about Breast Cancer Campaign or any of our fundraising events, just fill in and send back this form to:
Breast Cancer Campaign, Clifton Centre, 110 Clifton Street, London EC2A 4HT

Please print clearly in BLOCK CAPITALS
Title (Mr/Mrs/Miss/Ms):

____

Address:______________________________________

____

____________________Postcode: _________________

Daytime telephone number:______________________

Date of birth: __ / __ / ____

Email address: ________________________________

Please send me: (tick as appropriate)

☐ A copy of the charity's bi-annual newsletter FOCUS - includes updates on our research and fundraising

☐ A fundraising pack – with hints and tips on how to host your own event with the materials and support we can offer

☐ Information on becoming a regional volunteer – representing the charity's and fundraising in your local area

☐ An events leaflet – details of our national events and the time of year they take place

☐ Information about donating shares – get rid of those few shares that would cost more to sell then they're actually worth

☐Information about making a gift in your will

☐ A corporate fundraising pack – details and ideas on how your place of work/company can raise funds for BCC

☐ Breast Cancer Campaign does not share information with any other organisation, however if you do not wish to receive any further mailings please tick this box

If you have any queries please telephone: 020 7749 3700 or visit our website: www.breastcancercampaign.org

Breast Cancer Campaign is a company limited by guarantee registered in England and Wales. Company No. 05074725. Charity registration No 299758. Registered office Clifton Centre, 110 Clifton Street, London EC2A 4HT.

I want to make breast cancer a disease of the past.

If you would like to make a donation to the work of Breast Cancer Campaign please fill out this form and return to: Breast Cancer Campaign, Clifton Centre, 110 Clifton Street, London EC2A 4HT

Please print clearly in BLOCK CAPITALS
Title (Mr/Mrs/Miss/Ms):

____

Address: ______________________________________

____

__________________ Postcode: __________________

Daytime telephone number: _______________________

Date of birth: _ _ / _ _ / _ _ _ _

Email address: ________________________________

Donation amount: £ __________

☐ Please accept my cheque/PO made payable to **Breast Cancer Campaign**

☐ Please debit my Switch/Visa/Mastercard/ CAF card (circle as appropriate)

Card No: ☐☐☐☐ ☐☐☐☐ ☐☐☐☐ ☐☐☐☐

Switch Only: Expiry ☐☐/☐☐ Issue Number ☐☐ Start ☐☐/☐☐

Name on Card: _________________________________

Signature: ___________________________________

Date: ___________

giftaid it ☐

Increase the value of your donation by 28%. To make your donation go further, providing you are a UK tax payer, please tick the giftaid box.